Shoot
Albatross

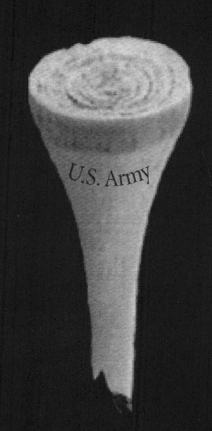

U.S. Army

A HISTORICAL NOVEL BY STEVEN R. LUNDIN

FIRST
EDITION

ISBN: 1-4392-2800-0
ISBN-13: 9781439228005
LCCN: 2009902211

Visit www.ShootinganAlbatross.com to order additional copies.

I dedicate this work to everyone daring to pursue a passion.

Steven R. Lundin

ACKNOWLEDGEMENTS

With special thanks to Kate Rosenthal for the art work, Pauline Benson, Jennifer, and Linda Hines for editing the text, Lisa for her encouragement, story ideas, line-edit, patience, and so much more, Roy Anderson for his skill with a camera, Nicole for shooting the course, the Martins for giving me the freedom to write, Slick for living so long, and to all of you who encouraged me to pursue my passion, especially family, friends, and complete strangers. Thank you.

DISCLAIMERS

AUTHOR BIOGRAPHY

Steven R. Lundin is the Marketing Director, Vice President, and co-owner of a foundation engineering company. He earned his MBA and holds actuarial enrollment with the departments of Labor and Treasury. His first short story was awarded top prize in the 2007 Authorlink® short story contest. A resident of Hillsboro, Oregon, the author recently completed the second book in his Albatross series.

CONTENTS

Chapter   **Page**

PART I: THE DRIVE

One   Finding Floyd   1
Two   Evan Wilkins, a Golf Course,   11
           and the Challenge
Three   The General's Visit   21
Four   Routine, a Watcher, and the   31
           Watched
Five   Where'd He Go?   43
Six   Dinner Engagement   49
Seven   Golfing without Instruction   57
Eight   A Reprimand and an Unexpected
           Encounter   67

PART II: THE FAIRWAY

Nine   The Dinner Party   83
Ten   Strong Emotions   97
Eleven   A Round of Golf   107
Twelve   A First Look   117
Thirteen   The Blind Spot in a Tree   131
Fourteen   Birdies, Eagles, and Albatrosses   139
Fifteen   More than a Look   147
Sixteen   The Briefing   153
Seventeen The Golf Tournament   163
Eighteen   The Back Nine   175

Nineteen	The Ball Plays Here	187
Twenty	Lifting and Lowering Glasses	193
Twenty-one	Till Death Do Us Part	203

PART III: THE HOLE

Twenty-two	Just One Day at a Time	217
Twenty-three	The Runner and the Arrival	229
Twenty-four	Some Sort of a Cruel Mistake	241
Twenty-five	Who's There?	253
Twenty-six	High and to the Left	263
Twenty-seven	Something Deadly Their Way Came	277
Twenty-eight	Live in You	287
Twenty-nine	Ancillary Passions	293

~~~ PART I ~~~
THE DRIVE

U.S. Army

"... but I shall kill no albatross ..."
Robert Walton in *Frankenstein*

CHAPTER 1

~ *FINDING FLOYD* ~

The best way to dispose of an old secret is to kill it with the old man who hides it. Take my word for it. When I tracked down Floyd Akerly, I found an old man still living with an old secret. I intended both to go. The day I found him, Floyd was ninety-four. He was thin, frail, shrunken, and entirely alone. Shame on someone! Such old men should never be left alone. Surprisingly, alone is how I left him, too, for on that first day, I left him still breathing. His words changed my intention. He unknowingly mesmerized me with what I craved to hear. He told me about Evan. Like an addict, I wanted more, and that is why I began a series of visits with him that lasted for several months. I got him talking and, in this manner, I became familiar to him. I gained his trust. With his trust came his words and, with his words, Floyd said it all. Well, he thought to tell everything, but he left out certain important parts. He spoke about what happened sixty-four years before, but he avoided revealing his darker secrets. My very existence told these truths.

I was at first alive with my find. I parked in my pearl Audi sedan about fifty meters from his house, and then simply sat, watching and waiting. Floyd lived in a mobile home on the rural side of the suburbs. A large open field led to the front of his house and continued around the back. Trees, shrubs, and bushes grew dense along both sides. What I could not see was Floyd. His windows were reflections of sunlight. Sunlight! Where was nature's fury? Where was her foreshadowing? Dark stormy clouds, angling rain, howling winds, thundering skies, a power outage, and downed telephone lines would have been more appropriate to my purpose. I imagined Floyd being frightened awake, his face appearing in his window between strobes of light, and his wide eyes catching only glimpses of me in the darkness, watching him. Instead, the day was a sensory contradiction between desire and reality, for the air was impressively warm, clear, and unmoving. Rather than an accomplice, the weather was indifferent. In my sedan, looking across Floyd's one-acre lot, I felt exposed, as though I were a forgotten prop left on a lighted stage. Floyd was there in his house, though, so like a predator lying in wait, I stared intently. Liquid fury flowed in my veins. I felt alive with watching and waiting.

Everyone has secrets, but at ninety-four, the most disturbing secrets have a way of becoming someone's truth. Before finding Floyd, I wondered if he remembered what he had done. Had he lived with his lies for so long that he no longer knew the truth? Who remembers his worst? After a time, no matter how terrible Floyd's actions might have been, no matter how sordid Floyd's behavior, he would have needed peace in his heart. There is no way he could have lived so long with a guilty heart. He would have gone crazy. Denial is the great source of peace for those with guilty hearts. Had denial created Floyd's truth? I also wondered if he might have forgotten. Old people do forget. At his age, legitimately, Floyd could have lost the truth in the synaptic abyss of old age. I was seeking Floyd with the intention of helping him both to remember and forget everything.

To see him inside of his house, I leaned against and peered through my car's window. I stared, squinted, rolled

down the window, and attempted a squint to find him
with only one of my eyes. This sometimes worked but, for
seeking Floyd, it failed me. Giving up my one-eyed squint,
I took a small pair of high-powered field binoculars from
a side-door compartment. I removed the binoculars from
their case, removed four plastic lens caps, unwound a
canvas neck cord, anxiously held the binoculars with both
hands, drew them to my eyes, and searched the front of
Floyd's house. I searched like a sailor seeking land. There
was no car sitting in his driveway, no movement anywhere in
front of, to the sides of, or behind his house, and nothing
to be seen in the reflections in his windows. I lowered the
binoculars and found a closer position from which I could
watch. With concern for neither the car's movement nor
the sun's reflection, I drove until I was only thirty meters
from Floyd's house. I again lowered my power window,
killed the sedan's throaty rumble, took the binoculars in
my hands, and found it much easier to see the inside of his
house.

I saw him. Right there at the tip of my eyes, I saw Floyd
Akerly. He was sitting at an uncovered window in a brown
rocker. I could easily see that. I could also see that he
looked as old as his age. From earlier photographs,
I knew that Floyd's hair had once been black. I also knew
he had dyed his hair during his fifties and sixties and that
it had looked unnaturally black back then. In his seventies
and eighties, his hair had thinned and grayed. Through
the binoculars, I discovered his hair was as white as an old
lady's. I also saw Floyd looking out of his window. From the
manner in which he stared into the empty field, I presumed
him to be looking to the past, like he was watching old
movies flickering in black and white in his brain. Were
scenes of El Rancho Golf Course in Los Angeles, California
playing in his memory? What about the big Army and Navy

3

golf game? During that unauthorized round, Floyd acted,
a Navy admiral responded, an Army general reacted, and
Floyd's entire life changed for the worse—for the much,
much worse. Did he remember? What about Evan Wilkins
and Amanda Nichols? What about them? They had been on
that golf course too. Did their images haunt his memory?

Although Floyd's look through his window was blank,
mine through the binoculars was not. Mine stalked. I was
surprised by feelings of anger. I found myself squeezing the
binoculars, furrowing my brows, pressing my lips, releasing
periodic heaves of breath, and slowly leaning closer at
Floyd. I nearly hung through the door window of my sedan.
He drew me the way a helpless animal draws predators.
I felt myself craving him. He must have noticed, for he
looked right at me. Perhaps I was too exposed where I was
parked, the sun reflected on a piece of the sedan's chrome,
or perhaps Floyd felt the intensity of my glare. Whichever
the case, he looked at me looking at him. Through the field
binoculars, at only thirty meters, I felt as though we were
eye-to-eye. I caught myself and resisted an urge to slam my
forehead toward his. I made a head-butting motion at him.

We remained staring at each other while I withdrew
back into my sedan and closed the window. He could not
have recognized me, for he never knew me. His expression
surprised me, though, for a happy sort of grin came with his
eye contact. Why the agreeable look of familiarity? Just like
when taken by surprise, when tricked by strategy, I sensed
a peripheral threat approaching against which I was too
late to react. I was startled by the sound of knocking on my
window.

The knock was, in reality, a soft knuckle-tapping. It
startled me. I turned and looked to find a small Hispanic
woman flanking me. She stood staring in at me. Her smile
was one of those half smiles in which suspicion hides

behind wonder. She was wearing a long brown skirt, a bright white blouse, and one of those wide leather belts that went out of style one or two decades earlier. She looked to be in her late thirties, and she appeared to be entirely uncomfortable about confronting me. She made nervous glances to her left and right. I answered her knock by lowering my window and speaking in the friendliest, fatherly tone I could manage.

"Hello," I said.

"Can I help you?" the woman said in broken English.

"Please," I said. "I am looking for ..."

I paused as though Floyd's name was lost to me. I turned in my seat, moved a map book from my lap, and turned back to her with a triumphant smile. "Yes," I said. "I am looking for Floyd Akerly."

I watched the woman's expression soften at the name. My binoculars lay in plain sight, so while holding eye contact and smiling at the woman's face, I carefully moved to cover them with my book of maps.

"Floyd lives there," she pointed. "Look, he was just smiling at me. See? He's waving now. I am stopped behind you. May I please get around you? You're blocking Floyd's driveway."

"Of course," I said. "Forgive me. I had no idea I was in your way." I glanced behind and ahead of me. "Are you going to visit Floyd too?"

"I care for him," the woman said. "I just went to the store for groceries. If you are coming to visit Floyd, I will take you. Look, there he is. He's looking out at us."

At my age, I was easily able to see the effect I had on the woman. My short gray hair, starched oxford button-down, blue blazer, leather-seated sedan, friendly demeanor, and harmless smile put her at ease. Young Hispanic caregivers bestow great respect on older businessmen.

"What is your name?" I asked.

"Mawdea," she said. I said her name back to her, she again said it to me—slowly articulating her sounds and rolling her tongue—and I tried again.

"Maria?" I asked.

"Sí," she said.

Her smile was meek. She looked uncomfortable, but she let me inside Floyd's house. From the moment I entered, I was surprised by its cleanliness and by the lack of odor. I expected the dusty, moldy, moth-ball odor that sometimes pervades the homes of the elderly. Most homes of ninety-four-year-old men smell of either medicine or approaching death. I was surprised to find Floyd's house smelling younger and cleaner than I expected. I had expected Floyd and his house to stink.

"What should I tell him?" Maria asked. She blocked my way from moving beyond his paneled foyer, smiling, and waiting for a reason to let me proceed.

"Tell Floyd I'm doing research," I said. "Tell him I would like to hear him talk about his experiences in the war."

"The war?"

"Yes," I said. "Say World War II."

The dear girl smiled. "He has no family," she said, "and he never gets visits. But he always wants attention. I know he will like talking to you about the war. You will give him—how do I say it? Life? You will give him life."

I nodded and smiled. I imagined that, at ninety-four, Floyd wanted nothing more than attention from me. I expected him to want attention for the memories I would wake in him. Because he had neither family nor friends, I imagined he spent his days either watching his television or peering from his window.

"You will be good for him," she said. "You will stimulate his mind and he needs that. But be careful. He gets tired easy. His throat gets dry when he talks for very long. Give him breaks. Give him water to drink."

"Water?"

"Yes," she said. "Water helps his throat, but do not give him ice. Floyd chokes on ice."

"I'll keep that in mind."

Maria led me straight to Floyd. She left me alone with him. I grin every time I recall her innocence, but how could she have known? The man she took care of had a past. When Maria saw Floyd, she saw only an old man in need of her services. She probably thought he was a cute little old man who was frail and deserving of peace. When I saw him, however, I saw someone entirely different. I saw an old man enjoying what he had denied Evan Wilkins. I saw a false dénouement awaiting a true climax.

Floyd must have seen me talking to Maria back at my car, but when I entered his living room, he did not turn to look at me. He sat still in his brown recliner and stared with neither expression nor acknowledgement of my arrival. Old men do that. They stare into emptiness, at nothing at all. I stood behind him and looked where he looked.
I thought he was watching memories of his younger days play in his mind. They would have been of his hopes, ambitions, travels, trials, and loves, the passions of his soul.

"Hello, Floyd," I said. He sat motionless, watching his memories. "Hello," I said again, but this time I shouted my greeting.

I watched Floyd start and turn to look at me. He smiled widely and happily, and his fingers went straight up and fumbled in his ears, as though seeking an elusive radio frequency. I made a mental note about his being unaware of my presence until I hollered my greeting. He was not aware I was watching him, even though Maria had informed him of my arrival and desire to visit. I noted, too, that my sudden appearance did not alarm him. When he spoke, it was in a forced, weak voice that sounded much too loud. This was his way of compensating for his hearing loss. Our greeting became a smiling shouting match.

"Hi," he said.

"Hi, Floyd!" I yelled.

I watched him for signs to indicate I had either spoken too loudly or too softly. I was certain he heard me, but he said nothing. He used his wrinkled index finger to point me to his sofa and watched as I took a seat before his recliner. I touched the sofa's two cushions. They were soft—soft enough to muffle sound. I squeezed both and smiled at him.

"I'm glad you came," he said.

His pleased, old-man smile showed in his mouth and his eyes. I knew he was pleased to have company. He was thin, wore a sweater that looked as old as he did, and wore glasses through which he once must have seen people and places now long gone. He was remarkably wrinkled, but his thin white hair, collared shirt under his sweater, loose slacks of some odd beige color, slippers lined with matted lamb's wool, and his animated character revealed a youthful eagerness for company. I found it ironic that my visit brought him to life.

I was careful not to give away my intentions by maintaining a friendly expression. I found this restraint difficult. In my sixty-three years, I had learned to let inner emotions make outward appearances. Expression is how we share life, but my smile hid my heart. Instead of sharing life with Floyd, I wanted to place one sofa cushion behind his head, let his lips kiss the other one, and then squeeze the two until he slumped, forever unmoving. It was fortunate for him that Maria was in the house, and it was fortunate for me that Floyd had an unchecked willingness to talk.

"Can you tell me about the war?" I shouted to him.

Old people die. I was anxious to hear certain details of his past before they died along with him. He spoke and I listened. His words took me back in time. Simply listening to what he had to say gave me a glimpse of the treasure he had denied me. I was captivated and wanted more to hear him than to silence him. I allowed this interest to show on my face, thinking he would understand, appreciate, and withhold none of his war experiences from me.

Floyd frowned at my words. I watched him again fumble with his ears, and I actually felt sorry for him. It must be frustrating when one is so old. Small objects such as hearing aids become tiny, and the dulled sense of feeling that comes with time makes tiny objects numb in old fingers. He looked frustrated as he fiddled, but after a moment of his frowning and making weak, throaty sounds, he looked up to me and smiled again.

"What was that?" he shouted. He used both his eyes and smile to indicate he had made a proper adjustment to his hearing devices.

"Can you tell me something about the war?" I said.

Floyd heard me. I saw his exaggerated smile again become a pleased, old-man grin. He shifted a thin arm from one side of his recliner to the other, allowing me to better see him. His eyes surprised me. Though they looked straight into mine, they appeared to be gone, as if he were looking somewhere in the distance. I became a screen on which he watched reels of old flickering memories. I had become that window through which he was staring earlier. The room became quiet. While he was gone watching his old memories, I observed him staring through me. His smile changed to a wistful grin. He shook his head, and his grin returned as a frown of embarrassment. I suspect he thought I interpreted his moment of silence as senility.

9

"The war?" was all I said, hoping to bring him back.

The smile returned to his eyes, and I could tell he was pleased with the opportunity to recall and share his memories of World War II. Rather than asking leading questions, I chose to sit back and listen when he started talking. He leaned forward in his chair, enlivened by my interest. His voice might have been loud and strong or quiet and weak, but I feared my mind would wander because his story would be devoid of color. I employed the trick of watching his words in my mind. I viewed them with the visual and artistic license of a paying moviegoer. The only sound in his room was his weak, scratchy voice, but its effect on me was like that of an indistinct background noise, like the sound of a bedroom fan spinning late at night.

I relaxed into the comfort of his sofa, squeezed the two cushions, and watched the old man's words play in my mind.

CHAPTER 2

~ EVAN WILKINS, A GOLF COURSE, AND THE CHALLENGE ~

"Millions of people were killed in the war. Some were innocent and others just had to die."

Floyd began speaking about the war as though it was something unknown to me. My interest was in much more than old black-and-white savagery. With his first pause, I changed his direction.

"I believe Evan Wilkins was in the 170th." I spoke as though the idea had only just then occurred to me. I pressed my lips, stared off toward his window, and returned my eyes to his while nodding quite certainty. "Yes," I said. "Sure he was. Evan Wilkins was in the 170th. Maybe you knew him?"

After he acknowledged that Evan had, indeed, been in the 170th, I was quick to tell Floyd that I knew nothing else about the man for, as I asked him, "How could I?"

Floyd did not answer my question. Instead, he did better. He recalled Evan.

"We had thirty officers in the 170th. There was a headquarters battery, a medical detachment, a service battery, and three gun batteries, A, B, and C. Private Wilkins was in Battery B. I'm not surprised you've heard of him. He was well-renowned for a time, but that was long ago."

Floyd repositioned himself in his recliner, took a sip of water, and then continued with growing recollection. I did not interrupt him. He needed to speak freely. I wanted to give him enough rope to hang himself.

"Yes," he said. "I believe you could have heard of Evan. A lot of people in the military knew of him back when I was in charge of Battery B and he was under my command. He was with us at Fort Lewis, at Santa Barbara and, after one of those typical military oversights, Evan was with us when the entire battalion moved to the Ojai Country Club in Ojai, California. Imagine that. We stayed at a country club."

"Incredible," I said, signaling encouragement with a turn of my head.

"It wasn't until after leaving Ojai," Floyd said, "that Private Wilkins came to my attention. Before then, he was only another young soldier. He was just another kid to command."

"Nothing happened at the country club?" I asked.

"There was a big military briefing held there," he said. I felt a sense of excitement by the way he leaned forward in his recliner to speak. "When we entered the country club's large ballroom, all of the officers were nervous. We were serious and solemn because we were certain we would get travel orders. We thought the entire battalion was being sent to fight in what everyone called 'Bloody Europe.'"

He laughed, shook his head, and continued by describing the great ballroom. "There were giant chandeliers, and these were surrounded by little ones. The lights were evenly spaced in the room. Everything looked big and bright, but it looked wrong for a briefing. The officers sat at round dinner tables where everyone could see everyone else. There was a row of straight folding tables at the head of the room, and those tables strengthened the rumors that had circulated among the officer staff that day. The rumors were the reason we assembled early for the meeting. We thought several of the highest-ranking members of the Army would be sitting at that head table. One, it was rumored, was to be a four-star general. Everyone knew important orders were coming, and we would not have been surprised if the president himself showed up that day."

I listened with great interest and envisioned the country club, an assembly of soldiers and officers, a general, and a sealed envelope containing some mysterious order. The order was to be delivered only at that briefing, but the meeting struck me as being out of place. I thought of a senator speaking in a movie theater. Round dinner tables were wrong for a briefing, and Floyd's description of large, floor-to-ceiling windows made it worse. The view of the club's lush grounds would have distracted the men, and the burgundy carpets would have been too plush for the soles of their boots. Floyd described polished mahogany wainscoting that ran from the floor to about five feet high around the windowless sides of the room. Wallpaper with thick vertical stripes covered the rest of the walls. The country club lent an air of pretension and loftiness to the meeting, as though it were a precursor to a large European invasion without horses, swords, sashes, lances, marching drummers, flying colors, and noble little boys ready to die for their king.

"We thought we'd get serious news that would send us to fight, but wouldn't you know it? They just told us about a 'secret mission,' and then they had our entire 170th sent to—now get this!"

He broke into a bout of frightful laughter. His humor came from his memory of an event lasting sixty-five years since that briefing. His eyes watered. He squinted and used his dry, wrinkled skin to wipe them.

"The first move of our secret mission," Floyd said, "if you can believe it, sent us from the country club in Ojai to the groomed grounds of El Rancho Golf Course on Pico Boulevard in Los Angeles, California. We couldn't believe it. That was back when everyone really loved the Army."

Floyd was grinning while he spoke, but after his last words, "loved the Army," he began laughing so hard he started coughing. He squinted his eyes closed and covered his mouth with an old cloth handkerchief. When frail old men laugh until they cough, they look especially vulnerable, like they are about to die. I squeezed the cushions when he made a hard, final cough, wiped tears from his eyes, and grinned when he looked at me.

"We stayed at El Rancho Golf Course for over a month," Floyd said. "It was while at the course that I got to know Private Evan Wilkins. Though he was one of my men, up to the point of arriving in LA, I really did not know him. There were just too many men in the battery. Besides, as an officer, I kept a professional distance between me and the men. Boys, I guess you could say. Evan was just twenty-one at the time. When I first heard about him, I had to go looking for him because I didn't know who he was. Ha-ha-ha."

I watched the wrinkles of Floyd's face bunch around his little glassy eyes. He used his arms to adjust his position in his recliner, reached for his glass of water, and laughed himself into several hard coughs. I saw water slosh from his glass and watched him use his yellowed handkerchief to wipe it.

When he looked up at me, he seemed to have much more to say. I nodded and listened to his brief explanation of how it was that the Army took the golf course.

"We just took it!" he said.

"How were you housed?"

"The Army housed Battery B," he explained, "in tents set up on the golf course parking lot, open areas of grass, and on the vacant fields across Pico Boulevard. I remember the evening I heard laughter coming from one of the tents and went to investigate. I stopped outside and listened before drawing aside the tarp door and peeking inside. I saw Sergeant Taylor with about forty men listening to him. They were all doubled over, laughing. One had his hands on his knees, and several were holding onto each other's shoulders for support. 'He broke it?' Taylor was asking the men. 'And then he threw it across the fairway? That's too much! Then he swore?'"

Floyd told me he listened and watched while Taylor and the men, again, roared their laughter. Obviously, something very funny had happened.

"What did the general say?" Taylor asked, gasping to catch his breath.

"Well," one of the men said. "The general shouted 'crap!' I think he was so mad he just might have."

The explanation refreshed their laughter, but Floyd's presence caused instant silence. A young soldier had been wiping tears from his eyes, and he was the one who first spotted Floyd watching them. The soldier stood rigid and made the loud call for attention. Floyd noticed the difficulty the soldier had getting his mouth, cheeks, and eyes to join his serious and erect posture. All of the other men snapped to attention, but they had similar difficulties composing themselves.

"At ease," Floyd said, but the laughter affected him too.

When he asked what had happened, everyone again began laughing, exchanging looks, and answering at the same time. Taylor's big voice silenced the men. He spoke with deep military authority, and it was he who gave Floyd the explanation, even though the story was one about which Taylor himself was just then learning.

A senior general was involved and, upon hearing that elements of his Army were encamped on the famous

El Rancho Golf Course, he was quick to challenge a Navy admiral to a golf game. The admiral accepted the challenge with only two words: "Damn right!" His simple acceptance reverberated like a handful of wet gravel rubbed between his palms.

Army and Navy pride were now at stake. Each had to win the game, but both the general and the admiral lacked the necessary skills to represent their branches with distinction. They decided each would partner with the best golfer he could find in his branch of the military and combine to form an appropriate foursome.

A large percentage of the Navy's personnel were already deployed, fighting a war far from the United States. Telegraphs went out to U.S. bases throughout the world and were not always favorably received. One admiral stationed with a carrier group near the Philippines crumpled and tossed the cable into a trash bin. After reading it, he had shouted, "Bullshit! This is war. We don't play. We fight!"

Another naval commander, perhaps one with a more finely-tuned sense of the Navy's high position within the hierarchy of the War Department—later renamed the Department of Defense—cabled the name of a golfer who could certainly win the game, beat the Army, and ensure the Navy achieved recognition as the best golfing branch of the military, a most distinguished recognition even today. The Navy already owned the military's highest position of golfing respect because of this seaman. The return cable was unambiguous about the Navy's choice. Bentley Knudsen accepted the honor and was relieved of his active duty responsibilities. He was sent to the naval academy in Annapolis, Maryland, where his newly assigned duties included golfing all day, every day, eating quite well, dancing with the ladies who were to attend the military ball planned during his four weeks of training, sleeping long hours, and doing whatever it was he wished. His sole mission became winning the golf game for the Navy.

When Floyd reached this point in his story, I thought Knudsen must have loved the Navy as much as Floyd had loved the Army back when it first moved the 170th to El Rancho Golf Course. I was struck by the thought that a wartime golf game had managed to inspire love, unlike war itself, which inspired hatred. Men loved their branches of the military, looked forward to the prospect of the upcoming game, and loved to think their side would win. I couldn't help but wonder if their love was more a distraction from the war. In 1943, everyone loved distractions from the war.

Unlike the admiral's quick success with finding his golf partner, the general had a problem. As soon as he'd heard the admiral's gravelly "damn right," the general sent telegrams throughout the Army. Several replies came back, and several men said the general had laughed out loud upon reading the first of them. A recent graduate of the United States Military Academy, a well-known and much-loved West Point icon, First Lieutenant Armstrong, was overwhelmingly proffered. The problem, however, was that Armstrong was no longer living. A gruesome crossing of his chest with a spattering of bullets, the perfect toss of a hand grenade—it was said to have landed just under his already lifeless chin—ended a promising future. Armstrong's body now lies in Arlington National Cemetery but, at the time of the general's laughter, it was in a rain-soaked field in Holland.

A second round of telegraphs produced a name that brought a smile back to the general's face. Private Carson, the Army's new hope, played two years before against Knudsen and soundly beat him. They had played on the crude, rough-cut course at Camp Callan, the naval training

ground in La Jolla, California, the course that became
the prestigious Torrey Pines Golf Course. The course was
known for being especially difficult, but the report said
Private Carson hit long that day, scored a string of five
straight birdies, and scored an eagle on the seventeenth
hole. The general gave the order, and Private Carson, who
had just taken part in the successful invasion of Sicily, was
recalled to the United States for reassignment to El Rancho
Golf Course in Los Angeles.

At this point, Floyd started to grin and frown at the
same time. I wondered aloud why he had stopped. He
began shaking his head back and forth, as though both
tickled and disgusted.

"The damn Navy," he answered, "arranged Private
Carson's return transport on one of their ships.
Unfortunately, it was hit by a German U-boat and that was
the end of Carson. It was stupidity, plain and simple."

I attempted a look of sympathy but felt bad for both
sides. When the Navy ship went down with Carson, it took
with it a large measure of the Army's certitude and swagger.

"We all thought the Navy had played a dirty trick on the
Army," Floyd said, "but when we learned that eight hundred
of the Navy's sailors also died as a result of the sub attack,
we just shook our heads. That's war. Innocent people die.
Still, Carson was supposed to have flown home. He was not
to have floated." He sighed before continuing.

"With war raging in the Pacific, Europe, Asia, and
Africa, you would have thought the greatest battle was
shaping up in Los Angeles, California. And wouldn't you
know it?" he laughed. "Private Evan Wilkins from McCall,
Idaho, Private Wilkins in my Battery B, a kid already
stationed at El Rancho Golf Course, was the one the general
partnered with to play against the Navy."

Floyd explained that Evan was given one month to prepare for the game that was scheduled for the last day of August in 1943. Knudsen would play with the admiral, and Evan would play with the general. The teams were set. Lines were drawn and a curious battle formed at the golf course.

"Professional golf was cancelled in 1943," Floyd said. "It was the only year in history the PGA canceled its season. But I'll tell you what. The secret got out. LA, Hollywood, golfers, and the news guys came to see the game."

"How is it that Evan was chosen to play with the general?" I asked.

Several other questions formed in my mind, but when too many unanswered questions accrued, I began to think more about answers than listen for them. I needed a break. The emotional cost of listening to Floyd's slow and labored recollections of his war experiences, hearing about Evan, and of being so near to Floyd wore on me. My senses were saturated.

Through his living room window, I saw evening had come. I gave Floyd a questioning look that suggested he should end his recollections, and he agreed. His monologue had exhausted him yet, in his drooping demeanor, I saw his unreasonable desire to continue, like a child whose parent calls an end to a day at the circus. He wanted to say more.

"You'll come back?" he asked. His voice was soft, and his throat was raspy. "I will answer your questions about Evan when you do. You will come back, won't you?"

"Damn right," I said.

I grinned because I used the admiral's acceptance words, and I left Floyd knowing I would return. Maria smiled. "You are always welcome," she said.

"The next time," I said, "I might come unannounced."

CHAPTER 3

~ *THE GENERAL'S VISIT* ~

During the summer of 1943, it was as Floyd said. No tents, artillery pieces, shells, vehicles, supplies, men, or anything else were allowed on the golf course while the 170th occupied it. All of these fighting staples were jam-packed around the parking lot, the clubhouse, empty open spaces, the maintenance sheds, and on the grassy fields across Pico Boulevard. It should be noted, however, that none of the 170th's equipment overflowed onto any of the properties on the far side of the golf course. Over there were large, well-maintained homes. These nearby homes were mansions, really, for they were massive structures with groomed lawns, clusters of tall trees, manicured gardens, mature bushes, and the large rhododendrons that were still colorful in August. The mansions had large driveways with large Bentleys, Royces, and Mercedes sitting in each. The exclusive little neighborhood sat like a diamond on the neck of the course.

The busy and crowded arrangements at the golf course, just next door to these homes, created the impression on the homeowners, and on their many visitors, that the golf course was remarkably busy. The neighbors wondered about the activity next door. The prevalent rumor was that something important had happened, was happening, or was about to happen, and several were seen watching from their yards and windows to discover just what it was they might be missing.

On the golf course, it was Evan's clubs that first caught Floyd's attention. Golf clubs in the forties were primitive things made of wood, iron, or both. There were no graphite or titanium shafts, bafflers, oversized heads, or any other modern improvement. Irons were so named because they were made of iron. Drivers were named for their effect on golf balls because, though they were also made with iron, they had formed blocks of wood at their ends that drove golf balls far down the fairway. The bags were bags, though, and Evan had been allowed to bring his bag of clubs along with him on every move he made with the Army. Floyd explained his reasoning for why it was that he allowed Evan the privilege of his clubs.

"A precedent had been set," Floyd said, "and I wasn't about to be the one to break a precedent for golf. The game was too important to the Army. In the beginning, I would never have denied Evan his clubs. That would have been stupid, but how could I have known what would happen?"

Evan was young and handsome. He always had a white-toothed smile or a playful, ironic grin on his face. Floyd described the subtle, charming influence Evan had on him. He explained that Evan reminded him of himself when he was younger. Evan was quick to help others, and as a result, everyone in the battalion liked him. In spite of being six feet tall, his brown eyes, short brown hair, and clean-shaven face gave him a boyish appearance.

"That first time I saw him," Floyd said, "I wondered if Evan knew something I didn't. He looked too confident. If there were twenty men at attention, in the full dress of their Army uniforms, with their eyes staring directly before them, their expressions sobered to the possibility of punishment, you would notice him first. He had a way of drawing your attention, especially when he wasn't trying."

While Floyd described Private Evan Wilkins, I allowed my glance to linger on an old Army photograph of Floyd, decked out in his full military dress. Floyd noticed my glance, and turned to look at the picture.

"That was taken about the same time," he said. "It was just before the golf game, back in Los Angeles."

I saw Floyd in the photograph, and I saw him as a young man of twenty-six, who also had short hair, only his was black. Floyd wore a stern military look that seemed threatening, and he appeared to be trying for a look of command. The 170th Field Artillery Battalion was comprised of the three fighting batteries, A, B, and C. There were four guns to a battery, and Floyd was the commander of the fourth gun in Battery B. I could easily imagine an order from him being quickly followed. He had one of those wedge-shaped faces that are so threatening on military men, as though it could be used to chop like the head of an axe. When I returned my eyes to his, the only remaining resemblances I could see between the soldier in the photograph and the old man before me were in the color of his eyes and his wedge face. His eyes were the same black. Only their expression had changed. In the photograph, his eyes had a serious, almost angry look in them. Now they held the look of resignation and acceptance, of peace. With years of retirement behind him, the scores that caused his stern expression in the photograph were long settled.

"Evan played golf twice every day," Floyd said. "He went once in the morning and again in the afternoon. The men rose early. They performed calisthenics, ran around the golf course—the only use of the course permitted to the men—ate breakfast in the mess tent, and then received

their morning briefings. While Evan played golf, they
tested, checked, cleaned, oiled, and rechecked the artillery
pieces for the two hours before lunch. They had an hour
for eating lunch but, at thirteen-hundred, they always left
the golf course. By that time, Evan had easily played his
morning round of golf."

I imagined the spectacle the Army created for the golf
course's wealthy neighbors. They would have seen men
running in the mornings, pulling artillery pieces in and out
of the parking lot, and filling every nearby open space with
equipment. They would have observed military vehicles,
their diesel engines rumbling and puffing black plumes of
smoke, coming and going at all hours of the day. At night,
when absolute silence returned, they must have puzzled
over the strangeness of it all.

"At twenty-two hundred," Floyd said, using what must
have been the same stern and uncompromising tone he had
used back at the golf course, "it was lights out. As simple
and easy as life at the camp became, we all knew what was
coming. I insisted on strict military discipline. I kept us
prepared for the real mission we all knew was coming."

It was normal for the battalion to live under a burden
of uncertainty, but the golf arrangement between the Army
and the Navy brought relief for a time. Floyd described how
they prepared for the possibility of waking up one morning
at the golf course, but then falling asleep the same night
at a base in Nevada, Arizona, New Mexico, Colorado, or
maybe Texas.

Uncertainty was the Army's certainty, but the pending
golf game relieved the men from any outcome other than
the 170th spending the entire month of August in Los
Angeles. They would stay right where they were. Also, no
one was uncertain about Evan. It had been Floyd who, once
the official word was out that the Army was looking for its

best golfer, brought Evan's name to the general's attention. The general, upon hearing about Evan's two-a-day practices in California, had frowned, doubted, telephoned someone at West Point, someone else in Washington, D.C., another in McCall, Idaho, and then dropped the receiver. Right then he ordered arrangements to fly him and his bag of clubs to El Rancho Golf Course Army camp.

When people fly from east to west, the planes arrive while several hours of daylight remain. This is especially true in August. The general used the warm afternoon to become familiar with the course. Like a celebrity, his entourage accompanied him. They walked along while he snuck in a practice round of golf, rushing to finish before the battalion returned from artillery practice. Intense moments of silence preceded each of the general's tee-shots, followed with loud roars of applause when his ball stopped just off a fairway. All was still while he selected an iron, then applause when his ball stopped well short of a green. On the green, all was once again quiet as he hit a couple of putts, and then everyone clapped while he stomped to his next hole.

"I'll find you some shoes," a lieutenant said, eager to say anything helpful to the general. "You won't want to wear those boots when you play."

A dogleg on a golf course occurs where a fairway makes a turn toward its green, and doglegs are said to either turn to the left or to the right. The dogleg's turn on the eighteenth at El Rancho Golf Course made a hard turn to the left. Strategically-placed sand traps lined the entire length of the 479-yard, par-five hole, one of which sat directly in front of the dogleg's turn and another which sat at the turn's far side. Well placed tee-shots targeted the center of the fairway, between the two sand traps, because from such a position, a wide-open view around the turn was available. Players could see all the way to the green. Most golfers at the El Rancho either landed in one of the traps or, for the same reason anxiety about trouble causes it, they erred by trying to stay too far from it. The trouble, in this case, was twofold. There was a cluster of tall trees past the sand traps, and there was another cluster beside the first trap. To miss the sand often meant searching in the trees.

When Floyd discovered Sergeant Taylor questioning the men about their hysteria, he learned the dogleg on eighteen was half of the answer. The general was the other half. The story was that, while the general was playing his quick practice round, there grew an unspoken tension between the general and his crowd. The tension was due to the general's desire to avoid being found practicing. He began repeating short glances over his shoulder, taking quick looks to the clubhouse, and making blatant stares at the tents that stood around the parking lots. As he proceeded, both his pace of play and his agitation noticeably increased. An older second lieutenant had the privilege of carrying the general's bag of clubs, but he also had the difficulty of keeping up with the general's pace of play.

"Here's your club," the lieutenant said. He rushed to catch up to the general and stood in the middle of the fairway, gasping for breath. He offered a two iron.

"Why in hell are you panting?" the general asked. "Is that sweat? You're hurting my game."

The general played the dogleg safely, for his tee-shot stopped well short of the turn. It was his second shot, however, a chip-shot, that was a bit wild. The ball went too far and found the dense cluster of trees at the far end of the turn. The general had shouted, "Crap!" and slammed his club into the fairway grass. He then threw his club into the tree cluster. The throw, as it was described to Floyd, was two-handed, included a powerful turn like an Olympic hammer thrower's, and resulted in the high-flying golf club colliding with the hard summer bark of a tree. Echoes followed the club's knock on wood.

"You would have laughed as hard as the rest of them," Floyd said. "The men were bent over with laughter. Mine was the only dry eye in the barrack."

"Sure I would have," I said. "I would have laughed myself to tears."

When the battalion returned from its training exercises, it was obvious to everyone in the 170th that the general and his staff had arrived. Still, the fact remained largely unspoken. The news traveled through the men like a scent. They quickly secured the vehicles and equipment, cleaned and dressed—taking extra swipes at buttons, boots, and buckles—observed strict military decorum by giving it extra snap, and then assembled in the mess tent where the general was expected to make his first appearance. The silent news of the general's presence was loud, played like a full-blast stereo without any speakers. There was electricity without sound. Eye contact told the fact, "Yes, sirs" were quick and crisp, and everyone seemed to be either doing, or on his way to doing, some important task. They walked with purposeful strides, carrying notebooks, scraps of paper, clipboards, and the many other visual excuses found on military bases.

The general first gave an officer briefing in the headquarters tent. He made the officers understand that his current visit was not about a secret mission, though secret it should remain. Instead, he called preparation for the Army's upcoming competition against the Navy a "special" mission. He described the role Evan was to play and gave orders for Evan's day-to-day activities. The orders were almost identical to those given to the Navy's

Knudsen. Evan's orders included his golfing all day, every day, eating quite well, resting when possible—when not playing golf—relief of artillery training, and working with two golf instructors the Army hired to help. The idea of a military ball was considered as a possible morale booster, but because the men were enjoying the leisure of camp El Rancho while so many others were dying in foreign lands, the idea was rejected.

The day following the general's arrival, while the battalion was again away for its afternoon artillery practice, the general stayed and golfed with Evan. It was just the two of them, but by "just the two of them," Floyd meant that the general and Evan were the only ones who played golf. There had been, of course, the general's entourage and the two golf instructors. The instructors acted as caddies, and the others followed along.

Each instructor tried to establish his credibility with a display of his depth of knowledge about the game, and they talked the entire eighteen holes. They gave tips like "try this," "aim toward the trouble," "open your club face," "close your club face," "lay-up short on this one," "go long," "loosen your grip," "chip it out," and "use your sand wedge here." After this last tip, the general tightened his jaw and squeezed his lips into a frown. The golf instructor from Florida, after noisily rattling around in the general's bag and failing to locate a nine iron, gave up his search with a complaint.

"You don't have a nine iron," he said in disbelief. "What is this? Did you lose it? You simply must have a nine iron for the game."

It was then that the general's frown changed in color from an angry white to a shade of amber. None of the entourage acknowledged the change. Instead, they became especially quiet after the instructor's unfortunate discovery of the missing club. No one told the instructor the club was then lying in a cluster of trees. Someone would quietly retrieve the club when they reached the dogleg turn of the eighteenth hole.

Par is the score standard for the game of golf. In 1943, shooting par at El Rancho Golf Course required an exact score of seventy-two. The general shot ninety-four that day, twenty-two strokes above par, but he remained in good spirits because Evan scored seventy-one. Evan played well, despite the instructors' chatter and the growing confidence of the instructor caddying for him. While play progressed, the man became louder, more animated, and more certain of the wisdom of his instructions. When they walked off the eighteenth green, the tricky par-five dogleg left where Evan's ball rattled in the cup after five strokes, the instructor from Arizona stood as tall as the Grand Canyon was deep, and the caddie yelped and jumped like a puppy.

The general headed back east, satisfied with the arrangements and, above all, impressed by Evan's ability to play. He scheduled his return for the following month, when he would play in the game against the Navy. He left Evan with five full weeks to enjoy playing golf.

"My orders were clear," Floyd said.

I stopped him from proceeding further with his narration of events. He was tired, and he had that quiet, labored voice that came with his speaking at length. He sounded like he had at the end of my first visit. His water glass was empty, several times he had taken his walker to the restroom, he drooped in his recliner, and he struggled with his memory. He was clear about his last words. He was to allow Evan to play golf.

I made up an excuse about some prior engagement. I could see he was anxious to keep talking, but he was done for the day. If he had been riding in an automobile just then, swaying with the vehicle's motion, he would not have heard the engine's hum, the tires on the pavement, or the air whistling around the car windows. He would have just fallen asleep. As I was leaving, Floyd called to me.

"Do you promise you will return?" he asked. "There is so much more to tell."

"Of course I will," I answered. "As long as you have information about Evan and the golf course, I will come back and listen to your every word."

"Good," Floyd said. "Then I will think about it. I plan to tell you everything. Did you hear that? Everything! I plan to tell it all, even if it kills me."

I looked at him and laughed.

"Great," I said. "Then you can count on me. I will come and listen to you talk yourself to death."

CHAPTER 4

~ ROUTINE, A WATCHER, AND THE WATCHED ~

Routine on the golf course was twofold. For the men, the days were spent drilling, training, and practicing. They worked to perfect the art of killing with artillery. They spent the mornings maintaining the equipment, learning artillery strategies, training with their gun crews, and practicing various speed drills for moving the guns while facing enemy fire. Evan, on the other hand, spent his time preparing to beat the Navy in the game of golf. His golfing twice a day became a regimen of golfing all day, every day. After an early wakeup call, he joined the men for calisthenics, running, and breakfast, but then he went off for a morning round of golf. He returned for lunch with the men, but then it was the battalion that went off. They went to beach positions along the coast, Evan stayed at the course to practice, and he returned with the men to share dinner every evening.

Evan chose to eat with the men because he liked them and they liked him. Their company provided him relief from the two distinguished golf instructors the Army hired. Chadwick and Fletcher spent their time following Evan, discussing golf, giving advice, and talking about what he could do to become a better player. Chadwick was from Arizona, Fletcher from Florida, they were in their fifties, and both looked equally out of place when surrounded by military men. They wore colorful outfits they assumed were

the height of golf fashion. Unfortunately, their clothes so
strangely contrasted with the drab-olive Army uniforms that
the two looked like circus clowns among men of war. They
wore knee socks tucked into knickers that flared at the
hip, sweaters crossed with a rainbow of colors, and brown
leather shoes with white laces.

Chadwick had greater self-confidence than Fletcher.
He carried himself with the air of assurance that comes
from knowing things that others do not. Were it not for his
golfing outfit, Chadwick could have been mistaken for a
professor residing in an ivy-covered building somewhere in
New Hampshire, Rhode Island, or Connecticut. He was the
bossier of the two, even going so far as to tell Evan what
to eat.

"You need red meat," Chadwick said during their first
meal together. They were sitting inside the mess tent, and
there were men sitting everywhere on rows of tables. Evan
sat across from the instructors, and he noticed the men at
the next table listening to the conversation, exchanging eye
contact and smiling.

"Is that so?" Evan asked. "You want me to eat meat? Tell
me why."

Chadwick first glanced at Fletcher, received a nod, and
answered. "Meat gives you strength. It gives you power. The
more meat you eat, the farther you'll drive your tee shots.
You want that."

Fletcher sat beside Chadwick and nodded. Though he
was the quieter of the two, Fletcher was more animated and,
as the men discovered during that first meal together, he
was the more entertaining. Fletcher took large bites of food
and chewed while listening to Chadwick. He kept his mouth
closed, eyes wide on Evan, and churned his jaws with the
slow motion of a grinder. At irregular intervals, he tongued
his food into lumps that showed as bulges in his cheeks, and

he nodded his head to indicate when he thought Chadwick made an especially important point.

"That's right," he said. "Eat meat and hit long drives. If you want power, strength, and distance, you have to eat more meat."

While chewing and adjusting bites, Fletcher extended his fork like a pointer. The men surrounding the group touched their neighbors and watched. They made a game of counting the time his fork remained pointing at Evan—the record was thirty-two seconds.

"What else?" Evan asked Chadwick, just to silence the men's snickering at Fletcher.

Fletcher never realized he was the brunt of their jokes, for each time Chadwick made what Fletcher thought was an important point, Fletcher put his left hand on his hip, stopped chewing, leaned his right elbow on the table, and stabbed the air with his fork. He would stare at Evan and nod his head like drips from a faucet.

After breakfast, Evan, Chadwick, and Fletcher chipped onto a practice green located just before the first tee. Next, they practiced putting and played a full round of golf. They took their time in order to re-emphasize instructions given the previous day. The threesome always returned to eat lunch with the men, after which they repeated the same routine when the battalion left for afternoon artillery practice. The timing resulted in the three arriving for both lunch and dinner right after completing the challenging eighteenth hole, with its dogleg, trees, and sand traps. Evan was able to relax and talk freely with the men while Chadwick and Fletcher ate in silence. Their silence reflected their scores, and their scores reflected their inability to conquer the dogleg on eighteen. They always managed to overcome their frustration in time to continue their breakfast instructions.

In 1943 the fields across from the golf course were referred to as a "tent city." As time went on, it became a confused cluster of buildings and houses, looking as though a neighborhood had piled up against the dam of the golf course. On the easterly corner of the course, at the farthest distance from the tent city, sat the neighborhood of mansions. The homes had mature trees on their lots, large swimming pools surrounded by brick patios, and bedrooms with dormers that looked out on the golf course. They were the homes of nearby Hollywood's wealthiest citizens and its most influential film moguls, all of whom were aware of the Army's occupation. By the first week of August, most had already seen Evan and the instructors out on the golf course, and one homeowner had even confronted the trio.

"I was there when it happened." Chadwick ran into the headquarters tent, wide-eyed and breathless, where he explained the incident to Floyd. "It happened just as Evan was about to pitch a ball onto the green."

"Slow down," Floyd said. "What happened? What in the world are you talking about?"

"Tell him," Fletcher said. He stood with one palm opened to Chadwick and the other flat before Floyd. He spoke with a tone of urgency.

"We were practicing with Evan," Chadwick said, "just as we were hired to do. Actually, we had him practicing his chip shot. You know those are tough shots to make, but they really pay off in tournament play."

"And so does putting," Fletcher added.

"Yes," Chadwick said. "Putting is important, too, but we never got that far. It was just as Evan made and held a perfect backswing that we heard it. He was poised to hit the ball, but we heard a woman scream."

"A woman?" Floyd asked.

"Yes. It was a terrible scream," Chadwick said. "She sounded surprised, scared, and angry, all at the same time."

"Where was she?"

"We were in the fairway, and we heard her calling from a nearby house. You know those really big houses. Anyway, after the scream, we heard her yell, 'Go away! Who are you? What do you want?' We looked in the bushes just as she called for help."

"Tell him what Evan did," Fletcher said.

"Evan? Did he do something?"

"You bet he did," Chadwick said. "He ran up a trail near us, carrying his pitching wedge like a club."

Chadwick described how Evan pushed through a thin line of foliage separating the fairway from the home. There he encountered the frightened woman standing beside a swimming pool full of water.

"When I caught up to them, I saw a young lady, well-covered by a towel, directing Evan toward where she pointed at the bushes on her left. She was obviously frightened, but our sudden appearance did not seem to increase her concern. I also looked where she was pointing to the bushes, and I saw Evan chasing after a man wearing a military uniform and running away through a cluster of rhododendron bushes. I followed Evan across the patio, through the bushes, and after the man, but I only saw what happened from back in the bushes."

"Tell him what happened," Fletcher said. "Tell him what happened when Evan caught the man."

"Evan never caught the guy," Chadwick said. "I came through a hedge of English laurel just as the man was jumping into the passenger side of a Navy-blue sedan. Evan caught the car as it began driving. He swung his pitching wedge, and the iron smashed into one of the car's taillights, shattering it. We watched the car speed away. I saw two

35

heads in the front seat, the broken taillight, and the license plate and colors of what Evan said was a Navy car. We were walking back through the foliage when we heard a man shouting at Fletcher."

"At Fletcher?"

"Yes, at me," Fletcher said. "When I got to the pool, I was alone. They left me. There was not even the woman, but I met a man coming out of the house and yelling at me. He wanted to know what I did to his daughter and, thankfully, that's when Chadwick and Evan returned. Evan looked annoyed. He had one of those angry, dangerous, and reassuring looks of a soldier. The homeowner saw him and stopped threatening me. 'He got away,' Evan said out loud, speaking to no one in particular and walking as though he intended to return to the golf course. Thankfully, though, he slowed and stopped when he reached me and the homeowner. The man asked what had happened."

"Evan talked to the homeowner?" Floyd interrupted.

"You bet he did," Fletcher said. "Evan told him that it was probably the Navy spying on him. The man asked if Evan had done something wrong, and he demanded to know Evan's name. Before he could answer, though, the homeowner turned to look at Chadwick and me. He was not happy."

While the instructors stood describing the event, Floyd remained sitting with his hands positioned as though he intended to push away from his desk. He pressed his lips so tightly that they appeared as a white crease in his face.

"You did not get us in trouble with the neighbors?" Floyd said.

"Not at all," Chadwick answered, frowning at Fletcher. "Fletcher told him we had heard a woman scream, but he also suggested we were not the ones being watched.

Fletcher said that maybe they were watching the woman, like the Navy would rather spy on a woman than spy on the Army. The man dismissed that idea."

"'You heard my daughter'," Chadwick said, pretending to be the man by lifting his shoulders and speaking with a deep voice of authority. "The man sounded like he was used to giving commands and receiving quick answers. When he turned from me to look at Evan, I got a chance to examine him. I placed him in his early sixties. He was leisurely dressed in patterned slacks, brown loafers, a buttoned shirt, and an unbuttoned sweater. His hair was short and black, with heavy graying along the sides, and he held a newspaper in his hand. He must have been reading the paper before rushing to his daughter's aid, but he stood there rolling the paper like he intended to hit a dog."

"What dog?" Floyd asked.

"There was no dog," Chadwick said. "There was only the man. Fletcher and I listened while the man spoke to Evan."

"'Who are you?' the man asked Evan."

"'Private Evan Wilkins, sir,' Evan told him. He apologized for barging in on him and mentioned hearing the scream. 'I ran over here and found your daughter pointing toward the bushes,' he said. 'I chased a man to a car that was waiting for him. He jumped in, and they sped away.'"

"'Why you? Why the Navy? And why in my back yard?'"

"Evan explained the Army's occupation of the golf course," Chadwick said, "but the circumstance was one with which the gentleman was already acquainted. He knew all about the Army occupying his golf course. Evan also explained his reason for being down on the course and introduced me and Fletcher as his golf instructors. Evan said he would be reporting the event to his commanding officer." At that, Floyd grinned.

"The man said he would be notifying the authorities," Chadwick said, "but then he looked at his house, at Evan, and said, 'I owe you. Thank you for assisting my daughter.'"

What Chadwick had not known was that during the poolside conversation, the young lady had disappeared without going too far. When he had departed with Evan, no one saw the window shade inside of the pool house falling like the lashes of an eyelid.

They had returned to the golf course where Evan had found it difficult to settle down from the poolside excitement. He was agitated and hit every ball too hard. His wild shots distracted him and compounded the effect of failure so that he should have taken a break instead of continuing to practice. Chadwick and Fletcher were even more distracted than Evan. They recounted the sound of the scream, the chase, and the homeowner's threatening approach. The word "Navy" kept coming up in their conversation and they rather enjoyed the thought of being the subject of a "spy mission." They were so busy watching the bushes that they quit watching Evan while he pitched his shots too high over the nearby green.

"Let's get dinner," Evan said, entirely failing to resuscitate his game. "Hey, you two," he yelled when they failed to respond to his first suggestion, "I said let's get dinner."

That evening in the mess hall during dinner, the place buzzed with the news of the encounter. When Evan entered, every man looked at him. He repeated the story twice, but then he referred continuing questions to the instructors. Chadwick and Fletcher were ready. They were eager to supply specific details. From the manner of their arm-waving, they appeared to relish the questioners' attention more than they enjoyed possessing the answers. Unfortunately, most of the men's questions sought answers neither instructor knew. Those most repeated were: "What was she wearing?" "What did she look like?" "How can we see her?" "What's her name?"

Floyd took the event more seriously than anyone. He required that a complete incident report be filed, interviewed the instructors, and ordered Evan to meet with him that evening at battalion headquarters. The meeting took place at Floyd's metal desk, in an area divided into several sections inside of one giant military tent where each element of the battalion was assigned its own designated area, including medical, supply, and headquarters. Battery B was located deep past these areas. There were desks with lamps, chairs, typewriters, black rotary-dial telephones, maps, drawings, file cabinets, garbage cans filled with used carbon paper, "in" boxes, "out" boxes, and everywhere there was paper written on, typed on, crumpled, printed, and sitting unused in stacks of boxes. There were people walking here and there, even though evening had come. They glanced at Evan on his way to Floyd's desk. He stopped and saluted.

"At ease, Wilkins," Floyd said. "Sit down. Tell me what happened."

While Evan described the details of the event, Floyd kept his head down writing notes for his report. He looked up when he had completed his notes.

"Did you talk with the girl?" he asked. "Did you see her? I mean, if she saw you again, would she recognize you?"

"I just ran past her to pursue the Navy man," Evan said. "She was gone when I returned. Who knows what she saw? What can you see in a blink?"

"So," Floyd said, "it is likely she wouldn't recognize you if she saw you again?"

Evan was surprised that his superior officer would ask about the girl. He expected the men's questions back in the

mess hall, but he assumed Floyd would maintain his strict
military demeanor.

"I doubt she could identify me," he said. Later that
night, after the lights-out call, he considered Floyd's final
question. He was sure the young lady would not recognize
him, but he was equally certain that he would recognize her.
He had caught a mere glimpse of her as he passed her on
his way toward danger, but he knew he would recognize her
if he ever saw her again. Any man would. He never lied to
Floyd. He simply failed to mention that he would recognize
her. Beautiful young ladies appear more so when they are
alone and frightened. He came to her rescue. Evan smiled
in the dark at the recollection of her dark wet hair, flushed
cheeks, alert eyes, extended arm, pointing finger, and
animated posture. He remembered her as tall and athletic.
He grinned to sleep with the thought she could have run
down the Navy man all by herself.

During the following morning's round of golf,
Chadwick and Fletcher kept a close watch on all of the
bushes, trees, and hedges. They played a nervous round.
When they walked down the fairway where they heard the
scream and call for help, both kept their eyes fixed on the
exact spot where Evan had run up to the swimming pool.

"Someone could be lurking in there right now,"
Fletcher whispered.

"You're right," Chadwick said. "Just because we can't see
them, doesn't mean there's no one watching."

Evan was unconcerned and pretended to be
disinterested. He did, however, make three quick glances
to the same spot Chadwick and Fletcher watched. He had
only eighty yards to reach the green with his approach shot,
and that is where he took his time selecting his pitching
wedge—the same club he used to hit the sedan. It was
then that he took his first glance toward the bushes, but

he looked for the same amount of time needed to draw a breath. He looked a second time just after hitting his approach shot. He was poised with his feet on each side of the ball, his weight balanced on the balls of his feet, and his club held loose in his grip. He made several checks for distance—looking at the ball, the green, and back to the ball—and then he hit. After watching his ball land on the green and hop with backspin, he took his second glance. He looked for the final time after repairing the dent his ball made on the green. He hit his putt first, retrieved the ball, used a wooden tee to loosen and fluff up the dent, and, just as he handed his putter to Chadwick, he looked at the bushes.

Evan never saw anyone watching him that day. Instead of the bushes, he should have looked to the high dormers of the home behind him.

CHAPTER 5

~ *WHERE'D HE GO?* ~

At lunch that day, when Chadwick and Fletcher were about to begin eating, several of the men approached and surrounded them with lunch trays. Before either instructor took one bite, the men started asking questions about golf and began a serious discussion of specific nuances of the game. It seemed as though they had developed a great interest in the game. With their lunch trays full and their questions unending, they brought their friendliest and most engaging attitudes either instructor had as yet encountered. The attention surprised the two, but it took no longer than a question before each was captured by the opportunity to talk. Like attorneys before the media, they spoke to be recognized as the professionals providing the most expert answers to the questions.

Chadwick and Fletcher were engaging. Neither sought to do anything other than provide answer upon answer, and they did so while giving animated and detailed explanations, remaining fully engaged until the men were called to depart for afternoon practice. The men seemed reluctant to leave the instructors' wise counsel and talked them into walking with them out to the trucks idling in the parking lot. The soldiers smiled, waved, and shouted goodbyes as the trucks pulled out with their heavy artillery pieces in tow. Chadwick and Fletcher waved back through the exhaust.

"That was priceless," Chadwick said, smiling like a grandfather.

"Yes it was," Fletcher agreed, but he did so while looking about and frowning. "I cannot find Evan," he said. "Where did he go?"

"He was just here," Chadwick answered, but he too began turning his head to search.

"Of course he was just here," Fletcher said.

"So where is he? When did he leave? Now that I think about it, he never showed up for lunch."

"Of course he did," Fletcher said. "Wasn't he the one who asked about divot replacement?"

"That was Campbell," Chadwick said.

"Then, wasn't he the one who asked about marking a ball on the green?"

"That was Savage."

"How to count strokes when your ball goes out of bounds?"

"Willis."

"What to do when your ball gets stuck in wet ground?"

"Lopez."

"When to use a two iron?"

"Morgan."

"How to play a dogleg?"

"Gill."

"When a mulligan is allowed?"

"That was all of them," Chadwick said. Turning to look at Fletcher, he added, "Now that I think about it, I'm certain I never saw Evan at lunch."

"Where'd he go?"

What the instructors did not know was that Evan and the men had earlier conspired against them. As soon as the men approached the instructors' lunch table, eager and loaded with countless questions about golf, Evan slipped out of the mess hall tent, retrieved his clubs, and spent the time practicing on a few of the holes on the very distant side of the course.

Golfers are never alone on the course. A group usually plays ahead and another behind, and the wind carries voices—people talking, cursing, laughing, and cheering. During the Army's occupation of El Rancho Golf Course, however, the course was empty, but it was far from quiet, for every golf course has its unique sounds of silence. The sounds are those that come without man, such as leaves rustling, birds singing, woodpeckers knocking, squirrels chattering, naturally-pruned twigs hitting the ground, and little flying things flapping and buzzing in the air. That afternoon, Evan was alone and playing with the sounds of nature.

His step was light while walking, driving, hitting, chipping, pitching, and putting around his short circuit of three holes. He addressed each ball, chose the precise club he needed, took great care while making each swing, and strode onward like a champion. His movements were not ostentatious, but he did seem to be performing a ritual meant to be seen by another. Were he asked under oath about his decision to replay one certain hole, a hole he played several times that afternoon, he would have admitted wanting—expecting—an encounter with the young lady from the day before. The men of Battery B were so sure of this outcome that they had little trouble convincing Evan to let them distract Chadwick and Fletcher. Because of their ploy, Evan enjoyed his time on the course that day more than any up to that point. He found himself desiring and anticipating an encounter with the young lady, and laughed out loud at his absurd wonder for the Navy's absence when he could have used them.

Evan just so happened to be close, again, to the fairway entrance that led to where he encountered the young lady.

After hitting a nice sixty-yard shot onto the green before him, he purposefully glanced over to the trail leading up to her home. He saw nothing moving except what was blowing in the wind. A chance encounter is what he wanted, but he grinned at the thought that their meeting would be unexpected only on her part. He again looked up to where the pool would have been seen, but all he saw were bushes, trees, and the highest peaks of her home. He saw no one, but it was then he became self-conscious for having looked—for looking long enough to make out a window or two. He felt embarrassed for peering so hard and for being so obvious about it. He had looked for her, and if she or anyone else had observed him, they would have seen in Evan a character he did not own. He was not a watcher. He was not lonely. He was not desperate. After fifteen months in the military, he had not had a single moment of female conversation or companionship. He had captured and preserved in his mind the image of the young lady by her pool, though it was only a flash. He favored the image like a painting of a beautiful woman. He wanted to see her again.

When his face reddened, the whites of his eyes appeared whiter, the brown of his pupils appeared browner, and the tightening of his jaw showed the distinct muscles of his face. He returned to himself by standing erect, looking ahead, and then moving ahead with his game. Just as he was leaving, fully intending to golf his way back to where dinner would be served in another hour or two, a new sound reached him. It was the sound of man.

Evan did not look. Unwanted visitors have a way of inspiring action on the part of the visited, and so it was for Evan when the two instructors hollered from the tee box behind him.

"There you are!" The voice was Fletcher's. "Evan. We're here. It's us."

46

He looked over his shoulder to acknowledge he heard them, but then he hit a putt that had "legs," for the ball traveled too fast, missed the cup, and rolled beyond the hole. In their rush to catch Evan, the instructors' clubs rattled in their bags until quieting when the two stopped on the green. Evan heard nothing except their heavy breathing until he was finished replacing the flag stick in the hole.

"We lost you," Chadwick said, winded from rushing to catch up with Evan.

"You two looked busy," Evan said. "All I did was play until you finished teaching. I thought you would be quick to come and find me."

"The men have taken a real interest in golf," Fletcher said. "We had to encourage them. We answered every one of their questions. Can you believe it? The men want to learn about golf. We intend to bring it up with your leader. His name is Floyd, right?"

"My commanding officer? Yes," Evan said, "his name is Floyd, Major Floyd Akerly. What do you intend to bring up with him?"

"The interest of the men," Chadwick said. "We think it would be a good idea if the men could take golf lessons in the morning. They have the interest, and we have the time. Lessons could help relieve the men from the boredom of artillery practice. They could use the distraction."

"You might wait," Evan said. "They showed interest today, but what about tomorrow? You had better wait to see if their interest lasts."

Following Evan's suggestion, Fletcher glanced about and saw he was standing near to where the seaman had spied on Evan. He looked up the trail where the young lady had called for help. He pointed up the trail, frowned, looked at Chadwick, and spoke to Evan.

"How can you be out here alone?" he asked. "I mean, wasn't it creepy? Didn't you feel like someone was watching you?"

"I never had that feeling," Evan said. "I felt completely alone."

CHAPTER 6

~ *DINNER ENGAGEMENT* ~

At times, the military line of command is less like a chain and more like a tree, just like that of a family. When a child in a family does not get what he wants from his immediate, his mother, he will make the same appeal to his father. Using the two for or against each other is an age-tested trick, but when the parents are united—as all couples should appear to be in matters of their children—the child might next reach for a higher branch. Here, though, the comparison of the tree and chain falters, for in a family, grandparent intervention between the parents and the child is little more than meddling. Higher branches are weaker than those at the trunk.

With the military, however, higher branches have much greater authority. The general's order that Evan be relieved from his regular duties was unquestionable, and so it was that Floyd found himself removed as Evan's immediate superior. He was removed, but not entirely. He did, after all, command that Evan report on the spying activities of the Navy. But that had been like residual authority, similar to how a teacher forever holds tenure over a student. Floyd internalized this anger by reasoning irrationally.

He felt as though he could no more order Evan to run, do pushups, clean latrines, oil guns, load shells, or fire at targets than he could order him to quit golfing. What had his authority become? Floyd asked the question over and over, but the answer he replayed to feed his offense was that he had become nothing. He knew it was the general who had taken his command, for the general was clear.

"No one tells Evan what to do," the general said. "Anything to do with him must be cleared by me first. Is that understood?"

"Yes, sir," Floyd answered, more so from obedience than conviction.

He forced himself to say what he was supposed to say because his feelings were rebelling against reason. Floyd was certain the general was wrong to trivialize his command. He laughed when he recalled how he ordered Evan to report and tell everything that happened at the Nichols' house.

"Give me a full report," he recalled saying to Evan, knowing full well that his command violated the general's order. It was a risk, he knew, but one he felt he could not avoid.

Who will complain? Evan? he thought. *No, Evan still respects me as his superior officer.* Floyd sat alone at his desk and allowed a grin to flash between two of his frowns. *Evan sure came when I called him. There is no doubt about it. Evan knows I am still in charge—regardless of what the general said. If the general thinks he can elevate one of my privates above me, then I will certainly obey.*

He stared at a nearby wall and grinned, whispering the words of his resolution. The decision was too easy, like swimming down a flowing stream. A current pulled him toward obedience, and he swam to go faster, thinking nothing about the possibility he was heading for what might be a deadly drop—one that crashes, thrashes, and froths at the base of a waterfall.

Everyone in the Army takes orders, and they know Evan takes them from me. I'll go along with it, but when his "special mission" is over, nothing will be the same. Evan will either be the private hero of the entire Army—someone I will have to treat with care—or reduced to something pathetic and humiliated.

Floyd smiled at the thought. He pressed his lips, lowered the ends of his mouth, narrowed his eyes, and looked for movement inside the tent. He reached a decision that made him laugh and nod his understanding.

I would know what to do with him then. A fallen Evan would be the first one I set to firing the artillery. He would clean every gun. His night watch would start at oh two hundred, and I would make him stay behind when the other men went on leave. Evan would go from the highest-ranking private in the Army to the lowest. I would make him a runner.

Still seated at his desk in the headquarters tent, Floyd ended his daydream with a throaty chuckle. He sat with his head on his fists, his elbows on the desk, and his thoughts gone with his plan. He never heard the orderly's approach.

"Someone to see you, sir," the young man said.

The voice surprised Floyd, and he reacted by jumping to his feet. Behind the orderly, he saw an older gentleman wearing a white shirt, wide tie, dark jacket, and gray hat. The man was a civilian. Beside him stood a young lady wearing short, white gloves. She grinned but kept her lips pressed and her eyes fixed on the man with whom she arrived. Floyd rotated his shoulders behind him, visibly inflating his chest, extended his hand with a thrust, and shook the man's outstretched hand like a knob.

"How can I assist you?" he asked.

Floyd fought his urge to look at the girl, but he lost the fight, for the scent of her perfume was already in the air he breathed. He had to look, and his quick peeks failed to make eye contact. He saw her pink sweater, white blouse, some sort of gold broach, brown hair, pretty face, and pure white teeth. He decided the scent of her perfume came from somewhere on the nape of her neck.

Floyd was captivated. He shook the man's hand without listening to his words, and he turned so the best side of his profile was positioned where she could notice it. His pose was that of a serious and intentionally friendly military man, but after Floyd failed to answer something the man had said, the gentleman cleared his throat and tried again.

"Excuse me," he said. "My name is John Nichols, as you may already know. An officer of yours came to the assistance of my daughter Amanda. We have come to formally thank him. I would like to favorably recommend the soldier to his superior officer."

"I know the incident," Floyd said. "The soldier is not an officer. He's only a private." Floyd's words came fast, his tone was defensive, and he gave both irrelevant and implied information. "In fact, Evan no longer trains with our battalion. His assignment is to play golf. Anyway, I'm his superior. My name is Major Floyd Akerly."

The man shook Floyd's hand, but Floyd turned to look more than hear the young lady's questions. "Did he leave?" she asked. "Is he here now?"

Floyd liked her tone. She sounded neither disappointed nor relieved that Evan might be gone. She really did not care. Floyd turned and looked Amanda full in her face.

"No," he said. "Evan is still here. The men should be finishing dinner. If you will wait, I'll send for him now." The orderly who brought Amanda and her father had not yet left. "Get Wilkins in here," Floyd commanded, believing authority impressed women. He was pleased by the orderly's snap in response to the command. Instead of grinning, he frowned at the back of the departing orderly. Though scowling, he took great care to keep the good side of his profile toward Amanda.

It was especially unusual for a woman to visit the camp, so eyes here and there took little glances to see her.

The scent of her perfume alerted every man in the headquarters tent of her presence. The aroma, her poise, the color of her clothes, the moist red of her nails and lips, and the sight of tan legs showing below her skirt stood out in the bland, homogeneous universe of the tent. Her face was fresh, devoid of anything but beauty. She was perfectly proportioned, with high cheekbones, large eyes, and long dark lashes that nearly reached her fine, well-shaped brows. Her lips were covered with a moist red shine and appeared to be swollen by innocence. Floyd liked the way they curved into a pleasing smile, a smile he saw she shared with no one but her father. Her ears dangled some simple diamond arrangement, and her face was surrounded by long brunette hair that fell with slight waves below her shoulders. A hint of pink showed on her face, and this color Floyd attributed to her being conscious of his attention. Floyd listened to Mr. Nichols, and every time he glanced at Amanda, he found her eyes on her father.

The orderly ran without stopping until bursting into Evan's barrack. The men of Battery B were talking, playing cards, writing letters, and performing other evening activities, but every one of them looked to the door. They saw the orderly's wide eyes and bent smile, and they watched him search until he found Evan. He then answered sixty questioning eyes.

"A woman is here," he said, winded by his run from headquarters. "She wants to see Evan."

The men's catcalls followed Evan from the barrack. By the time he crossed the large headquarters tent, stopped before Floyd, saluted, and waited for relief, he had already observed the young woman and her father. Of course he recognized her.

"This is Private Wilkins," Floyd said.

Evan turned to the father and nodded. "Private Evan Wilkins, sir."

"I remember you," Mr. Nichols said, shaking Evan's hand. "We came here to properly thank you for your assistance the other day. Please meet my daughter Amanda. She's the one you heard calling for help."

Evan turned, and his eyes met Amanda's for a second time. Whereas the first time he saw her eyes wide with fright, this second time he saw in them something like discomfort and embarrassment.

"Thank you for your help," she said. Before continuing, she grinned and glanced at her father. "I'm not sure what surprised me more, seeing the intruder or seeing you with that golf club. It all happened so fast. The man nearly scared me to death, but then you appeared and ran him off. Thank you again."

Amanda stepped toward Evan and extended her hand. He took it, met her eyes, and smiled. Her hand was warm in his, and it was soft. "You're welcome," he said.

Instead of returning her gaze to her father, she looked away to the floor, then back at Evan. Both laughed the way young people do when sharing curiosity. Such introductions are always better without the presence of others, especially the young lady's father.

"I'm having some people over on Friday," Mr. Nichols said. "We would consider it an honor if you would join us. It will be our way of properly thanking you, private."

Evan turned and looked at Floyd, respectfully asking permission with his eyes. Amanda and her father also looked and waited for Floyd to answer. He thought only a moment while shaking his head. "The men are not allowed off base alone. You know, with the war and all."

"Of course," Mr. Nichols said. "Then perhaps you can come too. Would that be allowed?"

Floyd took no time to answer. "Yes," he said, "that would work just fine."

The arrangement was made, and John and Amanda left. Later that night, long after Amanda was gone and long after the men stopped ribbing Evan, Floyd went to bed with his mind churning. He closed his eyes and thought about the coming dinner party, the approaching golf game, the war, Evan, and the possibility of spending time with Amanda.

Having Evan in the battery was not so bad after all. It was beginning to pay off for him. He was pleased with his quick thinking. On the spot, he had made up the rule that no soldier was allowed to leave the base alone. There was no such rule. If anything, no one was allowed to leave the base, period, except when they went to artillery practice. *I'm so clever,* he thought. *Because of my quick thinking, I'm now invited to Amanda's party.*

The last party Floyd attended was back in Ft. Lewis, Washington. He had just gotten his command, and stayed long enough to show off his new rank insignia. That was it—no mingling. He believed officers should never get too friendly with enlisted men, that they must maintain their distance and never let them forget who was boss. In this case, he intended to enjoy himself. He felt certain he could leave base for the evening without the general finding out, and he lay grinning at the thought that a night with Amanda was well worth the risk. Maybe he could find some reason for Evan to miss the party. Wouldn't that be something? Maybe he would make those two clowns—those instructors—give an evening golf lesson.

Evan had similar thoughts that night, but his excluded golf, the men, and the war. He went straight to thoughts of Amanda. Lying on his bunk, he closed his eyes, took a deep breath, and held it. He imagined he could smell her perfume. The scent of it lingered in his memory and evoked her image. He smiled before laughing, for despite the Army's ability to keep men surrounded by men, the sight of Amanda enlivened him. Everything about her became important—how she talked, what she said, how she sounded, smiled, blushed, laughed, took little glances, and how she held herself—everything about her. She was smooth and soft. He wanted to see her in more than his mind.

Evan wondered why Floyd lied. He knew there was no rule requiring soldiers to be accompanied when they left base. He knew they could leave only if they got permission from the highest-ranking officer on the base, but such permission was never granted. Were it not for Floyd's misrepresentation, he would have had to decline the invitation. As it was, though, he would be spending an evening with Amanda while her father entertained Floyd.

CHAPTER 7

~ GOLFING WITHOUT INSTRUCTION ~

The following day, just after their morning round of golf, Evan and the two instructors returned to the mess tent for lunch, as they had on the previous day. After sitting and eating for only a short time, several of the men arrived and again surrounded Chadwick and Fletcher. They asked questions about golf, but this time they did not seek tips and instructions about the game. Instead, they sought to learn just how it was that the two experts—for that is how they referred to the two—had mastered all of the complicated nuances of the game.

"You two know the game," Private Darrel Hansen said. Hansen was the oldest private in the 170th and his deep voice and southern accent added a tone of significance to everything he said. "But what we want to know is how you became experts and overcame all of the game's difficulties. How did you reach the point of perfection?"

Chadwick and Fletcher began speaking together, paused to glance at each other, and listened as Hansen continued. "You told us about the game," he said. "But we want to know about you. Tell us how you became instructors."

Men like to talk about themselves. This is especially true when they command an area of expertise, a high level of education, or a position esteemed by the general public such as doctor, lawyer, or politician. The pleasures they derive from talking about themselves come from an arrogance of ignorance and not from an ignorance of knowledge—for those who know, know. The mistake they make is with the men who fail to understand the impact their pedantic talk has on those near to them, especially those lacking in any such position or credentials. They talk with greater authority and about a greater breadth of subjects than those who have been formally educated. What unites all of these talkers, though, is their ready ability to discuss themselves, which is fine, if only they could understand that those listening—if, in fact, others remain listening for long—might desire to engage in the same enjoyment. An interesting experiment would be to disallow the word "I" from these talkers' vocabularies and see if confused silence follows.

Chadwick was the first to answer every question, which he answered the moment anybody asked one. Fletcher answered at the same time, but with less certitude and volume. The result was that he stopped talking at the beginning of his answers, frowned at Chadwick, and then waited for a pause before jumping back in. While waiting, though, he listened only so he might craft a more impressive answer than Chadwick's and, in this manner, the two instructors did not notice when Evan stood, returned his empty lunch tray, and then left the mess tent to retrieve his clubs to the sound of Chadwick's "The way I learned how to play golf was by playing golf."

There was quite a loud roar of laughter from the men. They nodded at each other, for such simple, insightful, and practical wisdom comes easily from talkers. Chadwick laughed, too, but he happened to catch sight of Fletcher frowning and waiting to add to the lesson.

"But playing is not enough," Fletcher said. "You need a good instructor so you don't keep repeating your bad habits." The men looked away from Chadwick. One pointed and nodded, several exchanged glances, and all ended with their eyes on Fletcher. "When I was young," he continued, speaking louder, "I had several bad habits. I opened my stance too wide, gripped my club too tight, and swung like I was hitting a baseball. I played with those bad habits for so long that they took me years to correct, but I finally did it. My father paid for golf lessons for me, and the instructor he hired was able to identify and correct all of the problems. Today I don't have any bad habits."

Everyone nodded their agreement and asked several more questions. Afterwards, the two instructors accompanied the men to the parking lot. When they stopped at the back of a large truck with a green tarp covering the back, Chadwick realized he had again lost sight of Evan. "Evan's gone," he said, frowning and glancing around the lot. "We have to go … now!"

"That's right," Hansen said. The men rushed to surround the instructors, grabbed them, deposited them in the back of the truck, and climbed in themselves. "We're taking you with us. You're coming to see our afternoon practice."

"No. How dare you. We are here for Evan." Chadwick saw Hansen bang on the back of the cab and felt the truck drive away from the golf course.

For the entire length of the drive out to their beach position at the coast, where the 170th practiced using artillery, Chadwick and Fletcher talked. Their complaints and threats were overcome by questions.

"You've just got to tell us that story about how you hit golf balls into the ocean from a cliff," Hansen said. "We loved that." The men nodded their heads in agreement.

Chadwick repeated his experience, and the discussion turned to creating divots. "Your artillery is the best divot creator," Fletcher said, laughing at the comparison between

59

playing golf and firing artillery. He surprised himself with the cleverness of the thought. "Both aim at a target," he said, describing the golfer and the artillery piece. "With golf, you shoot a ball, and with artillery, you shoot a ..." and here he faltered. He looked first to Chadwick for help and then to the men. Someone saved him by suggesting, "an artillery round," but at that moment Fletcher went on with, "A bomb. That's it. You shoot a bomb."

"Can't you just see it?" Hansen asked. "Here is our gun position at the beach. Compare this with the lawn back at Camp Golf Course. After only one round of artillery golf, the entire course would be cratered. The lawns would be destroyed and the greens would be smoldering craters. There would be splatters of dirt everywhere." Men who had not yet fought in Europe still laughed at such boyish thoughts.

While they were gone, Evan was alone and playing golf on the empty course. He had not solicited solitude, but the men figured he might wish to be free of Chadwick and Fletcher. After Amanda and her father's visit, the men, the majority of whom were in their late teens or early twenties, empathized with Evan and plotted to free him from the instructors. Following months and months of serious war training without free time or the chance to be with the opposite sex, they all would have loved to be on the golf course for an entire day. They envisioned playing golf with that tall, dark-haired, tan, smooth-skinned young lady instead of positioning, loading, aiming, firing, cleaning, yelling, repeating, and timing their maneuvers.

Artillery is loud. It results in a lingering numbness that rings in the ears. It also results in men spending much of their time daydreaming about where they would rather be or what they wish they were doing. That day, the men shared one scene in particular, one that included Evan,

Amanda, the golf course, and not a single golf instructor. The time was much better spent with such thoughts, for it was through Evan that each man was transported away from the noisy activity. They envisioned the quiet possibilities back at the El Rancho, and their visions manifested in smiles, whistles, hums, and chuckles. Each looked as though he very much enjoyed whatever he was then doing—happily training to kill.

Humor, too, was a staple of the young soldiers while training to kill. The instructors established themselves as reliable sources of humor, so the men naturally combined Chadwick and Fletcher with daydreaming and laughter. Later that afternoon, when the 170th was returning for dinner, everyone was anxious to find Evan and hear all the details of his assumed afternoon with Amanda. They expected to hear all about the romantic rendezvous they imagined during artillery practice that afternoon.

The eighteen holes of a golf course are split into two halves, with each half comprised of nine holes. The first half is referred to as the front nine, and the second half is the back nine. After playing the front nine, Evan's conflicting thoughts, given the unusual good fortune of his circumstances, frustrated him. He was both anxious and reluctant to play the back nine—the part of the course that passed within hearing range of Amanda's swimming pool. On the one hand, if he were to play the back nine, he would have at least some chance of actually encountering her. He would be in a position for thoroughly enjoying his afternoon. On the other hand, after what he considered his shameless effort the previous afternoon—making a short circuit within sight of Amanda's home—he felt he had been too obvious, like a lovesick teen, behavior that would be distasteful to a young lady of obvious privilege. After all, he reasoned, when a young man is too forward in his attempt for female attention, he more likely repels than attracts.

He was apprehensive about his previous day's actions. Though he had played past her home maybe five times and had not seen her once, he did not like the change in his character. He frowned for having acted so desperate and wondered at how Army life was changing him. He exchanged a club with those in his canvas bag, frowned, and made a subtle shake of his head. He identified the change and felt it as a dull sense of embarrassment. As an Army private, he was surrounded with men, and had allowed himself to become anxious to attract Amanda's attention. The absurdity of the thought came to him as he looked down the long fairway of the tenth hole, where he could see a red flag on a green flagstick at the very far end. The flag drooped in the still, warm air.

Evan understood that Amanda compelled the men's actions more than his own. He again frowned at his distraction, laughed, and shook his head sideways. Chadwick and Fletcher were paying the price for the men's attraction, and Evan's pride was paying for his own.

The truth of his situation was clear. He was to play golf, beat the Navy, and repay the Army with the victory. His repayment would be for his privileges. With his understanding, decision, or whatever else touched him, he resolved to restrict his thoughts and efforts to those of improving his golf game. As alluring as he found thoughts of Amanda to be, he relegated them to a much distant second place to his military responsibilities. He was so decided on the point that he actually spoke his resolve. "No," he said to the empty golf course.

The word dissipated like dandelions in the wind. When he said it again, he yelled, "No!"

Right after he did, he heard a sound behind him. He
turned to see a surprised bird, hopping from one branch
to another, and then he watched it take flight. He listened
to the flap of its wings and watched until it disappeared
somewhere in the distance. The peaceful quiet of the empty
golf course returned, leaving him alone, holding his ball
and his driver, and staring down the long fairway ahead
of him.

Because his decision steeled his resolve, he lost an
opportunity, for if Evan had played the back nine that day,
he would have encountered and spoken with Amanda.
She had seen him the previous day. She noticed him once,
then again and again. She was sitting in an upper room and
after noting his posturing, she abandoned the book she was
reading in favor of watching him. She saw him go around
the few holes in her view several times. She was certain he
could not see her because of the distance, the light, and the
distorting reflections of the window glass. She knew from
a lifetime in the house that he could see only reflections
in her window, and to him she was invisible as if she were
behind a one-way mirror.

She watched Evan's tall figure in earnest as he hit his
ball far down the fairway that approached her view. He was
not determined then, for his walk was more a stroll. He
swung his golf club in one of his hands while he walked.
She saw that he wore a light tan shirt with a collar and short
sleeves, and a white T-shirt underneath. Although she could
see the details of his clothing, she could not see that the
creases in his service slacks were much relaxed after the
walking, bending, and wiping activities of his practice, and
she could not see that his shoes had several tiny clippings
clinging to their sides.

She certainly could, and did, notice his several glances
to where he had encountered her by the pool, and smiled

to herself. At one point, the air in her lungs froze in a gasp of breath, the color left her face, and she stood up and took two steps away from the window. Evan had stared right at the window, and in spite of the distance, the possibility he might see her watching him frightened her.

When her father took her to thank the young man the day before, she had covertly watched him—watched him for those subtle silent words that all young women can read. There were so many male signs of interest inside the headquarters tent, however, that Amanda sought to notice little more than a polite kindness from Evan. Now, with her in the dormer and him on the course, distance, lighting, and reflections prevented either of them from feeling the fiery touch that comes with the first deep eye contact.

Without the instructors and with renewed resolve, Evan abandoned the back nine. Instead, he practiced on the front nine like a serious soldier. Metal drivers had been around for only ten years in August of 1943, but their distinctive clicks against well-driven balls were already established as a pleasing sound. The swoosh of a shaft cutting through air drew attention, but it was the club head's contact with a ball that drew looks of appreciation. He hit and followed each ball with a resolute stride, carrying his club gripped in one of his hands. The other end of his club rested on his shoulder, and if Amanda had seen him then from the distance of her dormer, she would have seen Evan looking like a soldier marching with a rifle. He strode to each ball and considered everything that might affect his next shot. He considered sand traps set before greens, well-placed trees that jutted branches over the fairways, flags that revealed a breezeless afternoon, slopes to the surfaces of greens, flagstick positions, and a thousand other little checks needed for play.

On the fourth green, he saw the flag placement would
be tough, because after hitting his ball, if the ball did not fall
into the cup, it would roll down from the top of the green.
He would then find himself repeating an up-and-down
rolling of his ball, just like a golfing Sisyphus. He decided
he could go long with a nine iron or go short with an eight.
Like all golfers playing alone, Evan changed his mind several
times until he reached his ball lying in the center of the
fourth fairway. He chose his nine iron, and then he used it
to place his ball high on the green. The ball went high, had
no backspin, and stuck like a little glob of mud on the green.
His putt was easy, and he scored a birdie, one stroke less
than par.

Evan spent nearly two hours on that fourth green. He
positioned his ball in various places and decided he would
have trouble if his approach shot landed low. There was
another sand trap he had not seen—up high—so he made a
mental note that the fourth hole at El Rancho Golf Course
could be a big winner, or an even bigger loser. When he
finished playing the green, he went back about one hundred
thirty yards and practiced reaching the green several times.
In this manner, Evan spent his entire afternoon alone
practicing his game, no longer seeking or considering
another.

By the time he returned for dinner, the men of
the 170th and the two instructors were well into their
meals. He put away his clubs and freshened up. When
he entered the mess tent, the loud sounds of dinner on
a military base—the clinking of thin silverware against
metal trays, tin cups sliding on long wooden tables,
heavy footsteps going for seconds, and animated men
talking and laughing—ceased. Everyone looked at him

and the instructors smiled. All watched and tried to draw conclusions from his face, but he avoided making eye contact and went straight for his dinner tray.

Evan walked tall. He looked the way a dashing hero would appear, right out of a bored soldier's imagination.

CHAPTER 8

~ A REPRIMAND AND AN UNEXPECTED ENCOUNTER ~

Floyd had four guns under his command, and each gun had a six-man crew. Forty-two men, including Evan, the two instructors, the gun crews, and the support personnel stood at attention, with backs stiff, chests lifted, arms straight at their sides, and eyes staring forward.

"Damn you!" Floyd yelled at them. "If Chadwick and Fletcher were in the Army, I would have you thrown in the stockade. I would have you court-martialed. You cannot kidnap civilian golf instructors."

Chadwick and Fletcher stood by the men, adopting their own versions of stiff and rigid attention. They exchanged eye contact after hearing Floyd spew his most significant threat when he accused the men of violating the general's specific orders. "It's out of my hands now," he had said, sneering and referring to a higher military authority than his own. "Your actions force me to write a report!"

The instructors were standing aside like affronted victims, but they widened their eyes and looked at each other when they heard the word "report." From each other, they looked at the men and then at Floyd. They looked like schoolboys before a principal. In later years, the word "report" lost all of its power and changed to represent a collection of bound pages few sought to read and fewer cared to write. In 1943, however, men took it to mean a citation, leave cancellation, extra duties, a mark on their

records, or some punitive measure. Their plan to relieve
Evan of the instructors' company each day disappeared
and, in unison, they all shouted their understanding of the
reality. "Yes, sir!"

Floyd scowled at Evan throughout his tirade. When he
finished, he walked straight up to him. "Get a report of your
activities on my desk by twenty-two hundred," he said.

"Yes, sir," Evan answered. He watched Floyd march
out of the mess tent like a race-walker; his torso was bent
forward, his arms swinging like scissors, and his legs taking
fast little steps.

The following day, Evan golfed, the instructors worked
on slicing and fading shots to Evan's advantage, and the
trio ate lunch with the men. All had been humbled, and the
mess tent was quiet. Even though the men were restrained,
Chadwick and Fletcher remained peripherally aware of
Evan. They did so to prevent being separated from him for
a third straight day.

Just as the men were to leave for the afternoon artillery
practice, however, Floyd approached. He called Evan for
a private conversation, and the two stepped outside of the
mess tent out of everyone's hearing range. Evan did not
see the same anger Floyd displayed the previous evening.
There was anger, no doubt, but Floyd appeared to be trying
for the attitude. The scowl, pinched lips, darting little eyes,
and choppy steps were normal for him, but his attitude
hinted of a covert subtlety behind his angry façade. Floyd
was conspiratorial, for he seemed self-conscious about his
intent.

"I read your report," he said. "Was it complete?"

"Yes, sir," Evan replied, "although I had no idea
Chadwick and Fletcher would be taken all the way to
artillery practice. I would have added that if I knew about it.
That fact goes in someone else's report."

"Of course," Floyd said. "I put it in my report to the general, but yours said very little. You said you only played golf. You golfed for the entire afternoon. Really?"

"Yes, I played golf," Evan said. "I played all day. Are you questioning whether my report is complete?"

"No, it's just that you reported playing only the front nine holes."

His tone held an unspoken question. He widened his eyes and waited, as though he expected additional information. Evan said nothing. An uncomfortable moment of silence passed while the two stared, and then Floyd could resist no longer. "Why didn't you play the back nine?"

"I plan to play it today," Evan said, "just as soon as you release me. I had to work on the fourth hole. It's a tough one. I played it over and over. You always tell us, 'Practice until you can't miss.' Well, that's what I did. Still, the fourth green is so tricky that I could still miss."

Following his answer, Evan made a humble little grin. Floyd relaxed and allowed a smirk to lift the left side of his frown. He liked to hear his men quoting his wisdom.

"Repeating the same shot works every time," Floyd said, "but is it true you did not play the back nine at all? You stayed and played on the front the whole time?"

"Yes, sir. That's what I said. It's in my report."

Floyd showed his kind side and white teeth, a sign of his acceptance, though his dark little eyes were too close together to appear content with, or accepting of, matters for reports. He smiled and put an arm around one of Evan's shoulders, like an older brother about to give advice. The two turned and walked toward the trucks that waited for his order to depart, but Floyd stopped where the crude rumbling of the truck's diesel engines would not drown his whispered words. "We have that dinner tonight, you know." he said. He turned to Evan and watched for a reply.

"At what time?" Evan asked.

"Artillery practice will end early today. I expect to return by seventeen hundred, and you should be ready to go at seventeen forty-five. I know it's just next door, but Mr. Nichols asked that we be there at six. I don't want to be late."

"Yes, sir," Evan said. "I'll be ready. I expect tonight to be our best night in LA. You can count on me to be on time to get off this base and enjoy some female company."

Floyd stopped walking. "Even at civilian dinners," he reminded Evan, "you are to act with the highest military decorum and professional reserve. We represent the Army, you know. My driver will pick us up at headquarters. Meet me there. We leave at seventeen forty-five sharp. Don't be late. Fifteen minutes is more than enough time to get there."

Floyd climbed into the passenger side of a waiting jeep and signaled its driver. The trucks followed the jeep, and from their high stacks, great plumes of black smoke covered their departure. Evan watched them depart, wondering about Floyd. The man spoke with tacit intent. He considered the questions to come from an unnamed suspicion, but he knew Floyd treated everyone under his command as though each were guilty of doing something he had not yet uncovered.

Leadership styles reduce to good and bad. Evan considered Floyd's bad. His leadership was a burden on the men. Good leaders motivate, inspire, encourage, challenge, and seek positive influences that stretch performance. Bad leaders do not necessarily discourage all people, for men of character do exist, and they endure through the burden of bad leadership, without grumbling and complaining or blindly following. But bad leaders fail to gain respect and admiration. Left alone outside the hearts of their men, their suspicions compound and cultivate an environment of low expectation that becomes their reality.

After the trucks departed and Evan turned to retrieve his clubs, he spotted Chadwick and Fletcher approaching, with Chadwick carrying Evan's bag. Neither instructor smiled. They wore their most sober expressions, as though they thought Floyd had further admonished Evan. The two appeared serious, and neither mentioned the previous day's incident or Floyd's resulting anger.

"Here are your clubs," Chadwick said.

"Thanks," Evan responded, and they all headed to the first hole without further words.

Following their morning practice of drawing and fading shots—the intentional, controlled, and strategic finesses of the hook and slice—the threesome began the afternoon playing the back nine's straight and easy par-four hole. Chadwick hit a nice tee-shot that landed nearly two hundred thirty yards down the fairway. Fletcher made similar contact with his ball, but after a straight shot, it slowly veered to the right. By the time it reached the ground, bounced, and rolled a good distance farther, it stopped just outside of a wooden stake. The stake had been painted white and placed to indicate the fairway's out-of-bounds mark. He frowned, turned to step away from the tee box, but then halted and looked at Evan. "What would you do?" he asked. "Remember, you're playing Army rush rules. When your ball goes out of bounds, you can either play the ball where it stops or hit another tee-shot. Either way, you have to count your next hit as your third stroke. You do it this way: count one for going out of bounds, the drop to get back on the fairway counts as stroke number two, and you count stroke three when you hit to go forward. Your ball will lie at three strokes. Say it like this: 'one out, one on, and one gone.' Really, though, it's better if you just stay in bounds."

Chadwick yawned. "If it was my ball," he said. "I'd just hit again. If you play the ball where it goes out of bounds, you're still about two hundred yards from the green and, either way, you add a penalty stroke. If you follow my advice, you will at least get your ball in play."

"I'll just try to stay in bounds," Evan said.

The two instructors quieted and watched Evan's tee-shot go bouncing and rolling another fifty yards past Chadwick's. Fletcher made the decision to hit his tee-shot again, and his second ball stopped at the left edge of the fairway, well short of the others. As the threesome walked to hit their next shots, they discussed remaining distances, sand traps, cup placement on the green, the surface of the green, the breeze that had picked up since their morning round, the flapping of the flag on the flagstick, and other considerations for playing well. In this manner, they completed the back nine in just an hour and decided to play it again. They returned to the tenth hole, but the instructors mandated that Evan play three balls on every green.

"Reaching the green," Chadwick said, "is not as important as getting your ball in the cup. Anyone can get on, but winners get in, and they get in with the fewest strokes."

On the green, Fletcher gave the most advice. "The trick to putting," he said, "is to leave your ball right next to the hole. When you miss, don't run your ball past the cup, turn around, and then do it again. Don't hit back and forth. Instead, stop your ball next to the cup. That way, the next putt you take will be your last. Your ball can easily fall into the cup."

Fletcher next bent down on the green, right behind one of Evan's balls, and studied the surface in order to advise about the line Evan should take with his putt. "It's straight," he said. "Just hit and stop your ball beside the cup."

Evan's ball might have stopped next to the cup, but it did not. Instead, it first fell straight into the hole.

"That's how to do it," Chadwick said. "When you can putt it in, don't leave your ball next to the cup. Fletcher is right, though. You should always hit hard enough to hole your ball, but soft enough so that, if you miss, your ball stops beside the cup."

Weather adds a bigger life to an empty golf course. Whereas a warm, unmoving day is calm—except for little flying things going here and there—a blowing wind forces branches to bend, straighten, and bend again. Leaves salute in the wind's direction, and everywhere wind stirs silence to sound. Occasional leaves fall, fly, and tumble across fairways, birds flap without moving, and, at the El Rancho course, fox squirrels raced, with their reddish-brown backs portending the inevitable end of summer. Both the fox squirrels and the Army were imports, but unlike the Army, the squirrels did not stay to thrive in Los Angeles. The native western gray squirrels—soon to be displaced by the foxes—remained hidden in their nooks. Only the imports ran with the wind.

The wind also carried sounds. Evan heard someone dropping a bag of clubs about a fairway over from where he stood. He glanced toward the sound, but his view was blocked by a buffer zone of trees meant to separate the fairways, protect golfers from errant shots, and keep players from distracting each other. He cocked his head and listened until he heard nothing except Chadwick and Fletcher arguing about what to do when one ball hits another's ball during play. They were arguing the same rule. "Are you two planning on arguing all day?" he asked, grinning before the threesome continued to play. They finished the hole, played two more, and stopped with a jolt. They were standing at the tee box nearest to Amanda's home, and they watched in silence while she hit a tee-shot.

It's a well-known fact that those living along golf courses make encroaching excursions when the course is empty. They first watch for straggling golfers and then for course monitors. Maintenance personnel are of secondary concern, for their care is for the ground. When the coast is clear, neighborhood adventurers play the few holes nearest to their homes. They stay where they can escape without notice to hide on familiar ground. Amanda was doing just that. She was doing what she had done since she was a little girl, back when her father still had time to golf with her. After the Army's occupation of the course, Amanda continued with her daily play without concern for being caught. No one watched the course. She had no idea, though, that three men were watching her play.

She wore a long white skirt and a dark blue sweater with a white blouse collar showing at the neck. Her hair was down and held off her face with a blue cloth band. There was something carefree and loose about her movements, as though she thought she was playing on an empty course. She was playing under the assumption Evan had already played through for the day.

The threesome stood there as Amanda made her shot. After she hit, Evan watched her and the instructors watched her ball. The ball went straight, Amanda held her swing position, and no one spoke a word. She stood facing her ball, her club high, one heel lifted, and her back turned to Evan. It was in that position that he noticed tan skin showing between the top of her socks and the hem of her skirt. She turned and found the men standing behind her, and she widened her eyes, drew a gasp of air, and lowered her club. She glanced left and right, took one step backward, and looked from Chadwick, to Fletcher, to Evan.

The instructors began apologizing with great alacrity. "Forgive us," Evan said after the instructors. "We were just watching your swing and never meant to scare you." Though she was clearly startled, he saw that after the apologies, she did not appear frightened.

"I'm sorry too," she said. "I knew you played out here, but I thought you were already gone for the day. It's only because you came back that you caught me."

Evan stepped forward without grinning. "We're the ones who should apologize," he said. "We should have warned you the moment we saw you. We wanted to see you hit." He grinned and added, "I have to say, you have an excellent swing."

With his words, her recent familiarity with Evan's face, the kind manner of his voice, the safe feelings engendered by the older golf instructors, and the penetration of his eyes, Amanda smiled. "You caught me," she repeated. Her face colored, and Evan smiled at the sheepish looks she turned to both her left and right. She laughed. "Is it okay that I'm out here?"

"Sure it is," Fletcher said. "We're the only ones besides you on the course. You can play all you want."

The three men nodded, and Amanda returned their smiles. Her initial look of concern was replaced by one of curiosity. She examined all three.

"Why don't you join us?" Fletcher asked. "We can play as a foursome. It's perfect. We have only an hour to play before we're done, and it would be our pleasure to have your company. Besides, it looks like it could start raining any minute. If you don't play now, you'll miss the day." He looked up at the sky, swept his eyes across the threat above them, and then returned to look at her. He restated his question.

Amanda looked up, too, and saw a dark bank of clouds bunched up in the west. Santa Monica would soon be soaked. She crossed her arms against the wind, looked up at the changing weather, and checked to see if the same question was in Evan's eyes. He answered her look with what she recognized as the nod of a polite, handsome, grinning young man.

"Please join us," he said. "You would make my day."

The four played together for the remainder of the afternoon, and it must be noted that their manner of play, conversation, seriousness, and pace slowed to one in keeping with the pleasures of the game. They abandoned the tedious and dull attitude of practice and enjoyed the afternoon. Chadwick and Fletcher stayed more on the sides of fairways, where they consistently played their balls, while Evan and Amanda walked straight down the middle. They proceeded like two acquaintances strolling along an unrolled, well-walked, green grassy carpet, which gave them an opportunity to speak freely. At one point, Chadwick and Fletcher stopped arguing to listen to laughter. They looked to find Evan walking backwards right in front of Amanda while she laughed and looked at his face—as though responding to some playful tease. The instructors smiled at each other.

When Amanda hit, Evan remained still, and she did the same when it was his turn. Both seemed aware that the other's silence included intent watchfulness, but when sneaking a glance, neither saw the other doing anything more than smiling and appreciating a shot. On the greens, their conversations ceased, and this worked quite well because the two instructors, imputing upon Amanda the want of instruction, did all the talking.

"The one farthest from the cup hits first," Fletcher said on one green.

"Don't move your ball, or you'll have to add a penalty stroke," Chadwick added, and then they both took turns with: "No one on the green gets the flagstick—it has to be pulled from the cup before a putt," "Mark your ball if it's in the way of another's," "Stay out of a hitter's line of sight," "If you have to talk, you should do so in a whisper." And on they went.

While the instructors chattered, Evan and Amanda watched each other from the corners of their eyes. They grinned while they played, and one of her looks made him laugh out loud. It happened at a time when she was about to putt. She noticed Fletcher was behind her ball on his knees and toe-tips, with his hands pressed flat against the surface of the green, judging the surface of the course Amanda's ball needed to travel to the cup. She saw Fletcher tilting his head left and right, making the long, sweeping motions of a pendulum. He finished and stood to share the wisdom of his assessment, eliciting her smile and Evan's laughter. When she hit, her ball rolled past the hole, and Fletcher repeated his earlier advice. "The trick is to leave your ball right next to the hole, just in case you miss. When you do miss, you want the ball to stop. That way, you're sure to make your next putt."

"Oh," she said. "I thought the trick was to hit the ball into the cup and not to plan for missing."

"That works too," Evan said in passing, whispering so only Amanda could hear him.

The foursome continued playing, with the two instructors playing along the edges of fairways and Evan and Amanda walking in the middle. The two asked initial questions that probed more for responses than information, and in only a short time their playful chatter elevated to a conversation of inquiry. Amanda learned why Evan was playing with the instructors, and Evan learned why Amanda played alone.

"It's the film business," she explained. "My father is just too busy these days. He never plays anymore. He taught me to enjoy the game, but then the films took him. Any time I want to play, I do so alone."

"Why do you play at all?"

"Hmm," she said, pressing her lips together. "Like you should ask me. It's the game, isn't it? How do you quit something you've been raised to love, especially in the summer?"

"You don't," he answered. "But surely you have friends who can play with you?"

"Young ladies don't play unless young men are playing too. None of my women friends can play, and the boys who play golf, well ..." She stopped when it occurred to her that she might say something insulting and make an unflattering stereotype Evan could take as applying to him.

"Yes?" he asked. He turned an ear toward her and grinned to let her know he was eager to know what it was she was reluctant to share about young men who play golf.

"Excuse me," she said, "but boys who play golf are just too impressed with themselves. They're tiring."

"Is that so?" he asked, exaggerating offense. When he teed his ball for his next drive, he did so with an air of great importance. "Just watch how well I hit this next drive. You will change your mind. You'll be the one who's impressed." He held his club poised to hit but paused and looked at her. "Don't you think I'm standing at the perfect distance from the ball? Watch this hit. You will be as impressed, I promise."

He took a powerful swing, missed, and exaggerated the effect of momentum pulling him out of his stance and spinning him along with his club. He wrapped the club behind him. Encouraged by her laughter, he said, "Maybe I should play alone too."

"Oh, no!" she said. "It looks to me like you need all the help you can get. I now understand. I do. I see why the Army gave you Chadwick and Fletcher."

Just as Evan was about to hit his real shot, the rain started. Rain on a golf course has a way of coming everywhere all at once. One drop does not hit first, and then another and another. Instead, a sky of drops falls together. The quiet of an empty golf course is suddenly the sound of rain everywhere. The sound begins as rain hitting dry grass, then becomes rain hitting wet ground, and finally rain hitting the many instant puddles. The sound could have been pleasurable if it weren't for the fact that the foursome was getting soaked. Puddles formed everywhere because the hot summer sun dried the ground, rendering it too hard to absorb water.

Golf bags in 1943, though still not restricted to the fourteen-club limit, did not include umbrellas. Golf was a man's game played in the sun, so the rain brought an immediate end to their practice and required the foursome to stand under the protection of a tree to say their goodbyes. Evan offered Amanda his light windbreaker as protection, and she accepted it with a polite "Thank you." He and the instructors watched her use the jacket to cover her head, and they remained watching her and her bag of clubs disappear up the path from the golf course to her house. After she disappeared from sight, they remained for a moment, silent and smiling.

"That was fun," Chadwick said.

"Our best day yet," Fletcher offered.

Both looked at Evan and found him nodding agreement. He said nothing while grinning and holding his eyes on Amanda's trail. When they began walking, they did so under a heavy rain.

"What do we tell Floyd?" Fletcher asked. He had to yell to be heard over the sound of wind blowing through the trees and bushes. "Do we say anything about playing with Amanda?"

"Don't even think of it," Chadwick said. "I'm not saying a word."

Both looked at Evan. "Are you kidding?" he said, laughing and turning his head. "I'm not saying a word. All we really need to do is figure out how to keep our grins from giving us away." He stopped to yell in the rain. "Let's keep this quiet. If Floyd finds out, he just might explode."

~~~ PART II ~~~
THE FAIRWAY

CHAPTER 9

~ THE DINNER PARTY ~

Floyd's anticipation grew throughout the day of the dinner party. Upon returning from his afternoon of artillery practice, he gave several tedious orders, most important of which was putting Captain Becker in charge of Battery B that evening. Floyd was anxious to attend the Nichols' dinner party, and he expected to be gone for as many as four or five hours. He shaved for the second time that day, showered, dressed, and made a final inspection of himself in a tall mirror that leaned against a wall in the officers' barracks. The reflection of polished boots, pressed jacket, stiff cap, notable rank insignia, and shiny buttons glimmering in the quarter's dim light pleased him.

He held himself taller, straighter, and with greater significance when he wore his dress uniform. After examining both sides of his cleanly shaven face, he grinned at his reflection in the mirror. He would make quite an irresistible impression that night. He further seated his cap, made a formal little click of his heels, and went out to the jeep that was waiting to take him and Evan to the dinner party.

Evan was just arriving when Floyd appeared at the jeep. The two smiled, greeted each other, and made quick assessments of the other's appearance. Their moods lightened to match their shared appreciation for the formal military attire and their expectation of an enjoyable evening.

A young Army private, waiting for them behind the steering wheel, whistled his appreciation as the two men approached. The private sat high in his seat as he drove and held his head with great significance, gripped the jeep's steering wheel with both elbows held high, and glanced about for anyone who might notice him in the presence of such important men. He knew others would be impressed.

The drive to the Nichols' house was short, covering the distance from the golf course to the big house along the other side of it, but it seemed much longer because Floyd ordered the driver not to exceed twenty miles per hour. The 170th had only a few of the little jeeps in its inventory, and all of them had open tops and no side doors. The openness allowed the wind to whip the passengers. If the speed was not limited, the passengers arrived at their destinations looking less impressive than when they began. The rain had stopped over an hour earlier, but the roads were still damp, and they glistened with a shine and cleanliness that was pleasing to see.

Floyd gawked at everything as they drove. When they turned onto the street where the Nichols lived, he saw it was lined with tall palm trees, unlighted lampposts, and massive homes that rivaled that of the Nichols. Lawns were green, shrubs and bushes were clipped, and fountains flowed at the center of circular driveways. The three-story homes were topped with rows of dormers, and high balconies looked like jewels lit atop each.

Neighbors tend to compete against each other on some basis, but here it would have been difficult to identify any competitive basis. The homes were all huge, immaculate, groomed to perfection, bordered by the golf course, and already brightly lighted for the coming evening. There were several large automobiles parked in front of the Nichols' house, however, christening their home the winner of the neighborhood competition that night. The driver of the jeep showed mercy on the neighbors, though, for he did not enhance the victory by parking. He stopped in the street out front, waited until Floyd and Evan climbed out, and then drove away. Floyd instructed him not to return until twenty-three hundred hours that night. On his return, he was told to park and wait for the two to emerge. He was not to come to the door.

Floyd and Evan walked toward the front door without saying a word, grinning and turning to look with their wide eyes. After they passed a pool into which water trickled, Floyd's reservation failed him and he spoke first. "What a huge brick house!" he said. "Can you believe it?"

He began laughing like he'd won the lottery, while Evan only nodded and grinned. He never expanded upon the obvious. The lawn, brick walkway, rose beds, the trickling of the water, brass lettering with the name "Nichols," and the twelve-foot wooden doorway surrounded by etched-glass windows impressed Evan. When first experiencing great wealth, people are either awestruck or they withdraw and study it. The latter allows for an observation of wealth's influence on others, its conveniences, and its revelation of some very fine possibilities. Evan receded into his thoughts, whereas Floyd expressed his.

"We're in for it tonight!" Floyd laughed. He moved his head by taking quick jerking glances at Evan, the door, the windows, the walkway, the cars in the driveway, and at nearly every other sight to be found in the direction of a spinning compass. He talked fast, as though his stream of consciousness was spilling out of control.

"The food is going to be great," he said. "Who are all these people? Where did they get all their money? I want a house like this. That pretty girl will be here. Amelia. She'll have friends here too. Evan, I get Amelia, and you can have one of her friends. Look at these cars. Whoa, that's a big door," he finished with a laugh, while Evan grinned, still saying nothing in return.

Floyd knocked hard on the door. When he did not hear anyone immediately come to answer, he knocked again. The door opened and the loud sounds of party conversation and laughter seeped into the evening air. An older gentleman wearing a black dinner jacket, white gloves, and shiny black shoes, stood at the open door examining the soldiers. He identified the older man with the officer's insignia on his jacket as the one whom he had been told to expect.

"Good evening," he said to Floyd. "You must be First Class Private Evan Wilkins. We are expecting you, sir."

"No," Floyd corrected, surprised at being mistaken for Evan, "I am Major Floyd Akerly. This is Private Wilkins," he said, throwing a thumb toward Evan.

"Of course," said the courteous butler. "Hello Mr. Wilkins. Please do come in, gentlemen."

The butler led them across an oriental rug and through a large, high-ceilinged foyer containing painted vases, a cherry table with cloth doilies, a curio covered with little knickknacks, a large mirror, and a massive grandfather clock. There were no portraits of the home's occupants, but the paintings on the walls were so huge and valuable that the décor was complete as such. Several arched entries to other rooms were visible from the foyer. The butler led Evan and Floyd into the room from where the greatest volume of happy conversation emanated. The moment the two soldiers entered the large room, all conversation dropped, eyes peeked, and then the voices picked up again. There were loud exclamations of: "Here he is,"

"This is the one I told you about," "These are our summer neighbors," "Come meet the First Class Private," and so on. Several times the name "Evan" was shouted, whispered, and repeated from all corners of the room.

A smiling Mr. Nichols came forward first, and with him were several men wearing similar white shirts and black bow ties. The ties were visible at the tops of their formal dinner jackets, just beneath their smiling, well-tanned faces, and several of them appeared to be quite well fed. Mr. Nichols shook hands with Evan and introduced him to the group surrounding him. He also introduced Floyd, but he did so as though it were an afterthought.

"Please allow me to introduce you to Claire," Mr. Nichols said to Evan.

He took Evan's arm and led him across the large room, leaving Floyd in conversation with the other men. They approached a group of well-dressed women who stared as a group, whispered without looking at each other, and smoked the cigarillos that were the fashion. They watched Evan approach and all rose as he neared. Mr. Nichols failed in his attempt to keep them seated, for these fifty-something women were determined to be seen. He made a formal introduction to his wife.

"First Class Private Evan Wilkins," he said, "please allow me to introduce you to my wife, Claire. Claire, Evan is the one I told you about who defended us and chased away that spy."

The woman reached out a slim, jeweled wrist, and offered her fingers to Evan. She smiled while he touched her hand, surprised at its softness. Evan saw Amanda in her mother, and with this recognition, his smile turned into one of those grins that friends share when they encounter each other by chance. "It's a pleasure to meet you," Evan said, but then he added, "It's not 'First Class Private' Wilkins. It's

'Private First Class.' Your husband has reversed 'first' and 'class.' But please just call me Evan."

"And please just call me Claire," she said.

She ignored his correction, and introduced Evan to the other ladies, each standing and awaiting her turn to meet the handsome young soldier. She stated his rank as her husband had. She preferred adjectives before nouns, and "First Class Private" sounded better to her. While introducing him to the ladies, Claire kept her attention fixed on Evan, and she noticed that despite his military bearing, the attractiveness of his uniform, and his practiced rigidity, he was self-conscious about his eager reception. She thought the coloring in his cheeks might have been darker than normal, saw the uncomfortable little glances he made here and there, and wondered at his fussing with the cap he held in his hands. She grinned with her lips together, and her large eyes narrowed a bit as she watched his behavior.

"Be sure to say hello to my daughter," Claire said to Evan, and the other ladies nodded their agreement.

The ladies pointed toward a group of younger persons farther back in the large room. The group included several of their daughters, a few young men, the greatest volume of laughter, and the greatest number of covert little glances, all in Evan's direction.

Floyd had been left talking with the men back at the entrance to the room, but he was not interested in their discussion about making some movie they were considering. Floyd, too, kept a subtle watch on Evan, who he then saw heading across the room with an elegant older lady. She was leading him to that cute young girl they had met at headquarters. After she and her father departed that day, the scent of her perfume had lingered. Since that time, whenever Floyd closed his eyes, he could smell her fragrance and see her image. He found both captivating.

Floyd excused himself from the group, and with purposeful strides, his arms swinging at his sides, made his way toward Evan. He looked at none of the people he passed until he caught up to and intercepted Evan and Claire Nichols. "There you are," he said to Evan, as though the two had been separated for some length of time.

He interrupted Mrs. Nichols at the moment she was introducing Evan to Amanda. She held her daughter's hand in one of her own, held Evan's in her other, and around them were several other young ladies. Mrs. Nichols smiled, turned her head, and looked politely at Floyd, but then she spoke to Evan. "Please introduce your friend," Claire said.

Floyd rejected the formality by turning to Amanda without acknowledging her mother. "Amelia," he renamed her, "it's nice to see you again. Do you remember me? I'm Major Akerly. We met at headquarters."

At that, Claire's smile changed from pleasure to propriety. She smiled with only her mouth, looking as though viewing him through the window of a passing vehicle.

"It's Amanda," she said. "My daughter's name is Amanda." She turned to Evan and added, "It occurs to me, though, that both you and Major Akerly have already met my daughter over at the golf course? Isn't that so?"

"Yes," Evan replied, exchanging a passing glance with Amanda.

The two sought to avoid each other's eyes. They looked away, but in their initial glance, in their brief visual touch, both laughed like friends with a secret.

"Amelia is it?" Evan asked, pretending he had not heard Mrs. Nichols' correction. "I thought you said it was Amanda?" He turned a questioning look to her mother.

Claire Nichols, well known in 1943 as Hollywood's social matriarch, was never one to miss subtleties. She nodded her agreement with her daughter's name, and she frowned as though she had glimpsed something in a fog. She did not enjoy missing little bits of information, but more so, she did not care to have others perceive the lack. Though she smiled, she allowed her eyes to rove from Evan to her daughter.

"Since you seem already to know Evan, you won't mind introducing him to your friends, Amanda. Why don't you introduce him and Major Akerly to all of your guests?"

The other young ladies were formed into a smiling arc behind Amanda. They seemed hesitant to look at Evan, so they stood like students waiting to answer their teacher's question. The young men were collected behind the young ladies, but they appeared to be much less interested in the soldiers. Some looked out at the gathering, others faced each other, and still others had their backs turned, looking in the opposite direction. Regardless of where their eyes were directed, however, they were all aware of Floyd and Evan.

As soon as Claire returned to her friends, Amanda introduced Floyd and Evan to all her friends, young men and women alike. Following introductions, the men mingled with the young ladies who were seated on an arrangement of maroon sofas and carved wooden chairs. A few young men stood to one side, aloof and smoking, watching the soldiers with feigned disinterest. One, wearing a thin, grey V-necked sweater with "UCLA Golf" embroidered in small blue letters on the left chest, strode in the middle of the group, as though he were lecturing the group.

"As I was saying," he began, but he stopped to look at Amanda the instant she interrupted him.

"Charles Ambrose," she said, "these two have no idea what you've been saying." She then turned to Evan and

Floyd and explained. "Charles was giving us a lesson. He believes there is a way for a golfer to tell just how good or bad he is by playing in the rain."

"It's not that I believe this to be the case," Charles whined in his nasal voice. "It's true. Everyone knows this. When you play in the rain, there is no middle ground. You're either good, or you're terribly bad."

When Charles spoke, he did not look at his audience, and he seemed to be forever picking at an invisible piece of lint on his sweater. He held his chin a bit too high and looked as though sniffing a scent in the air. Floyd became annoyed with him at once. "How do you know it's true?" he asked Charles, speaking with a tone of skepticism that exceeded mere disbelief.

Charles glanced sideways at Floyd, like the snap of a camera's lens, and then looked off in the opposite direction. "How can one explain the obvious to those who don't play?" he said. "If you were to play every day, like we on the golf team do, then you would have played at least one time in the rain. You would have realized that your play relied most on distance and placement. It relied on accuracy. Your play would need distance and accuracy. Rain makes fairways and greens soft, and this causes golf balls to stick when they land. Amateurs rely on their hits bouncing and rolling in their favor. This just does not happen in the rain. You can hit or you cannot."

He took a self-satisfied drag on his cigarette, glanced around at the other young men, allowed the smoke to wander from his mouth, and looked somewhere just above Floyd's head. He blew the wafting smoke for emphasis. The other young men smiled and nodded their agreement. One took two quick glances between Charles and Floyd, as though Charles' point had been well concluded.

91

"But golf always needs distance and placement. Isn't that what golf is—a game of accuracy?" Floyd asked, speaking at the side of Charles' head.

"Of course," Charles said. "I would never want to see you play without either."

Still not facing Floyd, but with his chin still held high, Charles bent his head sideways in Floyd's direction as he spoke, appearing annoyed.

"And the rain helps you achieve both distance and accuracy?" Floyd asked.

"That's not what I said," Charles replied. He gave an ironic grin to the others to indicate he thought Floyd a buffoon and as though all of them, except Floyd, understood this obvious fact of golf. "The rain teaches you how little you have of each," Charles said. "It makes you play your best and, as a result, it reveals just how good or bad you are at the game. I cannot say it any simpler than that."

"So you cannot learn distance and accuracy in the sun?" Floyd asked.

"I can," Charles said.

Amanda then interrupted their narrowing conversation. She stopped them just when they had reached that point in a conversation where certain trouble lurks, where tone, rate, and emphasis separates two speakers into antagonistic sides and they start to listen and watch with great interest, like the game point late in a tennis match, each choosing a favorite and despising the opponent.

"It's time for dinner," Amanda said with a smile. "Remember, Charles, this is a dinner party, not golf debate."

The group departed for the dining room, with Charles surrounded by the other young men and Floyd walking near to Evan and Amanda. The dining room was as large as the room they had just vacated and it was filled with fourteen large, round dinner tables. Each table was formally set with ten place settings, the usual forks on the left, knives and spoons on the right, dessert forks up top, salad and bread plates, water pitchers, folded white linen dinner napkins, goblets and stemware, and cups for after-dinner drinks with dessert. Lighted candle centerpieces shimmered when the air was stirred by the arriving guests. Ten servers dressed in white performed all of the necessities of the catered dinner. Nothing lacked at a time when much was lacking. The war had not affected the Nichols household, except for the occupation of their golf course and the inclusion of the two military men among the one hundred-plus dinner guests.

Charles sat with the other young men at a table just behind Floyd's. He turned his chair around so he was facing Floyd in order to continue their conversation. "Do you play the game?" he asked, fully looking Floyd in the eyes for the first time, even though his voice dripped feigned interest.

"No," Floyd answered. "I don't have time for games. When you're preparing for a war, where someone will lose and losing means dying, you prepare to win. Games are for idle times."

Everyone at Charles' table stopped talking. "That's too bad," he said, sounding defensive. "Peters here suggested we play a round. Since you don't play, I'll just accept that you can't and you'll have to accept that I was right about the rain."

Following these words, the clinking of glasses and the sounds of silverware scraping against plates became much more pronounced. Conversations from the tables around them took on a much louder aspect, and polite niceties about the party, the house, the dinner, and the guests ensued, but only for a moment.

"But don't you play?" a young lady turned and loudly asked Evan. "I thought I heard you did." She was seated at the same table as Floyd, Evan, Amanda, and several others. After glancing at Amanda, she added, "I mean, I thought you were practicing on the golf course. You play, right?"

"That's true," Evan agreed, speaking just above a whisper. "All I'm doing on the golf course, though, is practicing for a game. I'm not preparing for rain."

"Can you play? Really?" Charles said. He spoke loudly, as though he had not been able to hear Evan. For the first time that evening, Charles looked somewhere in Evan's direction.

"Sure I can, but not against civilians."

"That sounds stupid," Charles said. He turned back to his companions. "The Army has stupid rules." He turned back to Evan and laughed. "Why not?" He gave the other young men at his table one of his ironic, knowing looks.

"Good rule," he continued. "The Army doesn't dare play against civilians, probably because the Army knows it would be humiliated. How can they defend our country when they cannot defend their own golf course?" The college boys were alone in their laughter.

"There's a war going on," Evan answered. "The golf course is closed to the public for security reasons. The war is real, and the need for security is too."

"We could make an exception," Floyd said, surprising Evan. Everyone at the two nearby tables turned to look at him. "As a battery commander, I can make the allowance, so long as the game is played in the afternoon. It would have to be over before five." He looked at Evan. "By the time the battalion returned from afternoon practice, all civilians would need to be gone from the golf course."

"What do you say, private? Can you play now? Is your practice working? Would you care to play a round with a real golfer?" Charles taunted him.

Evan looked at Floyd, but Floyd was scowling at Charles. The young ladies' eyes sparkled, and they smiled at Evan. "You're on," Evan said. "As long as Major Akerly approves and arranges it, we'll play."

Floyd nodded his consent, and they arranged the game between Evan and Charles for the following Monday afternoon. Charles pushed to play as soon as possible. "I don't need any practice," he said, looking above all who were seated nearby. "I can play right now."

"No," Amanda said. "You cannot play right now. Don't you hear the music? It's time for dancing."

CHAPTER 10

~ STRONG EMOTIONS ~

With Major Akerly's permission, the round of golf was set. Evan would play against the supercilious Charles Ambrose, captain of the nearby university golf team. Once the arrangement was concluded, the evening's growing tensions defused before they could ignite. The group of young men settled down to enjoying themselves. This, in turn, eliminated the growing concern amongst Amanda and the other young ladies. When the group returned to the large party room after dinner, they did so with improved moods, and all engaged in laughter, music, drinks, conversation, dancing, and smoking. The evening progressed to the time that partygoers fondly recall the next morning after finding someone attractive, flirting, dancing until the wee hours, and whispering with friends—the kind of night that always ends too soon.

Charles distracted Floyd and he ended up staying near Evan instead of seeking Amanda's company as he had planned to do. The consequence was that Amanda remained near to Floyd, who mistook her proximity as a signal of her interest in him. As he flowed with the crowd back into the party room, he noticed the fast-paced music of the brass and string band had enticed several couples onto the dance floor. Emboldened by the three glasses of wine he had taken with dinner, Floyd decided to ask Amanda for a dance. He stopped where the crowd's flow ebbed just before the dance floor, but when he looked around, he saw only unfamiliar faces. On his left was an older woman who was following a man, presumably her husband, onto the dance floor, and on his right were three or four older men watching the dancers. The men held drinks in their hands and talked to each other while they watched. One of them noticed Floyd's confusion and smiled and nodded, but Floyd ignored the gesture. Instead, he turned around and looked in the opposite direction.

Where in the world did she go? he puzzled, and sought reassurance by looking for Evan. *They were just here. I can see that no one has gone back to those velvet sofas. No one but that damn Charles.* He frowned around the room.

Behind the sofas were several large windows. Through these, Floyd saw that nightfall had come. The darkness outside created a boundary that contained the light of the room. An open French door allowed light to create moving shadows of darkness, and it was there that Floyd saw Mr. Nichols and several of his men standing just outside. They were puffing on large cigars, and several of the men were glancing in Floyd's direction. They looked just as Floyd saw them, increasing his self-consciousness about being alone. He turned to search for Amanda.

While he was lost in thought, a young lady approached him and stood between him and the dance floor. He turned to discover her right in his face. "Ugh," slipped from his lips before he could catch himself.

The girl was tall—taller than Floyd—but her four-inch heels and the ankle-length dress that swallowed her thin frame made her seem much taller. The thick mascara on her lashes and the blue shadow on her lids added to her ungainly appearance. "Hello soldier," she said, smiling down into Floyd's face. "My name is Connie. Are you a general?"

Floyd attempted to look around her, but she was too close. He had no choice but to look up into her smiling face and then wished he hadn't when the overabundant fumes from her perfume struck him.

"Hi," he said. He shifted to his left for a breath of fresh air, as though he was being called, broke eye contact, and attempted to look out onto the dance floor. "Where did you come from?" he asked without looking at her.

Connie adjusted to again position herself directly in front of him, and she appeared to blush as she looked down at his eyes. She intertwined her fingers before her, and moved her shoulders so that her dress swayed as though it were on a clothes hanger, swaying in the breeze.

"Dinner," she answered. "I just came from dinner. I watched when you and that other soldier first arrived tonight. Afterwards I followed you here, but I must admit to waiting before approaching. Your uniform is intimidating. I saw you looking concerned and figured you felt uncomfortable being alone near the dance floor. I just had to come and rescue you."

"Yes, but have you seen Evan? I seem to have lost sight of him."

"I never looked at him," she said. "I was busy watching you. So his name is Evan? What's your name?"

"Major Akerly."

"Major, is it?" Connie smiled. "And is the major having a good time tonight?"

Floyd shifted to see around Connie, who again positioned herself in front of him, her dress shifting on her thin frame. She blushed down at him flashing a toothy smile. *Well, she's about as attractive as an unattractive woman could make herself, I guess*, he thought. "Of course," he responded. "I cannot seem to find Evan, though. I will repeat myself to you, have you seen him?"

"I suppose not," she answered.

She moved closer to him than he wished, resulting in the two of them standing and looking out at the thirty or so couples who were dancing.

"Doesn't that look like fun?" Connie asked. "Everyone's so happy."

"Why, there he is!" Floyd said, missing her question. "He's dancing in that group over there."

"Yes, he is," she said, "and he's a good dancer too. He moves well. He's very graceful. Can you move like that?"

"No, I never dance."

"That's alright," she said, as though feeling sorry for his shortcoming. "I'm the same way. I don't dance. It's a shame, though, because dancing looks like so much fun, don't you think? Look how your friend is enjoying himself, and look how much fun Amanda's having. She loves to dance."

Floyd scowled at the sight of Evan and Amanda dancing together. He felt Connie's shoulder bone bump his once or twice as he watched Amanda stepping and twirling and reaching for Evan's hand while she laughed and danced around him. The music included a piano, and the piano player was playing a collection of snappy Scott Joplin rags. Each vibration of the piano strings brought music to the air and further agitated Floyd.

Look at them dancing, he thought, frowning. *It's not right. They dance like they're the only ones in the room. Evan knows I'm just standing here. How obvious I must look, being the only one wearing a uniform and standing on the sidelines. I told him she was mine. I told him he would have to settle for one of her friends. He's becoming impossible. I'll fix him. Oh, no! Connie's poking my shoulder again. I have got to get rid of her.*

Charles had stirred up a competitive anger in Floyd, and this agitation was still with him. It had not dissipated with the golf challenge arrangements. Rather, it smoldered, like an ash-covered ember in a fireplace, but the flames flared up as he watched Evan enjoy the pleasure that he felt belonged to him.

"Let's go cut in," Floyd said to Connie.

Connie was delighted. "Oh, let's!" She did not quite understand his intention but thought he had decided to give dancing a try. She reached a long arm toward one of his and grabbed it as though hooking him with a wooden cane and trotted behind him, assuming they were about to dance. What she did not see was that Floyd was nearly dragging her along with him. They pressed through the crowd of dancers, and just as Floyd was about to knock on Evan's shoulder, the song ended. When the music stopped, Evan and Amanda looked at Floyd just as Connie grabbed onto both of his hands. She started making a strange movement that was probably the first few steps of a dance, but she stopped, smiling and chest heaving, as though she had just finished a waltz.

"Hi," Amanda said. "We were just taking a break."

Evan grinned and held onto Amanda's hand as she pulled him from the dance floor. The music began another snappy song, and Floyd then found himself standing alone with a dancing dress. Connie's awkward dance steps embarrassed him. At the instant she made her first turn, he headed to the open French door and went out through a cloud of cigar smoke, ignoring the several eyes that sought his, to the patio that surrounded the swimming pool. He walked past the pool, found the trail leading down to the golf course, and emerged onto the fairway. He walked in the darkness, his thoughts fueling his frustration.

Music and party conversations carry across golf courses, especially on summer nights. After an hour or so of walking and seething, Floyd heard when the band took a break. After dancing together song after song, Evan and Amanda

101

decided to take a break from the crowd, and they walked out onto the patio to cool off in the warm night breeze. Claire Nichols spotted them as they left, teasing each other and laughing. Her lips formed a quiet, subtle, sentimental smile. As soon as Evan and Amanda were out of her sight, she looked for her husband. She found him standing with a crowd of men, talking and laughing, and she lightly touched his hand. He turned, saw the look in her eyes, and smiled.

Overcast nights on a golf course are especially quiet, but that night, when the band took its break, the air filled with a symphony of another kind. Insects buzzed, crickets chirped, an owl hooted in the distance, wind rustled through the trees, and the indistinct sounds of conversation carried from the party. Neither Evan nor Amanda heard these evening sounds, for both walked lost in thought. Amanda was first to break the silence.

"Can you beat him?" Amanda asked. "Can you beat Charles at golf?"

"I have no idea," Evan said. "I suppose the question really is whether Charles can beat me. I have gotten to know this golf course and, because it has been raining, Charles will have to prove his theory." He looked at her in the dark and laughed. "Charles is right, you know. Playing in the rain really does let you know how good or bad you are."

Amanda was quiet for a moment, enjoying her thoughts and taking slow steps in the darkness. "How long will you be staying?" she asked. "How long will you be here at the golf course?"

"We're here only this month. We leave the first week of September. We never know too much about where we'll be going. We do know, though, we'll be traveling on a ship, going to Europe, and fighting against the Germans. We'll be going to help end the war. We'll go to win the war."

"Or to get shot," she said.

Evan laughed, giving the only response he could make. The two emerged onto the grass of the fairway, and the softer ground cushioned their steps. The nightscape was out of their view—coming only in shades of dark and darker—and so they moved closer together as they stepped toward the nearby green. They walked closely together in the darkness, enjoying each other's presence, talking with laughter. At first their hands made occasional, accidental bumping contact. Their shoulders were next, then their elbows, and then their arms brushed. Finally like taking the next breath—when it was natural to both of them that they should be touching—they brought their hands together. They became as quiet as the night was dark. Their fingers intertwined. Their hearts beat with increased rhythm and they slowed their pace. Amanda's shoulder's touch became more of a lean, and her breathing synchronized with his. They felt the charge and thrill a first touch brings, and remained hand-in-hand as they walked in the warm silence for the entire length of the fairway.

"What are you doing?" she asked.

"Having my best day and night in the Army," he answered. "You're the reason I enjoyed my golf practice today, and now you have continued your influence on me into this night. I need you to be around me more. Will you be joining us tomorrow? Will you play golf with us in the morning?"

Amanda could not see his face, but she could hear that he was happy. A man's heart can be heard in his voice.

"Are you asking if I can," she said, "or if I will?"

"If you will," he clarified. "Please join me, Chadwick, and Fletcher."

She was about to say something more, but when they reached the green, still hand-in-hand, something started going wrong. The change in the air was immediate, and they felt the same feelings of concern jolt like an electrical pulse to their nerves. One of the dark shadows had moved. There was a sound. There was motion. They felt each other's presence. One was fearful, the other felt a rush of adrenaline. Amanda tightened her hold on Evan's hand.

"Who's there?" he demanded, speaking in a tone of authority.

They had stopped walking and Amanda was pressed close against him. Evan never noticed her leaning, and he failed to notice her squeezing his hand. He leaned toward the darkness beyond and called. "Who's there?"

"Wilkins? Wilkins, is that you?" Floyd yelled.

There was a moment of relief, confusion, and understanding. Things happened more by feeling than by thought. Floyd recognized Evan's voice, discovered and understood that Amanda was there too, became more agitated, and commanded that he and Evan return to the base.

"We're leaving. Now!" he shouted.

The intertwined fingers separated and Amanda, Evan, and Floyd walked back to the house. Floyd did not thank or say goodbye to the Nichols for inviting him to the party. He strode to the door and commanded that Evan follow him. Outside, he went straight to the waiting jeep, and took his seat for the return trip to the golf course.

Before they left, Amanda ran up to the jeep, surprising them both. She was carrying Evan's jacket, the one he had given her for shelter against the rain earlier that afternoon. She did not know that her returning the jacket at that moment served to increase Floyd's agitation with Evan. Floyd looked without seeing.

Evan sat in the back of the jeep, bearing the brunt of the speedy drive back to El Rancho Golf Course. The driver noted Major Akerly's expression and remained silent and staring at the road before him. Unlike the trip to the party, Floyd ignored the windblown turmoil caused by speeding in an open jeep. He twice instructed the driver to go faster. When they arrived at the headquarters tent, Floyd jumped from the still moving jeep, said nothing to Evan, and stormed off.

His ill temper was lost on Evan, whose feelings occupied the other end of the spectrum. Though Floyd leapt from the jeep, scowling, Evan virtually floated from his seat, grinning all the while.

CHAPTER 11

~ A ROUND OF GOLF ~

Floyd spent the weekend before the golf game frustrated with the complicated situation he had created. He was the one who had permitted the arrangement between Charles and Evan, two men he disliked. He replayed scenes, conversations, and other little torments to feed his sense of offense. The result was an agitation that made him bitter, the natural outcome of such a diet. He did, however, expect to be relieved from all concern regarding Charles after the pending golf game, and he found himself pleased to think he would then be free to concentrate on his annoyance with Evan. Charles irritated him, but Evan touched something deeper, more unpredictable, and more distracting. Floyd needed to relieve his jealousy, which far exceeded his distaste for either man.

What was I thinking? he wondered. *That damned Evan has taken advantage of me. First, he's out playing golf every day, neglecting his artillery training, and then, to top it off, he cut in on me with Amanda. She was supposed to be mine! Damn him. It's just not right. I'll take care of this. I'll fix him. And what about that stick? What about Connie? It was Evan's fault I almost got stuck with her. I will get even. I just need to figure out how and when.*

He then recalled Charles saying, "I would never want to see you play without either." He further narrowed his eyes, pressed his lips, and frowned.

What an ass! Evan had better beat that guy. And why shouldn't he? He has distance and placement, and there's the irony, the sting. I have to watch Evan win before I can make him lose. He'll be like the mouse that nibbles at cheese before the spring snaps shut on its head. First things first, though. Evan needs to win at golf today. He needs to nibble. I'll let him have his moment. When the time comes, though, he'll feel the snap. He'll feel it alright. He'll feel more than a snap.

Floyd grinned and laughed aloud at his thoughts. He looked into the distance, saw nothing in particular, and stared to find shape for his unformed plan. Like all such plans hatched out of anger, his thoughts were not then forgotten, not put on hold, not refined, and not left festering like an open wound. Instead, they lay dormant under his active thoughts. He had to perform his morning duties. The practical demands of every morning required his full, angry attention. Following his meeting, planning, coordinating, and instructing the men of Battery B, he joined the officers from the other batteries for lunch. He was concerned they might discover the unauthorized golf game he was permitting that afternoon, so he never spoke a word throughout the meal. With his right hand holding utensils, his left arm surrounding his tray, and his eyes held fixed on his meal, he simply awaited the battalion's departure for its afternoon artillery practice.

Evan spent his Monday morning on the course with Chadwick and Fletcher. They played the entire eighteen holes, as usual, but the instructors added a new condition that morning. They required Evan to play faster in order to gain free time for extra instruction before the game that afternoon. Their plan did not require golf clubs, balls, fairways, greens, or activity. All they needed was time. When the three finished their round, they had over an hour remaining before lunch. They had Evan sit while they stood before him.

"You have an important game today," Chadwick said in a sober voice, taking a look at Fletcher.

His demeanor was serious as he peered through his glasses out of the only window in the small briefing room. He wore a buttoned shirt with the sleeves rolled up and his stance was thoughtful—one hand in his left pocket, the other extended before him, as though he were offering a handful of air—and he spoke in a wistful tone that lent to him a greater authority than usual.

"We have been," Chadwick continued, looking right at Evan, "merely practicing the fundamentals of golf—the basics. Before you play this afternoon, we would like you to try something new, something more critical. We want you to visualize the game in your mind. We want you to play the game in your head." Evan might have frowned, but the instructors took it as a look of uncertainty.

"Just sit somewhere, here or anywhere. The important thing is that you have uninterrupted quiet time. Close your eyes. See yourself drawing a club, positioning for your shot, addressing the ball, lightly gripping your club in your hands, and then feel yourself perfectly hitting each ball. Play every hole in your mind, and visualize playing the entire course exactly as you should—exactly as you will play it today."

After asking obvious questions and receiving answers more hypothetical than factual, Evan retired to his empty barrack, lay on his cot, relaxed, and then followed Chadwick's advice. He had difficulty staying focused, especially while visualizing his play on the first three holes. There was Amanda as he teed his first drive. She was there, too, when he putted, and she was watching, smiling, and clapping her hands when he retrieved his ball from a cup. It took the entire first three holes before he could visualize the game without his mind wandering. When he tried the fourth hole, he could see all of the traps, appearing to his mind like magnetic ponds filled with sand. If his ball got too close, he saw where it would be drawn into the sand. He was then able to visualize just how to avoid each sand trap. He imagined targeting his approach shot so that it landed hard on the upper part of four's sloping green. He visualized himself scoring a par on the eighteenth, with its tricky dogleg. When he joined the men for lunch that noon, he came with an air of profound confidence. He wore a broad, unconcerned grin, and turned his head left and right, as he acknowledged the men. He carried his lunch tray to a table where Chadwick and Fletcher were eating, sat down, and watched them look at each other and smile.

"You will win," Chadwick said to Evan.

Over the weekend, word of that afternoon's golf match had reached all of the men, and it was this knowledge that had them appearing more somber at lunch than usual. Rather than talking and joking, they spoke in hushed tones and took subtle glances at Evan while he ate. Several sat near him.

"Major Akerly says there will be no surprises today." John Michaels was in his thirties, making him the oldest enlisted man in the battalion, and it was Michaels who prided himself most on possessing information. "Akerly says you'll win," he continued. "He says you simply must win. He says you have no other choice."

Evan made no reply, but Chadwick could not contain himself. "Evan has already won," he said.

The men finished eating and walked to their trucks to depart for that afternoon's practice. Evan accompanied

110

them, and the group shook his hand, slapped him on the back, and offered their encouragement. Several wanted to stay behind for the game, but when Captain Becker, rather than Floyd, appeared and gave the order to load up for departure, they were quick to obey. They also had a clear understanding of what they were to do before they left. With military dispatch, they surrounded the surprised instructors, grabbed them as before, carried their protesting bodies to the back of the nearest truck, deposited them inside, climbed in, and banged on the cab of the truck, signaling the driver to go. Evan joined in Chadwick and Fletcher's protests, but Captain Becker blocked his way. A heated conversation ensued as Evan protested and Captain Becker commanded him to "stand down." Evan shouted until Captain Becker's anger reached a critical moment of uncertainty, and then he turned after the trucks and their artillery pieces were gone, taking the instructors. Evan was alone when he made his final protest.

"That's not right!" he yelled. The rear exhaust of Captain Becker's departing jeep coughed its agreement.

Evan next went in search of Floyd, where he voiced his complaint.

"I cannot allow those two to know what happens here today," Floyd said. "The general could find out. Because they're not here, they won't know. Though they might think a game was played, they cannot be certain. And you had better hold your tongue."

Evan swallowed his frustration and returned to his barrack to prepare for the game. About thirty minutes later, four automobiles pulled into the golf course parking lot and stopped in the area by the trucks. Floyd retrieved Evan, and together they went to find the same group of young men and women who had been at the dinner party. There was a quiet excitement about everyone assembled, heightened by the fact that they were doing something forbidden. Eyes glanced here and there, and everyone whispered. People acted as though they wished to avoid detection, as if discovery meant trouble. Floyd provided relief with the manner in which he strode about the first tee. It was obvious to all he was in control when he stood before them and took charge. He tossed a wooden golf tee into the air to decide who would hit first.

By 1943, there was no confusion as to who hit first on a hole. It was the player who had the fewest number of strokes on the prior hole. If someone won the previous hole, then he hit first on the next. It was simple. The practice had already become the rule, but the rule did not apply to the first hole of a game because no one had yet won a previous hole. The precedent at the first hole was for one of the players to toss a tee into the air. Upon its landing, the player at whom the pointed end aimed was extended the privilege of hitting first. When the pointed end of the tee landed and pointed between two players, however, as it did following Floyd's toss, an argument usually ensued. Charles was adamant that he was closest to the tee's aim, and Floyd was equally adamant that Evan was the target. Evan, with lips drawn and his head turning back and forth, looked down at the tee and stepped forward. He bent down, picked it up, and looked at Charles. "You hit first," he said.

Instead of protesting, Charles stepped right up to the tee. There was a strong swish as his club cut through air, and his ball flew off the tee with a solid click. He hit a nice drive that bounced and rolled farther, stopping dead center in the first fairway. The game was on.

The previous day had been wet, but the grass of the fairway that gray August afternoon had already dried. The surface of the ground had hardened in the heat, so Evan's first drive confirmed that both players would be hitting long that afternoon. Though his drive stopped shorter than Charles', Evan was the first to reach the green with his next shot—a long five iron—and he was the first in the cup with an easy six-foot putt. He won the first hole, won the second hole too, and both golfers scored par on the third. When there is a tie on a hole, the player who hits first is the one who had won the previous hole. Evan hit first on four, and his ball landed in a position from which he might approach the tricky green without first landing on the sandy beachhead of traps. Charles' ball landed near Evan's, but his next shot over-flew the green and managed to find the upper sand trap. He hit his third shot with a sand wedge that sent his ball and a swath of sand flying out of the trap. The ball bounced once on the green, well before the flagstick. It hung for an instant high on the sloping green, and then rolled all of the way to the bottom.

Sloping greens have a way of silencing onlookers, but Floyd reacted with a groan. "Ooh, that's too bad," he said, feigning disappointment. "Maybe you would like it to be raining right now?"

The Professional Golfers' Association, the PGA, cancelled professional golf in 1943 because of the war. Had there been a championship played that year, as the professional golfers walked along from one hole to the next, a crowd of spectators would have followed. The spectators were dubbed "the gallery," and it had been established as a goal of professional golfers to play so well that the gallery would rush up to hush and watch the professionals do their work. The greatest accomplishment, second to winning, or at least to earning money, was for a professional golfer to tell another that he "had the gallery running." Evan's small gallery did not run that day in 1943. Rather, it flowed like a slow-moving river without currents, rapids, or any other surprises. It simply followed the gradient of his consistent play. The flow was tee, fairway, and green, tee, fairway, and green. As play continued, Charles and his companions took labored strides, and Evan moved with such determination that he surprised Floyd.

"So that's his anger," Floyd thought.

The young ladies did not run in the heat that day, but they did rush to keep up with the play. Amanda watched Evan's every swing, and she counted each stroke he made and kept a mental tabulation of just how badly he was beating Charles. She held her breath when Evan was about to hit, laughed after his swings, and clapped when he birdied the tenth hole—the straight par four. She frowned on a hole where Evan's ball drew left, bounced on the dry grass of the fairway like a rubber ball hitting a hard surface, and rolled off into the rough. She did not notice how Floyd ignored her that day, except for the eight or nine quick glances he made and found her intense focus on Evan.

The eighteenth hole was the final hole of the game. In those early years of El Rancho Golf Course, that fairway—after the dogleg turn to the left—led straight to the green, sitting lush and groomed before the clubhouse. Charles had trouble with the far trees on his drive, but Evan faded his shot into the turn. When the players reached their balls and the gallery was assembled where they could see around the dogleg, everyone looked at Floyd.

"Oh, damn!" he yelled.

They saw his face was ashy pale, his eyes were open as wide as his mouth, and he was looking just past where the flagstick waved above the hole in the green. The group followed Floyd's eyes, and they observed exactly what it was he had seen. Several military vehicles were visible just past the green, and beside the cars stood the Army general and his entire entourage, poised like watchmen searching the distance. The general's pointed finger was proof they had been discovered.

"Damn!" Floyd repeated. "The game is over. Everyone leave right now!"

Charles started to protest, but Floyd's voice had such an authoritative, commanding, unquestionable edge that Charles checked himself and the game ended then and there. Floyd rushed ahead of everyone, and all of the young men and women followed at a reluctant distance. Those who did not belong on the golf course went straight to their cars and departed.

Evan caught Amanda's eye when she made her retreating, over-the-shoulder glance at him. Neither of them smiled. He stayed out on the course for another hour, putting. He returned to his barrack after seeing the battalion return from artillery practice. By the time he readied for dinner and arrived among the men, he found them to be a somber bunch. They had heard the news of the day's events and the general's arrival. Dinner talk was restricted to matters of artillery, but Evan saw questions reserved in every eye. Unsmiling glances, timely head turns, and the irrelevant conversations spoke enough about the day.

Floyd failed to appear for dinner that night, but he was ready for the following morning.

CHAPTER 12

~ A FIRST LOOK ~

Evan's training reached a point when there were only two weeks remaining until the late August date designated for the Army-Navy golf game. Military discipline had been restored on the base, and crisp saluting, quick obeying, and snappy yes-siring were almost overdone. Floyd's smiles, following his private meeting with the general, entirely vanished. He never spoke a word to Evan about the golf game with Charles, the general's surprise visit, Evan's artillery duties, or much of anything at all. Evan was instructed to practice with only the instructors, and he was assured the two would never again be prevented from attending a practice session. The certainty with which Floyd made his assertion did not sound like it came from an admonishment but sounded, instead, like it came from a severe punishment that Evan never felt.

The routine established at El Rancho Golf Course thus became even more predictable than it had been. For the men, it was instruction, lunch, offsite artillery training, and then dinner. For Evan and his instructors, it was golfing, lunch, more golfing, and then dinner. No one discussed the unauthorized golf game in public, and the knowledge that Evan was eight strokes ahead of the collegiate champion when they reached the eighteenth hole—the hole on which Charles' ball landed among a collection of trees—mattered not at all. Planning for the 170th Field Artillery Battalion's movements had begun. They would cross the Atlantic in the born-again Queen Elizabeth. From Liverpool, England, they would take part in the invasion of the continent to liberate France and help eliminate the Nazis.

Where humans are involved, when events return to normal, they do not necessarily return to what they once were. The passage of time softens rough edges, memories conform more with desires than with facts, nostalgia for what once was taunts what really is, and a tacit belief forms that the present can be made to resemble the past. Childhood memories, for example, can become more pleasurable with the passage of time. So it was that Evan played golf every day, Chadwick and Fletcher instructed him, and hours of strategies were adopted, tested, abandoned, refined, and practiced. The golfers were alone on the course while they played, and everything had returned to normal. Almost.

What changed was the addition of Amanda to the golfing trio. Every day the three men played the first hole, and when they reached the tee at the second hole, they would find Amanda waiting for them with her clubs. The second hole was well blocked from the view of the clubhouse, headquarters tent, barracks, parking lot, the area of parked artillery equipment, and all other vantage points where the men of the 170th might happen to be. The result was that the threesome could spend the remaining weeks practicing golf with Amanda, and she could play as though she were one of them. She was not taking lessons, she was not an instructor, she was not practicing for the purpose of improving her game, but she managed to become the most significant member of the group, just like the moon becomes most significant among a night sky of planets. The usual one or two August downpours had already fallen, so every day was warm and sunny.

Los Angeles' summer breezes had a coating effect on the golf course, like warm caramel oozing down a cone. Breezes caught the treetops and they trembled, air slid down their lengths, and then warm air covered everything on the course. The grassy tops of the fairways felt these breezes barely as a breath, but by the time they reached the foursome, the warm air was still. When they were quiet, the sounds they heard were simply those of nature, and when they were not silent, the sounds were those of the four: the swoosh of a club through the air, the appealing click of a club head against a ball, little phrases of appreciation, helpful suggestions, playful teasing, laughter of people enjoying each other's company. When a third member joins to form a foursome, a period of adjustment follows until the fourth becomes familiar, experienced, understood, assimilated, and then indistinguishable from the group. Amanda's case was different. The group accepted her at once. Her presence became a necessity, as though she had been with them all along.

Evan thought Fletcher enjoyed Amanda the most, because she was the recipient of his unending comments. Whenever he laughed, he looked to catch her eyes first. The two were often together watching Evan, and they scrutinized him every time he approached, addressed, and hit a ball. What Fletcher saw was never the same as what Amanda saw.

"Did you see that?" Fletcher whispered to Amanda, just after Evan's iron shot made in the middle of a fairway. "He did it again."

"No he didn't," she whispered. "Are you saying Evan moved his head during his swing? I didn't see it, but from where his ball stopped clear up there on the green," she smiled while pointing up the fairway, "Evan should move his head like that every time he hits."

Fletcher pursed his lips, tilted his head toward her, and peered at her with his brows raised. His eyes looked from the tops of their sockets. "Correction," he said, "must be immediate. I have to help him."

Fletcher called to Evan, who was about to return his iron to the bag, and had Evan try the same shot again, and again, and again. When Evan addressed each ball, with the heel of his left foot in line with the lie of his ball, Fletcher stood in front of him with his hand atop Evan's thin head, holding it like his hand was a cap. Fletcher would not move when Evan swung his club. If the military had permitted men to wear longer hair, Fletcher would have held a wad of it in his hand throughout every swing.

"Do you feel it?" Fletcher asked. "Your head remains still. Keep it this way every time you hit." Then he added, "I can't be there during your play, so you should just feel my hand there with you. Imagine I'm there holding your head still."

As soon as Fletcher was finished with his lesson, he returned to Amanda with the serious look of a professional, a look of someone who had just completed something quite important. Amanda smiled at him, and he nodded without meeting her eyes, as though using his head to drop a silent exclamation point at the end of his lesson.

"Keep your head still throughout your swing," Fletcher said to Amanda.

"To be sure," she said, "I will."

As she moved on, she exchanged one of those familiar, understanding, shared glances with Evan, and he returned to her a sideways grin. The two quickly developed a manner of looking at each other after every one of Fletcher's lessons, and their eye contact was soon enhanced with smiles and subdued sentiments. She would occasionally pass close enough to Evan to add some quiet little comment that Fletcher could not hear.

"Fletcher's right there holding you," she would say. "His hand is on your head. Can you feel it?"

One day, Evan's ball landed in the middle of a short fairway, still about fifty yards away from its green. He stood beside the ball and selected an iron from his thin canvas bag as Fletcher rushed up and stopped him from hitting.

"OK," Fletcher said, "here we go. This is the perfect distance for practicing your approach shot." Fletcher exchanged a look with Chadwick and a glance with Amanda. "There are three different approaches that work well. First, I want you to try a bump-and-run shot."

Evan's clubs had metal heads, but Fletcher's vocabulary excluded golf evolution. "You do the bump-and-run by using a wood to run your ball up onto the green. For this approach, position your ball in line with your right heel, take a medium swing, and make your ball roll onto the green. Just pop it. There's one more thing. When the ground is this hard," he said, banging the head of his club on the ground, "rolling your ball up onto the green is the best idea. Now give it a try."

Evan made one, two, and three such approach shots. His ball went too far, too far, and then not far enough.

"Just keep practicing the shot," Fletcher suggested.

Chadwick wrinkled his brow and squinted, then approached Fletcher. He placed an arm on Fletcher's back and looked at Evan.

"Let's try a second approach shot," Chadwick said. "Use a middle iron to land your ball about three-quarters of the way to the green. Then let it roll. Swing your club back until it is pointing at the three o'clock position, then swing forward and let it end pointing at the nine o'clock position."

Evan used his eight iron to take three such approach shots, and two of his balls landed on the green and one landed just short. "That's better," Chadwick said, speaking more to Fletcher than to Evan.

"How about I just use my normal shot?" Evan asked, while retrieving his pitching wedge from his golf bag.

This time, all three of his balls flew high and landed hard on the green, each one landing with a slight bit of backspin. He placed all three balls within close putting range of the cup.

"Hmm," Fletcher said, "your approach shot has been working for you. Maybe we should not change it just now. Go ahead and use what works." Looking at Amanda, he added, "It's the lesson that's important. Knowing you have options makes you a better player."

"Fletcher's right," Chadwick added. "Of the three approach shots, you should stick with the one that works best for you."

Amanda exchanged eye contact with Evan, and she laughed out loud, drawing the attention of both instructors. They watched her try the same three approach shots.

"That doesn't work at all," she said.

The instructors laughed, Evan smiled, and then he introduced to her a fourth way of reaching a green. He picked up a ball and simply threw it with his hand. Because the ball landed early and rolled onto the green, Chadwick named the new method the "toss 'n run," and Fletcher laughed as though at a great joke. With her among them, the instructors loosened up, and Evan and Amanda became ever more playful, teasing, and flirtatious. They laughed, walked together, and developed their own language of subtleties and eye contact.

"Of course you know," Fletcher said, "you cannot do that in real play."

"Isn't this real play?"

"No!" he said. "This is only practice. All it does is ready you for the real thing."

"I think she's ready for the real thing now," Evan said, drawing her eyes to his.

"Is that so?"

In this manner, a whole week passed in what felt to the group like a few short days. On Friday of their first full week of daily-doubles golfing, Chadwick and Fletcher were again searching through the back nine rough and Evan and Amanda were walking together down the middle of a fairway. Their pace was slow as they strolled along the grassy carpet, albeit dry and worn this late in the season. Evan noticed Amanda's hesitating and turning toward him, as though she had something to say or to ask of him. She said nothing until she stopped walking and turned to face him. He was carrying her bag of clubs, and he stopped with her, thinking she would want to make her selection.

What is she doing? he wondered. He offered her the bag of clubs. *Clearly she's thinking. But, no. She does not have the need of a club. She's nervous. She's avoiding my eyes. I think she wants to ask me a question, but she doesn't seem to know how to begin.*

Evan watched and waited while Amanda looked at the ground. He noticed how her feet lightly shifted, the palm of her right hand caressed the back of her left, her drawn-back hair showed the full of her face, her forehead creased slightly, her lips were held closed, and she seemed troubled by some resolution she had yet to make, as though she was crafting words to put to her thoughts. After pausing in this manner long enough for Evan to notice her discomfort, she lifted her eyes and gave him a nervous smile.

"Can I see you this weekend?" she asked.

"Yes," he said, answering more quickly than he expected. He sought to recover himself by adding, "I would like that."

They smiled at each other without considering the "how" behind Amanda's question or about the speed of Evan's answer. There comes a time when a young man first looks a young lady full in the face, in broad daylight, and allows her to view in his own eyes, to see clearly, a reflection of the same emotions she also is feeling. This is honesty's most innocent moment, honesty's most unabashed, for after this first revelation, all future relations grow. They can look back and pinpoint the moment their interest was openly shared, and they can say, "That's when we knew," though such little moments fade with a couple's first kiss. The first kisses receive all of the attention, recognition, and later recollection. Even a first touch, with hands held together, fingers intertwined, stirs more emotion, but it is the first deep look that permits these others. It was just such a first look for Evan and Amanda. It was the spark that ignited, but does anyone return from riding in an automobile and care about the engine's first spark?

After that first look, Evan and Amanda's relationship changed. Fletcher noticed an increase in their enjoyment of the practices, more frequent laughter shared between the two, a greater amount of lingering eye contact, and a new familiarity and closeness in their manner. They teased each other in a private way that excluded everyone else, and it was as though the foursome had again become a threesome, with one of the new trio comprised of Evan and Amanda. On one hole, Chadwick and Fletcher stood watching and whispering. They were huddled together near the edge of a fairway, and Evan and Amanda were out in the middle.

"Look at them," Chadwick said. "They look like they're in their own world."

Their first look, though only a spark, opened for them a private experience where they experienced everything together. Driving, pitching, chipping, putting, bunker play, drawing, fading, and all other facets of the game of golf became autonomic functions to Evan. He started playing rather than practicing.

"We'll be here tomorrow, Amanda," Fletcher said just as the foursome broke for the day. "See you on two?"

"Yes," she said, but she took her eyes from Fletcher's, found Evan's, lingered as though asking another question, and returned to look at Fletcher with resolve. "I'll be there."

"I don't have a choice," Evan said. "I have to play tomorrow." Turning to the instructors, he added, "But you don't have to play. You two have been playing a lot. Why don't you take a day off? I'll be fine for one day."

His suggestion caught their attention just as it had Amanda's. The following day, after lunch and the usual round of morning practice, the battalion left for artillery practice. Chadwick stopped Evan just as he was preparing to leave to meet Amanda.

"Hold on," he said. "There is a town Fletcher and I have wanted to see for years. It's called Pasadena. We were thinking about going right now, but that would mean you are on your own this afternoon. Are you okay without us? We would be back before the battalion returns from practice. What do you think?"

"I would practice alone with Amanda," he said, pressing his lips to suppress his smile.

"You would be alone," Chadwick said, "but get back in time to meet us for dinner. Don't let Floyd catch you."

Evan found Amanda waiting for him at the second hole of the empty golf course. When she saw he was the only one approaching, she asked about the instructors.

Evan explained their decision to go to Pasadena. "We're alone today," he said. "I have to be back by dinner, though." He saw that she understood what he said, but he noticed, too, that she avoided making eye contact.

During Amanda's hesitation to look at him, she developed a half smile, tugged at a blouse sleeve, smoothed her skirt pleats, and glanced here and there as though she were being watched.

"We don't have to play golf this afternoon," he said.

"Really?" she said, looking him full in the face and smiling. Her eyes revealed a lively sparkle of pleasure. "Do you mean it? But I thought you had to play golf."

"I do," he said," but that's all I've been doing. I sure could use a break. An afternoon away from the game would do me good."

"Alright," she said, sounding relieved, nervous, and excited all at once. She took Evan's arm by the elbow, pulled him so that he was compelled to follow along, and the two walked together the length of the fairway without hitting a single shot. She next led him past several other tee boxes, across fairways and greens, and emerged through the brush and trees separating her home from the golf course.

"Can we have a day at the pool?" she asked. "Will you get in trouble if you spend the day here?"

"I don't know. No. Probably," he said. "But who cares?"

They both laughed at his sudden indifference. Amanda went inside to change into her bathing suit while Evan changed in the pool house into a pair of her father's swim trunks. When they emerged minutes later, they slipped into the cool water for a quick swim, then sat poolside on thick terry cloth towels, sunbathing, talking, teasing, laughing, and enjoying an afternoon of getting to know each other. They were both aware of being entirely alone, but much of their conversation began with words like who, what, when, where, why, and how. After several hours, they separated to change clothes before meeting back by the pool.

"Would you like to have lunch?" Amanda asked. "It's all ready for us." She led him to a patio table where, to his surprise, Evan saw a small weathered table with two wooden chairs. The chairs had cushions with an auburn print that matched the cloth napkins and placemats up on the table.

"How did you manage this?" he asked.

"We have help," she said. "You remember the night you came to our party and the butler met you at the door? His wife Maria cooks and cleans for us. She did all of this for me."

Like a wisp of air, Maria flowed through the house, following Amanda's hasty instructions. The spread she prepared included sandwiches, potato salad, pudding topped with whipped cream, and a serving pitcher with ice cubes floating in pink lemonade. They sat at the little table and ate together, talking about Floyd, Chadwick, Fletcher, the young men from UCLA, and Amanda's parents.

"What about your parents, Evan? Where are they? Please tell me about your childhood."

Evan swirled his glass of lemonade, watched two ice cubes knock about in the liquid, and spoke without meeting her eyes.

"I grew up in McCall, Idaho, and I played a lot of golf. How's that?" He looked up and grinned.

"And your parents?"

"My mother passed away before my first birthday, and my father died before I was born."

"I am so sorry," she said, frowning, drawing her hands together, and holding them under her chin. "Who raised you, then?"

"I lived with my grandmother," he said. "Edna was alone. I was alone. She was good for me, and I was good for her. She had several old men who liked her, and that is how I learned to play golf. She made every one of them take me golfing."

"Where is she now?" she asked, meeting his grin with hers. "Is she alone in Idaho?"

"No," he said, "When she died, I joined the Army. That's everything. Really, I am my family."

Next they talked about the golf course, her home, the Army, the Navy, her mother's frequent parties, but not of their being together. The conversation moved from people and things to ideas. They talked about the upcoming competition against the Navy, about the Army, the war, and the growing film industry, but not about the time they were sharing.

When the subject of the conversation finally touched on the matter of the two of them, they looked toward the pool, at nearby trees, at a loose thread in one of the napkins, at their hands, and then, with self-conscious grins, at each other.

"What happens after you leave here?" Amanda asked.

"You know I'll be going to Europe to fight the Nazis, or maybe I'll end up fighting on some island in the Pacific. I'm not sure. Wherever I go, I can only be sure of fighting and trouble."

"That's not what I meant. When do you suppose you'll be leaving?"

He saw her twisting her napkin like she was trying to wring water from it. With her question, she reached the end of the napkin's give, but she squeezed further while awaiting his answer.

"Wiiilkiiinns?" came a faint call, carried from somewhere out on the golf course. They both heard it. Evan snapped his head toward the voice, and she followed his look with wide eyes of her own. He looked at his pocket watch and saw it was past dinner time by over an hour.

"Someone's looking for me," he said. "I have to go. Now!"

They jumped up at the same time and stood facing each other while holding hands. They reacted as though the surprise and alarm the searcher caused brought them closer together. When the voice came again, Amanda squeezed. While she appeared to be frightened, he looked helpless. He released her hands and turned to go.

"Thank you for a beautiful day," he managed. "I'll see you in the morning."

Evan took his bag of clubs and rushed down the darkened pathway and emerged on the golf course. Once there, he hid behind a large tree that stood beside the fairway. He remained behind the tree while scanning the course and the nearby fairway for any movement, carefully listening for sounds. Then he saw someone on the fairway coming straight toward him. He pressed closer against the tree, watched the man stop to cup hands around his mouth, and then he heard him call again.

Evan had no trouble putting together the approaching figure with the voice. *Oh, no,* he thought. *It's Floyd. He's coming right toward me.*

CHAPTER 13

~ THE BLIND SPOT IN A TREE ~

Evan made a quick assessment of the area where he stood. The pathway behind him was surrounded by the tall foliage of the trail. He peeked from behind his tree and saw Floyd in the remaining light of the summer evening. He knew Floyd would see him if he moved from behind the fat trunk. Pressing his hands against the rough bark, he stared and thought about Floyd's finding him hiding so late and so close to Amanda's house. He froze at the prospect.

He heard Floyd's brisk footsteps getting louder. Floyd took large strides, turned his head left and right, and furiously watched for every motion. Evan estimated that he would soon be opposite the tree. He took careful little side steps and peeked around the trunk, taking care to stay silent, hidden, and unmoving.

He thought of his golf clubs. A rattle would give him away. He took one hand off the tree trunk and, with a snake's slow and deliberate movements, slid his arm behind him and wrapped it around the bag of clubs. Rather than strike, knocking the bag and rattling the clubs and giving away his position, his arm squeezed the loose clubs together like a boa constrictor crushing its prey. He killed both the bag's ability to move and to make any sound.

At a critical point, Evan lost sight of Floyd. Compensating for the blind spot in the tree took care, good timing, and his ability to anticipate Floyd's movements.

He imagined the speed at which his pursuer was moving and adjusted his own movements around the tree accordingly. As the sound of footsteps grew close, Evan synchronized his baby steps behind the tree in order to remain hidden. He held open his eyes and listened. Suddenly, nothing moved on the opposite side of the tree.

Evan held his breath, squeezed the bag of clubs tighter, listened more intently, and remained motionless with his face pressed flat against the bark of the tree. He still had one arm wrapped around the bag of clubs behind him. He looked down and realized that the bottom edge of the bag was poking out to one side behind him. It would be visible to anyone standing beyond the base of the tree. If Floyd happened to look at the tree, he would surely see it, and no doubt he would investigate and easily discover Evan. He considered his options and found them to be few. He resisted the instinct to jerk the bag back, knowing the sudden movement would give away his position. His mind went into a heightened sense of alertness. His thoughts came in bursts. *Quiet. Be careful. Don't move. Listen. Breathe.*

Emotions came like words. Though panic was the dominant feeling, he also felt the greater instinct of self-preservation. He sought to remain hidden. Rational thought often becomes scattered in such situations, and decisions then made tend to miss important considerations such as "If I move, what might I step on, snap, and then give myself away?" No one is exempt from the need for clear thinking, though some are better under stress than others. Evan possessed this ability. In the absence of footsteps, he considered what to do next. His heart set the pace for his racing thoughts. He decided to completely withdraw the bag and remain entirely hidden from Floyd.

Floyd shouted again, and it sounded impossibly loud. Evan pressed closer against the tree, retracted the bottom of the bag at the speed of a clock's hour hand, but gained little comfort when done. At once, the silence struck him as being entirely too pervasive. Floyd broke it by again calling his name, but Evan did not move.

Floyd resumed sweeping his eyes from here to there across the golf course. At one point, he fixed his eyes on the trunk of Evan's tree. The moment was brief, though, for Floyd sought to see farther than the trunk. He stared up the pathway that led to Amanda's house.

"Damn him!" he said, yelling at the empty golf course. He scowled, took another glance about, turned, and proceeded to walk away from the tree. "Damn him," he said again.

Evan again made careful little side steps around the tree, and he watched Floyd walk away, turning his head to see both left and right. Floyd stopped, cupped his hands at the sides of his mouth, and filled the air with another call. Evan relaxed by releasing his breath, lessening the tight squeeze he held on the bag of clubs still squeezed against his back. Clink! One iron club knocked against another. The sound was minute, but Floyd heard it. He had been listening for a reply to his call—listening carefully—and he stopped, turned back, and looked for the source.

Evan again adjusted himself into the blind spot of the tree, tightly squeezed his bag of clubs behind him, pressed his cheek close against the bark, and looked to the bottom position of his bag. Satisfied that it was hidden, he froze, listened, and heard the call of his name break the silence.

Floyd again stood unmoving, listening and watching. Hearing only the quiet sound of the empty golf course, he made a closed-mouth grunt of frustration and turned to depart for the second time. He left intending to continue his search for Evan elsewhere on the course. He felt relief that his suspicion was not confirmed—he had expected to find Evan at Amanda's—but the comfort was imperceptible in the manner in which he frowned. He grunted again, heaved an exhale, and turned his back to leave. For a moment, he considered abandoning his personal search in favor of delegating the job to the battalion's lowly runner.

It was then, however, that Amanda Nichols appeared on the edge of the fairway. She had come down the pathway from her home just as Floyd was leaving. Evan saw her first, but he did not give her a wide-eyed look of wonder, did not turn his head, and he did not mouth words of caution. He remained pressed against the tree trunk, looking at her and grinning for how ridiculous he must have looked to her. He watched as she purposefully avoided giving away his position. When she first walked several steps out onto the course, her look was a passing, furtive glance. With one of her hands, she attempted to make some sort of signal to Evan, while at the same time keeping her eyes fixed on Floyd's back. She held her arms at her sides, with one hand extended flat, and she made subtle patting motions of the air. Evan understood her to be indicating that he should remain where he was. She then drew a deep breath, looked out toward Floyd, and pretended not to see Evan.

"Major Akerly," she called, "is that you?"

Floyd stopped, turned, and saw it was Amanda calling for him. He looked both ways and came forward to meet her. The agitation of his expression changed to a smile. He rushed to where she stood.

"Amanda!" He spoke as though he was surprised to see her, and he used a familiar tone normally reserved for family and friends.

"Where is Private Wilkins?" she asked. "I thought I heard you calling to him. Is he out here with you?"

"No. I'm looking for him now," Floyd said. "He's late. He did not return from practice with his instructors. He missed dinner, and I thought I'd better try and find him. I don't suppose you've seen him, have you?"

"It's evening," she said, "and I neither golf during dinner nor walk the course alone at night. You must be searching for him in the wrong place. If Evan is out here, then where do you suppose he is?"

Floyd looked at her eyes, searching them deeper, but he looked too deep. He became distracted. Her eyes, the sound of her voice, and sight of her there alone with him gave him the perception she was speaking to him with an equal tone of familiarity. The sight of her tall figure, the light patio dress she still wore, the intentional smile she gave that added unintentional animation to her eyes, her pretty face, the manner in which she had walked out to meet him on the golf course, and the manner in which she made one or two nervous glances off to her side, entirely distracted him. It pleased him to see her there with him.

"No worry," he said. "I'll find him, but I much prefer finding you. What a pleasant surprise. We never did get to talk at your party. There were just too many people. Besides, Evan and those college boys distracted us both. Maybe we can get acquainted now. Will you walk with me? We can talk."

Young ladies have the uncanny ability of showing a smile while they are frowning inside and, with Floyd, Amanda was an expert. She did so while taking a small step backward, bringing her hands together before her, twisting her fingers, and again making a quick glance to Evan's tree. She just barely smiled when she answered Floyd.

"No," Amanda said, hesitating not a bit. "It will be dark soon, and I'm expected back at the house. My parents have important guests coming tonight. I simply must be going."

Floyd adopted what he thought to be a gallant posture. He contorted his eyebrows and small eyes in an attempt to appear compassionate. Several lines appeared on his forehead. He took two steps toward Amanda and lowered his voice. "Then," he said, "I will at least make sure you make it home safely. You must allow me to escort. I insist."

Amanda glanced at Evan's tree, but she never saw him. When Floyd moved closer to her, Evan side-stepped farther behind the tree, but she gave a small start upon seeing the edge of the bottom of his golf bag showing from behind the trunk. She recovered by smiling at Floyd.

"Of course you may escort me, major," she said, ensuring his attention remained away from the tree. Floyd saw only her pretty smile.

They walked toward the path that led up to the Nichols home, with Floyd determined to play the part of a gentleman. He felt his presence to be especially helpful because, as he reminded her, a seaman had once spied on her from behind these same bushes—near the same path she would be otherwise walking alone. He determined she see him as brave and chivalrous. When they reached the swimming pool, he stopped.

"It looks like you already had your dinner," he said, pointing. "But it doesn't look like you ate alone."

Amanda checked her surprise when she followed Floyd's finger to the wooden table where she and Evan had eaten their late afternoon lunch. The table was in post-meal disarray, and it was obvious that only two people had eaten. The napkins were wadded and tossed onto the empty plates, no ice floated in the lemonade, and the serving dishes were half empty.

"Oh," she said, "my parents often eat lunch out here. They must have done so today." She shrugged and continued walking. When she reached her back door, she took the knob in her hand and looked at him. "Thank you, major. Have a good night." She went inside and closed the door behind her.

Floyd protested her quick departure. He planned to suggest that she stay out and talk a bit longer. He had crafted words for mentioning the possibility of seeing her again. By the time he articulated his thoughts, however, he was met by the window glass of the closed door. She had not been unkind, just firm. She knew most men understood rejection, but decided Floyd needed a closed door to get the message.

Just as soon as Floyd and Amanda passed the tree, Evan took off toward the golf course. He ran with the bag of clubs rattling on his back. He stopped when he reached a par three hole just before the eighteenth, pulled out his nine iron, and began swinging and hitting balls at the green, as though he was unaware of the time and still practicing. Not surprisingly, his nerves affected his shots. The first ball sailed clear over the green, the next did the same, another went right, also too far, and several more proved to be magnetically opposed to the surface of the green. He attempted to calm himself by looking in his bag, and withdrawing and examining several additional golf balls he intended to hit. As he looked into the bag, he laughed. He thought of his day spent with Amanda. With his iron, he manipulated the collection of golf balls he had dropped right there in the grass. He thought of Floyd, too, and his smile was reduced to a frown. He hit the remaining balls without a single one landing on the green.

Evan replaced his club in the bag then heard his name being called. He looked back as though surprised and saw Floyd approaching from across another fairway. He caught up to Evan in a flash.

"There you are," Floyd said. "Do you know you're late?"

"I thought so," Evan said. "I'm getting hungry, but I thought it would be better for the Army if I stayed to practice."

"That's not your decision."

"Of course not," Evan said. "Should I wire the general?"

"Don't get smart with me. Pick up these golf balls and get back to base."

Floyd waved his hand at the scattered balls. "Look at this. What's going on? This hole must have the most difficult green on the course. You did not hit a single ball on the green. Is something wrong? Is the Army in trouble?"

CHAPTER 14

~ BIRDIES, EAGLES, AND ALBATROSSES ~

Evan's day with Amanda compared with an ocean wave cresting, crashing, and rushing ashore. His early morning round of golf with her and the two instructors was the smooth swell, always so pleasing to see way out in the ocean. His afternoon at her home was like the swell blown by warm winds, gaining size and becoming unstoppable as it approaches its own inevitability. The wave's crest was the sound of his name coming to him on the wind, as though it had been carried a great distance. His eluding discovery by Floyd was the breaking wave's violent tumbling, noisy crashing, and confused rushing that had him hiding behind a tree, running across fairways, and finally returning to the Army camp where Floyd soaked him with salty, frothy reprimands. As ocean water slides back into the sea, though, it reshapes the shore and wipes clean its sandy surface. What then remains is not what was. Forever is changed, and so it was for Evan and Amanda.

When Evan first saw her the next morning as she waited with her clubs by the tee box at hole number two, there was that instant familiarity that comes with shared experience. He went straight to her. They looked directly into each other's eyes, laughed out loud, and just as they had done prior to their surprise parting the previous evening, they held each other's hands. Their approach that next morning was so immediate, and so familiar, that Chadwick and

Fletcher stayed off to a side unzipping pouches on their
bags, wiping golf balls, examining wooden tees, writing on
the morning's scorecard, discussing the morning's plans,
and performing as many little nothings they could find.

"Are you alright?" Amanda asked Evan. "Did you get
into trouble?"

"I'm fine," he said. "I was found doing nothing more
than practicing golf. Major Akerly was upset, but he's always
that way. What about you? I didn't mean to leave so quickly.
We didn't have dessert. How about we try again next time?"

Evan never waited for her to answer his first question
before lingering his "next time" suggestion. His words were
a challenge, emphasized with slow up-and-down nods of his
head, without laughing, and with a grin he made with his
lips pressed together and his eyes narrowed.

"Yes," she said after returning his smile, "but do you
really think there will be a next time? Do you dare? Do we
dare?"

"Sure. Why not?"

"Well, first there is Major Akerly. He really wanted to sit
and get to know me last night. I had to be rude to him just
so he would leave. He's nosy, and then there are those two
over there."

Evan followed Amanda's nod toward Chadwick and
Fletcher. They were standing face-to-face, comparing
how each gripped his driver. Chadwick dangled his club
before him in his left hand, and Fletcher was showing
his grip while squeezing his club with both of his hands
pressed together. They appeared to be engrossed in their
conversation and unaware of Evan and Amanda.

"You did a fine job of being rude to him," Evan said.
"From what I could tell, Floyd got your message loud and
clear. So loud and clear I think it echoed through him to

me. He was especially mad at me last night. At me! And all I was doing was what I have been ordered to do."

"So, how can there be a next time?" she asked.

"As long as we're both willing, we'll find a way."

They again laughed together, then spent the entire morning practicing with greater attention to the game than either had shown before. Evan drove his shots farther than ever, and on one par four hole, he drove onto the green, a first for him at El Rancho Golf Course. He next made his putt and scored an eagle.

"What does that mean?" Amanda asked. "Why is it called an eagle?"

"It's a way of recognizing a difficult accomplishment," answered Fletcher. Both Evan and Amanda looked at him, but he said nothing more.

"Fletcher is talking about slang," Chadwick said, casting a frown at Fletcher. "Just forget about an 'eagle' for a moment. The answer to your question resides in the past. At the beginning of the last century, the word 'bird' was used to mean 'neat' and 'nice.' Today's new word for the same thing is 'cool,' but in the early eighteen-hundreds, the word was 'bird.'"

"So I would say 'bird' if I thought something was cool?" Amanda asked.

"You would say it was a 'bird,' yes. That was the word for 'cool' back then. Anyway, putting your ball into the cup in fewer hits than par was seen as being cool. Back then it was said to be a bird. Because the use of slang words always changes with time and, because beating par by one stroke remains something cool to do, the slang changed a bird into a birdie."

"So if a birdie is a cool shot, then what is an eagle? A really cool shot?"

"Exactly," Chadwick said laughing, clearly enjoying his being in possession of knowledge, like a pedantic instructor. "The same effect that gives us slang also affects slang. A bird is just a bird, but an eagle, now that's a bird. Beating par by two strokes is called an eagle."

Fletcher, Evan, and Amanda smiled and watched Chadwick as he explained the golf terms.

"Is anything better than an eagle?" she asked. "I know an ostrich is a bigger bird. Do you score an ostrich if you shoot three under par?"

"Good point," Evan joked, laughing.

"No," Chadwick said, looking from Evan to Amanda. "An ostrich is a bigger bird, of course, but it does not soar like an eagle. Birds soar, eagles soar, and so do sea eagles. An albatross is what you score if you shoot a double eagle, three under par. Hit one of these, and you'll be the one who soars."

"An albatross?" she said loudly, frowning, and honestly interested. "What is an albatross?"

"It's a sea eagle," Chadwick answered. "They fly out on the ocean." He saw Amanda's skepticism and continued. "Their wings can span over ten feet, and if there is enough wind out on the ocean, they can glide for hours. They dive for food."

"Who can hit an albatross?" Evan asked. "I've never heard of anyone shooting an albatross. To shoot an albatross, you would have to score a hole-in-one on a par four hole or hole your ball in only two shots on a par five. Who can do that?"

"It's been done," Fletcher said, finally finding an opportunity to join the conversation. He spoke with wide eyes, using that same emphatic manner insecure men use to reinforce their logic.

"Have you seen a player shoot an albatross?" Evan asked.

"I have not seen it," Fletcher said, "but I have heard it's been done." He spoke as though defending a fact. "I have seen the scorecard of a guy who hit one. I saw the scorecard myself!"

"The scorecard?" Chadwick reacted. He turned his head and spoke quietly to Evan. "Fletcher's seen an albatross on paper."

"So," Amanda said, distracting them by pretending she was confused. "If shooting an albatross is scoring three under par, then how do you shoot an albatross on a par three hole? Three minus three is zero. If I don't play the hole, I get an albatross. Right? Anyone can do that."

Fletcher laughed as though he had heard a great joke, and Chadwick turned away, frowning and shaking his head. They moved along, playing, laughing, and chatting about golf.

On one par four hole, Fletcher and Amanda sliced their tee-shots, and their balls rolled off the fairway grass. They went off together to find where the balls had stopped. As they approached a line of brush running along the rough, Fletcher jolted to a halt at the sound of Amanda's startled moan.

"Oh!" she said. "Poor bird. You're hurt, aren't you?" Her voice was like a coo.

She bent over to examine a small bird. The frightened creature was injured and had pressed itself against the bottom of a bush. It chirped repeatedly and pressed away from Amanda until there was no more give in the bushes.

"Its wing is hurt. It can't fly. Oh, no. This is so sad."

Fletcher approached and dropped his bag of clubs, which increased the bird's agitation, and it released a rapid burst of chirps. He bent down beside Amanda, reached his hands under the brush, surrounded the bird with his fingers, and lifted it while using his two thumbs to prevent it from falling and further injuring itself. He and Amanda knelt while examining it for injuries.

"It's been shot," Fletcher said. "Look right there."

He pointed to what appeared to be a small black hole in the feathers on the bird's chest. The injury prevented it from flapping its wings and flying away.

"The wings are fine," Fletcher said, "but it will never fly again."

"Who would do such a thing?" Amanda asked, as though she had never imagined something so helpless could be the target of a man's gun.

"It was probably some kid," he said. "It happens all the time."

"What does?" Evan asked, arriving with Chadwick.

"Shooting," Fletcher said. "Someone has shot this bird, and I told Amanda that it happens all the time."

"It's true," Evan said. After examining the bird, he added, "We should just leave it under the dark brush over there. His survival is out of our hands. It's all we can do. It's an injured bird, and it's going to die."

Chadwick and Fletcher agreed, and they left the bird huddling and chirping deep in the brush. Two holes later, Amanda still had not forgotten the incident.

"Have any of you ever shot a bird?" she asked Evan.

"Forget birds," Fletcher added. "Evan is training to shoot men. That's what the 170th does. It uses its artillery to shoot men."

In wartime, little thought goes toward the actual purpose, mechanics, or results of artillery—the blood, bone fragments, and splattered guts. Less, still, is the thought a young lady gives to the deadly side of a soldier's work. Amanda had given no thought to it until Fletcher brought it to her attention just then. The bird was such an innocent little creature. With her emotions still unsettled, she looked at Evan as though realizing the purpose of his soldiering for the first time.

"Of course we shoot men," Evan said. "We shoot men who are trying to kill us. War is kill or be killed."

"Darn right!" Chadwick interrupted. "If you don't hit them, they hit you. In fact, they're the reason you're shooting. The Nazis seek to eliminate certain people, and they have been doing it with a great measure of success. I'm thankful you're going over there to stop them. I can't imagine any civilized person feeling otherwise."

"If we don't stop them," Evan said, "We'll at least give them hell."

"What a messy thought," Amanda said. "And I thought shooting a bird was bad enough."

"What's worse, shooting a bird or shooting a man?"

"I should say, 'shooting a man,' but birds do not harm anyone. They're helpless."

"What if we shoot Nazis?" he asked.

"Then that's good, I suppose. Since you have to, though, you should be sure to do it well." She looked at him and her frown became a smile. "Just try not to shoot their birds. I suppose the Germans have birds that are just like ours."

"Just for you," he said, "I will not shoot any birds. Although it occurs to me now that I might be forced to shoot a few here. To beat the Navy when I play against them, to win the golf tournament, I will need to shoot as many birds and eagles as I can. What if I need to shoot an albatross? Will you approve?"

"Fire away if you must. Go ahead and shoot an albatross for me. But do you think you can do it?"

"Unlikely," he said. "It's nearly impossible."

"Let's hope your competition knows that," she said.

"I hope he's not that good."

CHAPTER 15

~ MORE THAN A LOOK ~

After finishing their afternoon practice session, Evan and the instructors prepared to say goodbye to Amanda. This particular day, Chadwick and Fletcher did not behave in their usual manner. Their actions were more deliberate, and each spoke in a purposeful, mechanical manner, as though they were reading lines from a script. Amanda noticed the change in them at once. She became suspicious, but Evan met her furrowed brows with a grin and a shrug of his shoulders. He looked at the instructors. "What's happening?" he asked. "What are you two up to?"

"Happening?" Fletcher repeated. He looked over at Chadwick as though he sought assistance to answer Evan's simple question. "What do you mean?"

"I mean, you're acting strange, Chadwick. What's going on?"

Chadwick was bent over one of the several packed pouches of his golf bag. He put away the ball marker he had been using that day, zipped the pouch, and lifted his bag onto his shoulder.

"Nothing's the matter," he said. "Well, nothing except that eighteenth hole. It's too damn hard."

"Then why won't you look at me? And Fletcher, look how he is rushing to leave."

"We both have to go. We have no time for goodbyes today. Say goodbye to Amanda for us."

Though she was standing beside Evan, Chadwick and Fletcher departed without any further explanation, and Evan and Amanda were left standing alone. Neither said a word. They, too, went through the actions of ending their afternoon of practice. Evan put away his putter, and Amanda retrieved her ball from the cup of the seventeenth green. They had skipped the eighteenth because it was too visible. She returned her putter to her bag, and both finished stowing their gear.

Evan brushed his hands, Amanda smoothed her blouse, and then they had nothing left to distract them. They were confronted with the uncomfortable reality of being finished and standing alone at the threshold of goodbye. At four-thirty, the summer sky still held well over four hours of sunlight. The air was warm and calm, all of the little flying things around Evan and Amanda were nowhere to be seen, and all sound seemed to cease. They stood, unmoving, facing each other amidst the remarkably quiet atmosphere. The critical moment of their pending separation heightened their feelings and their hesitance. Each refrained from telling the other of a strong reluctance to part. Both looked expectantly, shifting feet, and smiling uncomfortably as they waited for the other to speak the obvious. Words were wanting.

"Tomorrow on two?" Evan asked, though his question was more of a statement.

"Yes. Do you really have to leave so early? It's not yet five o'clock."

"Maybe I don't," he said. "It's approaching our mealtime, though, and if I'm missing for long, Floyd will come looking for me, as we learned yesterday."

"Let him," Amanda said, and then she added to her words one of those challenging grins to which Evan could not help but react by straightening up and wrinkling his brow. He would do whatever she suggested.

"Do you understand what you're saying? The Army exists with discipline. Without it, there's chaos."

"Of course," she said. "But what about you and the Army?"

"We are also chaos without each other," he said, "for now at least. Look what happened yesterday. Major Akerly came to find me but, instead of me, he found you," Evan teased her.

"Actually," she said, "I came to find him and to distract him from finding you."

"It worked, but you may have done your job too well. He became much more interested in finding you than me. You had better watch him. He could become a problem."

"Yours or mine?" she asked. "It would be impossible for me to care less for him, but what can he do to you? Should I care?"

* * *

Floyd climbed from the seat of the small Army jeep and spotted Chadwick and Floyd walking with their golf bags over their shoulders. Evan was not with them.

What is this? Floyd wondered. *Where's Wilkins now?*

Floyd frowned like a sour, hostile, bitter old woman. An involuntary twitch and muscle flex under his dusty uniform registered his displeasure. His clothing was wrinkled from the day's artillery practice, and the short and choppy steps he took toward the approaching instructors brought life to the wrinkles, like thin wires convulsed by electricity. "Where's Wilkins?" he demanded.

Still over a hundred feet away, the instructors stopped and turned to look at each other. Both wore questioning expressions and mock surprise.

"My goodness. Where is he? Chadwick, did we forget to bring Evan?" Fletcher exaggerated the questions and grinned with his mouth wide open.

"Evan wanted to rework his approach on one of the greens," Chadwick shouted to Floyd.

"Which green? Where is he? You know he missed dinner yesterday by over an hour?"

"It's a good thing he practices so diligently, isn't it, major?" Chadwick said.

"What? No! I ordered you two to watch him. One of the orderlies swears he saw a woman on the course golfing with Wilkins the other day. He cannot sneak off alone." To emphasize the depth of anger Evan's absence had evoked, Floyd ended with the greatest threat in his vocabulary. "I'm writing a report."

"You ordered us?" Chadwick asked with a questioning tone of voice that carried its own answer. "You ordered us? We're paid instructors, not members of the Army under military orders. We're being paid to help Evan win a golf tournament, not to babysit him."

When an older man speaks in an affronted tone of certainty, regardless of being faced by a uniform or being nearly double the age of the other, there is always a moment of hesitation in the younger man, and so it was with Floyd. When such authority is merited, though, as in the case of an officer of the law or a soldier in uniform, this hesitation is no more than a pause. Like fireworks, Floyd's fuse burned for the briefest of moments. "Damn you!" he responded. "We'll see about that."

He brushed past the instructors and bumped Fletcher with his shoulder. The two watched him lengthen his stride as he headed up the fairway of the eighteenth hole. He would search the course in reverse. After he had gone only as far as to where the eighteenth's dogleg made its turn, he looked into the distance. He could see past the tee box to the green of the previous hole. He saw two figures and stopped, squinting, and staring, as the two persons melted into one.

* * *

"Chaos without each other?" Amanda again asked, repeating Evan's words.

Neither missed the tacit subtlety in her question. Again they looked into each other's eyes, smiled, laughed, and turned as though to go nowhere together. They left their clubs lying on the ground, and slowly walked about the surface of the seventeenth green. Evan reached for her hand and she readily extended it. They looked in opposite directions while walking together, going here and there, but going no farther than the edges of the green. Their conversation was filled with the fun, flirtatious language of youth that excludes third parties.

They took slow, lingering steps, and halted, laughing, all the while pushing and pulling the other. They stepped sideways at times, walked backwards, and smiled at the smooth surface of the green, at each other, at the flag stick, and again at each other. They teased each other and talked without saying anything in particular. Evan tugged Amanda's arms while she alternately resisted and yielded, finally twirling to a stop in front of him. They were face-to-face, separated by a distance much more intimate than either had expected. Their laughter ceased, but their smiles remained. In one smooth motion they tensed. They widened their eyes while narrowing their focus. A moment of breathless silence followed. Both saw only the other, and they sensed what would happen next. He drew her close, she leaned toward him, their arms circled each other, and they came together. Her heel lifted as though drawn by a string, and they crushed together in a kiss. It was then that their earlier first look was wonderfully relegated to its proper place of insignificance. With his arms around her waist and hers around his neck, they kissed for the first time. The moment was theirs. It could never be taken or forgotten. A first look had opened the way for a first touch, and the touch had further opened the way to their first kiss. They established an intimacy that excluded all others.

"So that's it," Floyd said, whispering to himself from back up the fairway. "We'll see about that."

He tightened his eyes and pressed his lips so tightly that a jaw muscle twitched as he watched. Red blood vessels bunched on his forehead, crimson burned in his face, and he seethed with anger, like a construction foreman giving instructions to an insubordinate crew. He went toward the two at the pace of his heart rate. The longer it took them to separate and the longer Floyd took to reach the green, the angrier he became. His emotions were like steam in an over-heated pressure cooker, only he had no release valve. He simply gushed with anger.

"Wilkins!" he yelled, entirely lost in his emotion.

Evan and Amanda jumped apart and looked like they had been caught stealing. Both watched Floyd with open mouths and wide eyes as he rapidly approached. Amanda's hot cheeks reddened, and she quickly picked up her clubs and walked away.

Evan's cheeks, on the other hand, whitened to the same color as the frothy spittle that formed at the outer edges of Floyd's chewing lips. The moment changed forever.

CHAPTER 16

~ THE BRIEFING ~

"It's amazing," Fletcher whispered to Chadwick. "This place is ready." The instructors were sitting alone at a rectangular briefing table set up in a grassy area between the Army headquarters tent and the clubhouse. The Army had ceded the clubhouse to the Navy, and both sides agreed to the wisdom of holding the briefing on the neutral ground between them. This way, neither could claim to enjoy any advantage.

The admiral arrived for the briefing with the much-celebrated Bentley Knudsen. They came in a large black sedan with a Navy insignia painted on both front doors. Two red, white, and blue flags flapped and snapped as the car approached, and then hung limply when it stopped at the front door of the Navy's temporary El Rancho Golf Course headquarters. Two military jeeps, another sedan, and three large transport trucks arrived behind the admiral's car. The Army had placed a large wooden sign reading "Navy Headquarters," outside of the clubhouse, and the sign was flanked on both sides by large U.S. flags. The Navy men pointed and smiled at the perceived welcome.

"I've never seen anything like it," Chadwick whispered back. "You saw all the people. They did the best job I've ever seen getting a golf course ready for a game."

"Amazing," Fletcher agreed, keeping his head down as he watched people arrive and take their seats for the briefing.

The Army had called back the regular golf course staff earlier in the week, and all of the maintenance and administrative workers, instructors, caddies, groundskeepers, marshals, and course management, along with over one hundred eighty Army and Navy personnel, had worked everywhere all at once. The maintenance men hand-watered the greens and tee boxes, as was the manner of the day, and privates mowed fairway grasses, clipped bushes, pruned hedges, trimmed trees, and raked sand traps. Everywhere, men swept, wiped, polished, and cleaned. The Army took responsibility for repairing any and all divots. Where these were found on tee boxes and fairways, the soldiers removed the offensive patches of ground and replaced them with fitted squares of grass. The men used their military boots to stomp the patches into place, and they carefully watered each repair as though expecting them to take root before the game the following day.

"Look at all the people," Fletcher said. "They keep staring at us. They must think we're in charge."

"Enjoy it while it lasts," Chadwick said, "and, please, stop waving at them. Look, though, the place is starting to fill up. We'll most likely begin any minute."

The lawn before the briefing table was still quite green. Rows of wooden chairs were arranged on it so that two sides of chairs were separated by a center aisle that led to the briefing table up front. The arrangement looked more appropriate for an afternoon wedding than a military briefing. The Army sat on the right—the groom's side—and the Navy sat on the left. Every chair was occupied, and those who could not sit stood in groups beside the chairs and talked amongst themselves. The golf course staff grouped together in the back, the UCLA golf team stood close to the bride's side, and Amanda and her friends huddled together near the groom's side, whispering and taking furtive glances at the soldiers. A curious group of men and women, dressed in the latest fashion, stood in the very back behind the many rows of occupied chairs. Their clothing, hair, and attitudes were those of celebrity, which added to the sense of importance among all present. Amanda frowned when she saw her mother and father standing among the back group.

"Who are those two over there?" Fletcher asked, nodding his head toward two men who stood in the back holding notepads and cameras. "That one just took a picture of us."

"They're newsmen," Chadwick said. "I thought they would come. News of this golf game has circulated for only one month, but look, there must be three hundred people out there."

"But Army and Navy golfers are not that good," Fletcher said. "I mean, they're not professionals."

"Three reasons," Chadwick answered. "First, I think they came to see golf. Because the PGA canceled professional golf this year, no one has gotten to see a single game. The second reason is the location. Los Angeles is a city filled with gossip. You've heard it. Everyone knows the Army took over the golf course, and they know about the game. That's why those two news reporters came all the way from downtown. And the third reason is, well, that's obvious."

"Because everyone loves golf?" Fletcher grinned and drew laughter from Chadwick.

"True," Chadwick said, "but the real reason is the war. Everyone has seen the films, and they're sick of the bad news. People want relief. They need a distraction. They're coming to forget about the war. Mostly they're coming for golf. Ah, here comes Evan."

The two men watched as Bentley and Evan arrived and took their seats in the front rows on their respective sides of the aisle. Everyone at the briefing got their first good look at Bentley Knudsen. It was reported that Bentley had always enjoyed a life of privilege, and his demeanor showed it. He was just over six feet, but he appeared taller because of the manner in which he lifted his nose. He appeared to observe the world through drooping eyes that were forever looking at something off in the distance. When he walked, he flowed, as though he had all the time in the world to arrive. His Navy dress uniform was impeccably pressed with stiff creases. He walked to the front row without noticeably seeing anyone else, and there he sat like a ruler on his throne, being seen more than seeing. He did not look over at Evan, but this was fortunate, for it allowed Evan the opportunity to observe Bentley without also being observed himself. Evan turned with the intention of greeting him. Instead, he saw Bentley already sitting on the opposite side of the aisle, straight-backed, head cocked high, shoulders rotated behind him, and his hands resting together on his crossed leg. Bentley's shoes, buttons, and buckles shined as though new, and his short, black hair, the lightly colored skin of his shaven face, and even his nails appeared spit-shined. Whereas Evan's face and arms had tanned from his month of golfing, only Bentley's hands and forearms looked to have gotten any sun at all, and his untanned face indicated he wore a hat when he played golf.

The general and admiral joined the instructors at the briefing table, and each sat so he faced his own men. Both appeared imposingly stern, serious, gruff, and angry, as though they felt self-conscious about having relegated the war to second place behind a golf game. The commanders hated their enemies, lamented the losses of their troops, and sought to play a decisive role in helping to win the war. The mood at the briefing was infectious, though, and so it was that the two senior fighters became engrossed in the festivities and for the moment, at least, they forgot about the war. They smiled and nodded agreeably to each other, started the briefing with introductions of the players, and gave a serious explanation about the purpose.

Chadwick and Fletcher were seated at the table between the two, and the civilian instructors waved when they were introduced as golf experts. Chadwick then stood to identify the members of the two teams and to give an explanation of the rules of play.

"They will play a modified version of Best Ball," he proclaimed, speaking slowly and enunciating his words. "Each member of a team will hit a tee-shot. Team members will proceed to the location of the best shot. Both will hit from there. Team members will continue to do the same until both reach a green. Once on a green, the players will count their own scores. We will record the lowest individual score as the team score." He paused while smiling at Evan, looked down at Fletcher, and ended with his eyes finding Amanda's. "The team with the lowest total score for eighteen holes wins the day," he finished.

The crowd remained silent while collectively considering how this form of play worked. Further, all appeared to be considering which team would be advantaged by playing this version of Best Ball. Fletcher had sat quietly while the others spoke, but he wanted to have a part in the explanation. After all, he reasoned, Chadwick had enjoyed the honor of speaking to the large crowd. He would too. Wearing a yellow V-necked sweater that matched the color of only a few of the ribbons worn by the two commanders, Fletcher pounded his elbows on the briefing table, spread his hands before him, and looked out at the crowd. At the sound, the general turned so quickly his chest medals tugged against their ribbons.

"Do you have any questions about these rules of engagement?" Fletcher asked, smiling and looking out at the men. No one raised a hand. He then made the blunder that started it all. "Then," he said, speaking with the enthusiasm of a politician closing a speech with a passionate line meant to elicit roars of applause, "let the battle begin!"

Fletcher's mouth growled into a grin, revealing his delight with his clever use of the new military phrase, "rules of engagement." He was a happy man who expected to elicit roaring cheers after his emphatic call for battle. He had clenched his fist, widened his eyes, and swung his right arm in the manner of a punch across the front of his body. The crowd's reaction, though, was not at all what he expected. The golf game was not to be an engagement, and neither the admiral nor the general cared for a battle—not there on the golf course. The competitors were from separate branches of the military, but they fought on the same side in war. For Fletcher to suggest otherwise was unfortunate for him.

During the moment of silence that followed, he realized his mistake. The admiral, however, reacted before Fletcher could say another word. He pushed back his chair in an aggressive attempt to get to his feet. The chair legs did not scoot, but instead caught in the grass, and the chair and the admiral began tipping backwards. The crowd experienced the slow-motion effect that accompanies misfortune, watching the admiral's eyes widen, jaw drop, and arms flail. He made a wild grab at the receding table. On his way down, they saw a moment of uncertainty. Along with his arms, the admiral flailed his legs, and his polished boots slammed into the bottom of the briefing table. The toes caught a metal edge under the table, and then, for just a fraction of an instant, the admiral appeared to be balanced between the table going one way and his chair going the other.

The crowd's response was immediate. Everyone jumped to their feet and rushed forward in a surge. Groans, gasps, exclamations, and other sounds of chaos filled the air. The general reached the stunned admiral first, but it was Fletcher whose hand tugged the most urgently on the admiral's arm.

"Let go of me, you buffoon!" the admiral yelled. "Damn you! You're wrong! That's not right. Let go of me!"

Too many people were moving, talking, and helping at the same time, but they all heard the admiral's shouts for silence. He regained his feet but not his composure. He grabbed onto Fletcher's sweater and yelled in his face. The admiral proved he was an expert at admonishing men.

"We are on the same side," the admiral said. "Rules of engagement are for war, and damn it, this is not a war!" He poked his right index finger against Fletcher's chest and turned down the corners of his mouth. "You never should have said that! We are only playing a friendly game of golf."

"But you're playing against the Army," one of the reporters yelled from somewhere.

"Of course we are."

"Don't you want to win?"

"We will win!" the admiral shouted, without first considering the possibility of an adverse reaction to his conviction.

Chaos ensued. The men in the Army collectively hooted their disapproval of the admiral's "We will win!" declaration. This, in turn, resulted in all of the Navy men turning and shouting back at the Army men. The reporters exchanged glances with each other, the UCLA boys laughed, the young ladies stepped backward, the Hollywood set stood stunned, and the golf course personnel looked dumbfounded. It appeared as though the bride and groom sides would come to blows before the end of the ceremony.

The dangerous state of uncertainty reached a zenith of hostile chaos, but then came the sound of a thundering boom. Silence was immediate. Some placed their hands over their unprotected ears, others looked wide-eyed and frightened, and still others appeared staggered by the sound. Everyone turned toward the two MPs standing beside the upset briefing table, and they saw one of the MPs pointing a large forty-five caliber weapon into the sky. While a puff of smoke was still dissipating above the gun, he fired a second shot.

Officers called together their units, and the men responded with the immediacy and silence of military obedience. The briefing area emptied, and units assembled in the distance. The admiral and general stomped off, Bentley trailed the admiral, and the MPs followed right behind the departing soldiers. The briefing area was left looking like the remains of an outdoor church service devoid of sound, parishioners, and a pastor. Though the military vacated the area, the civilian groups remained. They skirted the rows of empty chairs, and once the confusion dissipated, they walked their eyes up the aisle to where the empty table stood like an abandoned altar. To everyone's surprise, they saw Evan and Amanda standing alone in front of the table.

Crisis has been known to relegate prudence to second place behind concern, as it had for Amanda. Her concern far outweighed her sense of discretion, for during the height of the confusion, just moments before the MP fired his weapon, she had rushed to him. The two were left standing alone up front, facing each other, holding hands, and seeking the comfort of the other's eyes. They found what they sought. In their world of silence, each spoke volumes without saying a word.

Evan's expression broke first. His lips lifted at the corners and parted into a smile. He stood directly before her, laughed, and nodded his head. She, too, allowed a smile to curve her lips, but color came to her as she recalled the speed at which she had rushed to him.

"Are you okay?" Evan asked.

"We're both fine," she said.

"After what just happened, I think we are in for quite some game."

"I'll say."

"Will you still come and watch me play?"

"What do you think?"

"I'm not sure what to think. You were out of your chair and up here so fast. What happened to you?"

"You happened to me," she said.

Amanda looked away and squeezed her lips until dimples appeared in her cheeks. She frowned at how quickly she had run to him. Her reaction came from concern for him, she knew, but she knew also that her reaction came from the more intimate feelings she had for him. When she returned her eyes to his face, she forced a smile.

"I came to you." She tensed at her honesty, kept her gaze steady, and watched, holding her breath. She did not wait long for his reaction.

"I like that you did," he said.

At the same time, both experienced the sensation of being watched. They saw it in the other's eyes, and realized they were not alone. Still holding hands, they turned and looked up the empty aisle. Though all of the briefing chairs were empty, they were far from alone. Amanda saw her father first, then mother, her friends, and the civilian group behind where the chairs stood empty. A camera flashed the moment she returned to exchange a confused look with Evan.

"Let's get out of here," she said, seeking to avoid the smiling faces watching them. "Don't you just want to get away?"

"I do," he said. "You want to go too?"

"I do," she said.

"But do you hear that? I'm being called. I have to go." After turning to leave, he added, "Please be here tomorrow."

She agreed and he departed, leaving Amanda standing alone like she was abandoned at the altar. Those remaining watched her walk slowly down the empty aisle. Most were reluctant to leave, but did so knowing they would return the next day to watch the big game.

Major Floyd Akerly skipped the briefing, but no one noticed his absence. The following day, everyone would know how he used the time to get ready for the game.

CHAPTER 17

~ THE GOLF TOURNAMENT ~

The first official sound of the game was the sweet click of a driver connecting with a golf ball. The club's swoosh cut through the air, but its click brought smiles from the crowd. Uncertainty went flying with that ball, and Evan, the general, and all of the other spectators watched in a moment of appreciative silence. The first ball lifted, flew off the tee, and disappeared in the distance. Knudsen neither smiled nor frowned as the Navy men cheered his shot. Rather, he stood unmoving, facing his diminishing ball, his driver held high and pointing behind him. His back heel was lifted, the toe pointed like a dancer's, and the outside edge of his front foot was torqued and supporting his weight. He held the position until the ball was gone, stopping somewhere way out there—somewhere in the middle of the fairway over three hundred fifty yards away.

Gone with that first hit was all uncertainty about Knudsen's ability to hit a golf ball. The general and Evan exchanged glances, and while Evan's expression revealed appreciation for the impressive shot, the general's look registered concern.

"Did you see that?" Cedric asked, handing a driver to Evan. A random assignment of El Rancho's regular pool of caddies had Cedric working for Evan. He was the youngest of the pool, but Evan accepted the boy because of his experience and love of golf. His enthusiasm was unrestrained. Evan kept his eyes fixed on the distance while listening to Cedric and nodding his head. "That was perfect," the boy said. "Do you see how he's set up for his second shot? From where his ball landed, Knudsen can avoid the sand traps on the left. He has an open shot to approach the green. You had better go where he went. Now hit it hard."

"I was thinking the same thing," Evan said.

He hit a drive that made the same sweet click, brought a similar moment of silence, flew off in the same direction, elicited the same cheering response from the Army, but his ball stopped eight yards short of Knudsen's. Amanda had watched Evan hit hundreds of times throughout the month of August, so she allowed her unimpressed gaze to linger on Knudsen. She first observed him just as Evan was teeing his ball in preparation for that first hit. He stood behind Evan, on a far side of the ball, and she saw him staring at Evan like a stalker. He peered from beneath his brimmed hat, and he kept his head down so that he appeared to look from the top half of his pupils. His lips formed a straight line as he studied Evan. Amanda noticed how he ignored Evan's ball to watch the intricacies of his swing. He never looked to see where the ball landed, either. His gaze remained fixed on Evan until the very moment the general stepped onto the tee box, carrying his driver like it was a club. With his free hand he patted Evan's back. A broad smile covered his face.

The general hit a fair shot that first started going left and then faded to the right. When his ball came to a stop still touching fairway grass, he received a cheer that was louder than those cheers given to both Evan and Knudsen.

The admiral was the last of the foursome to take his first hit of the game. When the last of a foursome finally tees-up his ball and stands ready to take his first swing, following three well-hit balls and surrounded by a crowd of onlookers, he cannot help but feel a touch of self-consciousness. The reaction is natural, but the admiral never showed any such feelings. It was when his ball smacked against a nearby tree that he let loose with less refined reactions. He scowled at the Navy men who cheered his shot, and he banged the ground with the head of his club. "Dammit!" he yelled.

"It looks like the battle is on," a grinning Chadwick whispered to Fletcher.

"Shh," Fletcher reacted, placing a finger to his lips and looking to see who might have heard. "That's not funny," he said. "We cannot use that word. Golf is not a battle."

"Okay, okay, then the game is on."

The relentless August sun had dried the fairways and changed them to crunchy walks of grass. These were outlined by the dry yellow and brown grasses that farmers see following harvest. The sky was clear, the air was warm, and there had been no wind. There were, however, regular seismic rumblings that only the admiral and the general felt that day. They felt these tremors after each rupture of the hard ground with their clubs, when vibrations traveled up the steel shafts they gripped in their hands, resulting in fissures that cut the skin at the tight edges of their convex lips. In golf, once all players have taken their initial tee-shots, the player hits first whose ball is farthest from a hole or, as the rule appeared from the admiral's play on the first four holes, the player hits first whose ball travels the shortest distance.

The crowd walked and ran behind the players, cheering, hooting, and laughing as the foursome progressed. Knudsen and Evan played the entire day on the gold-colored fairway grasses, while the commanders played brown. Onlookers discussed this latter point—and the violent clubbing of the ground—without using words. Instead, they spoke with their eyes. By the end of the first three holes, the big men had made so many hard bangs on the ground that they appeared to be knocking seismic energy into the earth—energy that would return in the future and rumble Los Angeles. Aggressive men play aggressive golf.

The foursome walked in teams of two, but with the addition of Chadwick and Fletcher, the two teams appeared to be lopsided in favor of the Army. By August of 1943, golf course etiquette already had evolved for over two centuries. Each player remained quietly behind the hitter's ball, and everyone remained perfectly silent when a player was hitting on a green. Away from a green, people could talk.

"Do you see it?" Fletcher asked. "Something's wrong with the admiral."

"Yes," Chadwick answered. "He should not be out here. He's leaving a trail of divots just like that Gretel girl who left a trail of bread crumbs in the woods. The Navy's team score will consist solely of Knudsen's score. The admiral added nothing."

"The same is true of the general," Fletcher said. "Evan's score will be the Army's score. The general added nothing, either."

"Watch what they do here. They've reached that tricky fourth green."

"This will be fun to watch," Fletcher whispered, struggling to contain his grin as Amanda approached.

"What's so funny?" she asked.

"Nothing," he said. "I was just telling Chadwick it will be fun to watch the teams play this next hole with its sloping green."

Golfers say anyone can hit a nice shot, but the good players are those who can put these nice shots together, one after another. Bad players cannot. Both Knudsen and Evan played well, but Knudsen established himself as the leader from his first drive. He scored a birdie, a par on the next hole, another birdie, and then he stood two strokes ahead of Evan, who scored pars on the first three holes. Both were about to hit their approach shots onto the sloped green of the fourth after hitting long, straight drives that seemed to roll forever on the hard ground. Each had to make his next approach shot from about the same one-hundred-twenty-yard distance to the green. When two players hit approach shots from about the same location on a fairway, the second to hit always watches the first in an attempt to glean any advantage before he takes his own shot. What club did the first player use? How did the wind influence his ball? Did the ball bounce? Slow green or fast? Any number of such questions might be answered simply by watching the first player hit.

Knudsen was first, and he hit with a nine iron that sent his ball flying too high and too long. Unfortunately, the back sand trap was waiting. Knudsen's ball came down hard, and it landed the way a rock lands on the dry sand of a beach. Evan had an advantage here, because he had practiced taking this approach shot until he had nearly perfected it. He turned down Cedric's offer of a nine iron, agreed that going high was the right strategy, and requested a pitching wedge instead. He approached and addressed his ball, setting up for his shot, and took a hard practice swing. When he stepped away from the ball, he surveyed the crowd until he found Amanda. Their eyes met and then it was done. If the crowd of onlookers had noticed his look, they would have seen his grin and might have thought he was happy. Had anyone noticed Amanda, they would have seen her turn and whisper to one of her girlfriends.

Evan returned his attention to the ball. He hit a high-flying shot that would definitely clear the three front sand traps, but it was uncertain as to whether it would stop short of the back trap. While he hit the ball high, everyone drew and held their breath and no one said a word. The silence of the four seconds the ball took to reach the green seemed to last for minutes. On its way down, some of the Army men and two or three of the UCLA golf team were first to break the silence. They made long, drawn-out sounds, as though encouraging the ball to go and stop at the same time. The ball stayed high. It looked long, but then it hit.

Even though fairways were not irrigated in 1943, greens remained lush because of daily hand watering. Evan's came down on the back edge of the green, and onlookers feared it would bounce and roll into the back sand trap. It did hit straight down on the green, but it did not roll off toward the bunker. Instead, it hopped with a backspin that sent it rolling away from the trap, toward the hole.

Throughout the ball's flight, the onlookers made "O" sounds groaned in a low tone. As it rolled toward the hole, they switched vowels to utter the higher tones of the letter "A." It slowed its roll, the crowd groaned its vowel, but still the ball continued moving toward the cup. Afterwards, people described its motion as having a dream-like inability to move, for it slowed as though being drawn by a magnet. Evan would have an easy putt for a birdie, but his ball never stopped moving. It crawled in millimeters until nearly stopping on the edge of the hole. There, it teetered for an awkward instant, and then it fell straight into the cup. One-half of the crowd broke into a frenzy of shouting, cheering, back-slapping, smiling, and hand shaking. He grinned as he retrieved his ball and tossed it to Cedric. The young caddie was unable to contain his laughter.

"That was amazing," Cedric said. "You tied the game."

"We're even," Evan agreed, "but Knudsen still has to finish this hole. He is much better than I thought he would be. Let's see how he plays the green."

A score of two under par is called an eagle, and with that one shot—with Evan's eagle—the team scores were tied at two under par. They would not remain that way, though, for Knudsen's ball was still lying in the upper sand trap. Everyone hushed and watched when he hit his ball from the sand. Half of them wore smiles.

"Quit bumping into me," Chadwick said to Fletcher, who was standing beside him like an excited little boy. "Stand still. He's going to hit."

Knudsen accepted a sand wedge from his caddie and advice the admiral whispered. When he nodded to the admiral, he did so in the dismissive, matter-of-fact manner of those who are over-confident. He knocked his ball out of the trap with a blow of sand, and it landed on the green well before the hole. Unfortunately, though, it had legs and rolled right past the hole. It slowed down by the cup, but the slope had such an effect that it drew the ball onward and downward. It rolled almost forty feet to the bottom, where it stopped just short of rolling off the green.

"Oh man," Fletcher whispered. "We've got him now."

Trouble on golf courses comes all at once. Whereas a player might be several strokes ahead on one hole, he could fall behind by several strokes on the next. Knudsen made a hard hit of his return putt, but it was not hard enough for the ball to reach the top of the slope. Instead, it reversed directions somewhere near the top and rolled right back down, stopping close to where it had begun. The men of the Navy were now the ones making the 'O' and 'A' sounds, but they ended all of their vowels with a unanimous groan of "O."

"Look at him," Fletcher said. "He's staring at the green and shaking his head. He knows he made a mistake."

"Shh," Chadwick said. "The admiral will hear you. Besides, Knudsen is hitting again."

Once his ball stopped rolling after his first attempt, Bentley again stood at the bottom of the green and judged the slope of its surface. He again hit a putt that made a solid "click." Though he hit the putt harder than he had on his first attempt, the ball still did not have enough behind it to make the hill. It again went up, only to roll back down the slope. Even the Army supporters groaned for Knudsen. As though he was a determined soldier instead of a sailor, Knudsen made a third assault on the hill. It proved successful. His ball stopped at the top, and then he needed only one more putt to finish the hole.

Chadwick clapped and smiled, but only until he saw Fletcher frowning, pointing to here and there, and moving his lips without making a sound. He was counting Knudsen's strokes. Fletcher noticed the attention and gave up his effort.

"Do it again," he said.

"Alright, but listen this time," Chadwick responded. "That was one for the shot from the tee, two for the shot into the sand trap, three for the shot out of the sand and onto the green—the one that rolled down the hill—four for the first putt that rolled up and then down, five for the second putt that came back down, six for the putt that stayed up, and seven for the putt into the cup. That was a seven, a triple bogey."

"Terrible," Fletcher said, grinning and shaking his head. "Knudsen just blew his lead. That is, unless the admiral can do well on this hole."

Chadwick laughed and looked over at the admiral. "That is not going to happen," he said. "The admiral just scored a twelve. Look how mad he is."

They watched the admiral stomp his way off the green. Though neither he nor Knudsen exchanged any words, both shared frowns. In only one hole, the Navy had gone from being ahead in the game by two strokes to being behind by three. Their confidence became concern and, as in every situation where flattery flows from repeated success, the Navy men felt the check of capable competition like a slap of discouragement. There would be no easy win. There would be no rout. The game suddenly held the importance of a tournament, and every shot became significant.

Knudsen started wiping dirt and clippings from his golf balls, and he examined them for nicks, cuts, or scratches. He dropped blades of grass in the air to test for wind and stared before every shot like a surveyor looking at terrain. He began taking more than one practice swing before each hit and, on greens, he started kneeling to assess surface slope. He performed all the details that facilitate championship play.

By the time the foursome walked off the last green of the front nine, the Navy had evened the score. Knudsen finished his first nine holes with an impressive string of three straight birdies, and as he, the admiral, their caddies, and the crowd of followers made their way to the first hole of the back nine, Bentley's composure returned. He strode like a man with a mission, with his club held tightly in his hand and his expression devoid of humor. A reporter chased after him and asked several variations of only one question, but Knudsen ignored him. In a move that foreshadowed the more complicated relationship to come between the media and the military, the admiral sent an aid to Knudsen's assistance. The reporter's expression went from determination to defeat, and he quit Bentley and talked to the aid, understanding that any information was better than none.

Evan and the general walked to the tenth tee with a crowd following behind them. The general was all smiles.

Chadwick, Fletcher, and Cedric followed and chattered like children, two hundred men wearing Army uniforms followed like a foaming stream of olive-drab, the young men from UCLA moved like a raft on the edge of that stream, Amanda and her female companions followed them, and then came the Hollywood set. This latter group was impressively casual in their sport jackets, sweaters, and dresses. Though they brought up the rear, they walked as though they were leading, rather than following, the procession. They watched for who was observing them. Evan twice looked back from where he led the gallery, but he was unable to locate Amanda in the mass of movement.

The area around the tenth tee was packed with people. All of the individual groups had become a unified crowd that talked, laughed, and looked as one. They stood watching and whispering. At the beginning of the game, the end was still too far away to anticipate. Back then, their excitement had come from hope. After all, the end was still forever away. By the tenth hole, though, everyone seemed charged with an increase of suspense and excitement. The game was close, there was only one half yet to play, and someone would win. Viewing became serious. Hushes were obeyed and cheering was unrestrained. The noise was louder than it had been earlier in the competition. Silences, too, were different. Like a tank needing only one liquid drop before reaching its static limit, supporters needed only a look or a laugh before gushing forth with emotion.

"What's going on?" Evan asked, approaching the tee with his driver in hand.

"Look over there," Chadwick said. "Those two are discussing something important."

"Those big men walked away together," is how Cedric would describe the moment to Amanda. "They stood by themselves just talking. Everyone was ready to go. I mean,

172

we were all just waiting for the players to tee off on the back nine when we noticed that they were discussing something important, well out of the crowd's hearing range. It was obvious the admiral and general were conspiring about something. I just followed along with Evan and Knudsen. The two players were going to find out what was happening. Anyway, when we approached them, they at first continued their discussion. Just as we arrived, they shook hands, pretended to be happy, and patted each other on the back. It was Knudsen who demanded to know what was happening."

"We've both decided we've had enough," the admiral said. "We're calling it off between us. Our game is done."

"What!" Knudsen shouted, thinking the admiral's inclusive use of "we" and "our" applied to him and Evan. "I cannot quit. I will not quit! I can win!"

"This is a gentlemen's game," the general said. "Nobody's talking about you or Evan quitting the game. Gentlemen never quit, and neither does the Army or Navy. We do, however, accept the truth of a situation, and we make adjustments as conditions require. This is precisely what we're now doing. It's what we just decided to do." The admiral exchanged a look of agreement with the general, and they smiled with lips, teeth, and cheeks, but without the accompaniment of their eyes.

"I have little doubt," the admiral said, "that both of us could continue playing this course for hours, maybe for days. But several truths have emerged from our play on the front nine, and we've agreed on all of these truths except one. The first truth is that neither one of us has contributed a single stroke to the game. Our scores don't count. The Navy's score is yours, Bentley, and the Army's score is Evan's. We hit, our men clap, but our continuing to play will have absolutely no bearing on the outcome of the game."

173

"The second truth," the admiral went on, "is that our continued play is only slowing the game. Both of us have much more important matters needing our attention. There's a war going on, for crying out loud. We're done playing. The third truth is that the real competition is between you and Evan. Everyone knows this." The admiral released a heavy sigh. He looked from Knudsen to Evan and back at his man, like he was a father counseling his sons. "We're at the halfway point in this game and the score is tied. You two play without us. The general and I played enough for one day. Let's get this thing done. Bentley, go and win for the pride of the Navy."

Knudsen's expression changed from disbelief to understanding. He took a step closer to the admiral and exhaled in relief. "Oh! So it's not me. You mean Evan and I will continue to play. You two are the ones who are done."

"That's what we decided, what I said, and exactly what we meant. We're done playing."

"But you said," Bentley added, "that you and the general agreed on all truths but one. What was the one? What is the truth you disagreed about?"

"We could not agree on who's going to win the damn game."

CHAPTER 18

~ THE BACK NINE ~

Man likes simplicity in his fights. He wants one side to support and the other side to despise, especially in time of war. History has countless examples of the dashed hopes, confusion, uncertainty, surprise, unexpected defeat, chaos, and accidental victories that result when the number of competitors is greater than the tidy little number of two. The Prussians taught this lesson to Napoleon, and by World War II, every leader on earth accepted the truth as easily as accepting the spherical shape of the planet. The cluttered field of competitors—Japan, Germany, England, Italy, the Soviet Union, the United States, and all of the others—was welcomingly reduced to the binary neatness of the Axis versus the Allies.

The general and the admiral joined the crowd assembled to watch play continue on the back nine. With this reduction in the number of players, from four down to just two, the competition was reduced to its basic element of us-versus-them, Army-versus-Navy, Knudsen-versus-Evan, and all the way down to the perennial favorite of one-on-one. In its simplest terms, one would win and one would lose. It was easy. All seemed pleased with the simplicity of this fundamental building block of competition.

Such neatness has the consequence not just of focusing support on one favorite, but also of permitting squinted eyes to focus clearly on only one opponent. When Bentley

Knudsen hit his first tee shot on the back nine, every Navy man hollered, and those on the Army side remained silent. Evan hit next, and when he did, Army supporters cheered and the Navy men milled about in silence. Amanda and her friends cheered for Evan, the golf course staff politely clapped for both sides, as though playing the role of a neutral Switzerland, and the two reporters just wanted action, appreciating both the good and bad shots. The Hollywood set cheered for no one at all, as though waiting for cheers rather than giving them, and the young men of the UCLA golf team cheered for the game of golf, in the same way mercenaries cheer for a good fight.

Microscopes allow viewing small images, whereas the opposite is true with a telescope. The big picture view of play on the back nine showed Evan and Knudsen tied as each prepared to hit his final drive on the eighteenth hole, the last hole of the game. The eighteenth would decide it all. A small picture of play on the back nine, though, showed both players hitting long drives on the tenth, landing their second shots on the green, making their putts, and scoring birdies on the hole. The score then remained tied after the tenth, eleventh, twelfth, and thirteenth holes. Through an ensuing series of pars, birdies, and bogeys, hope for victory swung to one side, back to the other, and then finally settled in the uncertain middle with the action of jostled water in a glass. The stillness of water in a glass, though, has nothing in common with the calm on the eighteenth that day. Rather, the onlookers' excitement more resembled water boiling in a pan as the crowd bubbled with anxiety.

Evan found an air of expectation surrounding the final tee box. Those watching him drew breaths of hot air, rubbing, picking, wiping, and busying their fingers with movement, glancing to make short eye contact with each other, and looking everywhere in expectation. Several used humor to release tension, and others stated obvious facts as a means of relief. The entire crowd looked poised to take some radical group action, like wildebeest on the Serengeti, paused and huddled, waiting for the first chance to jump into the river that blocks their migratory path. All who watched awaited the start of what would be conclusive action.

"You saw his last drive," Fletcher said. The instructors were standing together and watching Knudsen as he prepared to hit his final drive of the day. Fletcher took quick looks from here to there and returned to look at Chadwick with wide eyes and a toothy grin. "Evan made that shot just like in practice. He'll do it again. He knows how to play the dogleg."

"The score is now even," Chadwick responded, ignoring whatever point Fletcher sought to make. He laughed, nodded his head, and narrowed his eyes like one peering into a light. He spoke without pause and much more quickly than was normal for him. "The eighteenth will decide it all," he said, nodding his head and seeing Knudsen stand before his ball. "Evan knows how to play this dogleg. It's tough, and par five holes are long. Still, I think he will win."

"You need to settle down," Fletcher said. "Evan knows how to play this hole. He's done it a hundred times."

"Settle down? Me? I should say the same to you. I agree with you that Evan has already played this hole a hundred times this month. Still, I wonder. What will Knudsen do? Par fives are so long, and he has plenty of room to make a mistake. It would be nice if he made one with his first stroke."

Fletcher laughed at the thought of Knudsen hitting a terrible drive. He turned his narrowed eyes and residual grin to where he watched Knudsen place his ball on a tee. Bentley stood tall, held his club loose in his hands, and stared intently down the fairway before him. From the tee box on eighteen, Knudsen appeared to be looking to the far end of the dogleg at the trees lining both sides approaching the turn, and at the sand traps that the course designer had strategically placed to increase difficulty.

"Look how dry the grass is," Fletcher whispered, still not looking at Chadwick. "If Knudsen hits hard enough, his ball will roll and roll. It will roll right off the fairway and all the way into those trees."

The eighteenth hole was well known as the toughest hole on El Rancho Golf Course. A player's ball needed to travel four hundred eighty yards in only five hits to score par on the hole, and all players had to decide early how they intended to play the sharp dogleg turn to the left. Men like to hit long, but with the hard August ground, the players also had to worry about their balls rolling past the turn and rolling into the far trees. Knudsen saw the trouble. He stood at the tee box, pointing to the far trees with his driver, and whispered about strategy with his caddie. Their conversation went for so many minutes that the admiral approached and whacked Bentley on the back. "Let's play," he said.

While he walked off the tee box, Knudsen's caddie followed and nodded his head in confident up-and-down motions. The watching crowd recognized that a decision had been made, and the result was that everyone held their voices in their throats and fixed their eyes on Bentley. They returned the area to immediate silence. Everywhere around the tee box, the anxious crowd waited. Knudsen finished staring down the fairway and readied to hit. Every voice was held wanting, like balls in a cannon waiting for the touch of a spark.

Just before Knudsen approached, addressed, and hit his final tee-shot, he caught sight of Evan approaching him. Knudsen's caddie later explained his view of the incident to Floyd.

"That Army kid just wanted to get inside Knudsen's head," the caddie said. "Evan walked right up to Bentley and said, 'Good luck,' like Bentley needed luck. Then he extended his hand as if he could interrupt Bentley's concentration at such a critical time. I think that kid was being obnoxious. Bentley just nodded, without breaking his concentration, as if he were shooing a fly. He didn't need luck, especially the wish for it from someone he was about to defeat. The kid must have been playing some kind of mind game."

Knudsen did not accept Evan's extended hand, causing quiet murmurs to grow into shouts of protest. Half of the onlookers simply laughed out loud. Evan shrugged his shoulders and departed the tee box, returning silence and leaving Bentley standing alone with his driver. The smiles and frowns turned to neutral lines of anxiety when Bentley addressed his ball, took a practice swing, glanced into the distance, repositioned his feet, and then took his real swing. He hit hard. The click was just as sweet as the one he had made when he started the tournament, and for the first time that day, all who were present cheered together. Knudsen's ball lifted at about a fourteen-degree angle, flew far, came down evenly, made a long, low bounce, rolled, and then stopped in the middle of the fairway. For his next shot, he would have a clear view around the dogleg. He had placed his ball in a perfect position.

Evan walked to the tee box carrying his driver in one hand and his ball and tee in the other. Cedrick, Chadwick, and Fletcher followed close behind, and Chadwick whispered so loudly that Evan was compelled to address his complaint. He stopped on the tee and turned to face him.

"I know you don't like it," Evan said, "but you do want me to win, right?"

"What I don't want," Chadwick answered, "is for you to lose."

"That's not an answer," he said. "I don't want to lose, but I also want to win."

"Don't you see?" Cedric added without looking at Chadwick. "This gives Evan a chance to win the game right here and now. He can do it!"

Cedric spoke in a tone that was neither an appeal nor an argument, just a defense of Evan's pending tee-shot. Chadwick ignored Cedric when he continued his appeal to Evan.

"The young are always willing to take unnecessary risks," he said, "especially when others are to bear the consequences. But I advise against it. Just follow Knudsen's shot. He has a good lie. You can too. You'll get him on the approach."

"The way you're hitting," Cedric said, "you can make it. This will ensure you win!"

At issue was how Evan should play the dogleg. On the one hand, he could hit his tee-shot and place his ball so as to gain an open view around the turn to the left, just like Knudsen had done. Alternatively, he could "cut the corner" by hitting over the dogleg's thick, tall, dense cluster of trees. He could take the hypotenuse of the dogleg.

"Look," Chadwick said. "If you make it, you can win. If you get caught in the trees, though, you'll add a devastating number of strokes to your score. Cutting corners is always risky."

The general, after perceiving the curious edge of tension on the tee box, walked up to the group for an explanation. "What's happening?" he asked, frowning.

"I'm going to try to win the game, here and now," Evan answered. He made direct eye contact and spoke with a tone of confidence.

"Very good," the general said. "The rest of you can just get out of here. Let him hit."

"But ..." Fletcher said in protest, assuming that the general needed more information to stop Evan from cutting the dogleg's corner.

The general cut off Fletcher's protest at the first word. He then led the others from the tee and left Evan standing alone with his number three driver in hand, the driver he used when he needed both loft and distance. Everywhere around him the crowd returned to watching in silence. Evan ventured a quick glance over to where he knew Amanda was. Their eyes met, he held the contact, but then he was gone. She had never seen him looking so distant, as though he saw her face without feeling her support. His expression was vacant, though he did not appear nervous.

He looks so focused, she thought without speaking, *concerned, confident, and withdrawn. Where did he go?*

Amanda brought her hands together and held them under her chin. She watched him intently until after he hit, wearing an outward expression of concern.

Evan, on the other hand, saw Amanda by looking straight through her. He wanted no more than to know she was there, but when he saw her drawn lips, searching eyes, and creased forehead—saw her concern—he was struck by the irrelevant thought that she was beautiful. Young men will have the oddest thoughts at just such moments, but Amanda was, in fact, poised as just described. Her eyes were piercing, her usually animated laughter was missing, the smooth skin of her forehead wrinkled, and her hair surrounded her face the way an ornate frame enhances an artist's painting. She was uniquely beautiful.

Evan placed his tee and ball but, instead of addressing the ball as though he were to hit it straight down the fairway, he turned to his right about twenty degrees. He placed his feet farther apart than his usual shoulder-width stance and looked up at the top of the tree cluster that blocked the path his ball would take. He lifted and lowered the head of his club several times, as though seeking something in its balance, and then he tightened his usually light grip. His looked up at the trees, down at his ball, up at the trees, down at the club head positioned behind the ball, up at the trees, and down again. While he quadruple-checked his position, people in the crowd murmured. Someone far away asked, "What's he doing?" another said, "Oh-no!" and still another added, "He'll never make it." The voices served only to intensify the moment.

Bentley Knudsen heard the murmuring. He turned back to look over his shoulder, and there he saw that Evan was positioned to cut the corner with his drive. He halted, stared, grinned, and nodded with the enthusiasm of a dare. He, too, glanced toward the tree tops, but the prospective outcome had him laughing and shaking his head in outright disbelief. When he returned to look at the admiral, he smiled and repeated sideways turns of his head. Both spoke without saying a word.

Evan took his practice swing. He swung hard so that the slant of his club cut the air with a powerful swoosh. Knudsen heard the sound and stopped grinning. He exchanged another glance with his caddie, but his look held a question instead of ridicule. He and the entire crowd rushed a glance to the tree tops and back to Evan. He stood ready to hit his ball.

His position was farther from his ball than usual, which made him appear to be using his club to reach for the ball. He made slight adjustments with his feet and

knees, searching for an equal distribution of his weight.
He balanced his three wood in his hands, gently held the
club's face behind the ball, and drew back the club until
his left arm was high, straight, and pointing in the opposite
direction of where his ball would travel. There, he paused
his backswing and cocked his wrists so that the club head
fell behind him as though he was trying to scratch an
itch on his back. Throughout his backswing, the crowd
seemed to draw and hold the same breath of air. Evan
broke the moment of silence with the cut of wind from
his club and the pound of the club head against his ball.
The hit sounded more damaging than sweet. Instantly, life
returned. All heads turned to follow the ball's path. They
saw it lift, fly, lift some more. When they saw it was on a path
to hit the top of a tree, they groaned in unison.

Evan watched with his club dropped behind him and
his face turned toward the back of his diminishing ball. He,
too, watched it climb toward the tree top, and he reacted
by leaning like he could influence the ball to a side of the
limb in its way. Fade is the wrong word, though, because just
before he had swung the club, just before he had taken his
backswing, he had made a small movement to close the club
face. The result of this movement was that his ball, after
flying off the tee and traveling one hundred or so yards,
began to draw smoothly to the left, oh so slightly. He leaned,
the ball kept going, it tended left, voices raised, soldiers
yelled, and when the ball appeared on course to hit the
tip-top of one of the trees, the groaning sounds of wonder
changed to the roaring sound of groans. By no more than
the width of a leaf, the ball missed the limb. It kept right on
going and descended behind the dogleg's thick cluster of
trees and bushes, where it disappeared from sight.

The crowd reacted like a startled herd of deer. Evan
collapsed backwards onto the grass of the tee box, laughing

and listening to the rumble of the herd as it ran off to
discover where the ball had landed. He could feel and hear
the deep pounding of their flight, but the comparison
with a herd of deer soon gave way to the excited sounds
of humans on the move, like sports fans rushing a field.
The soldiers and sailors were fastest and loudest, but the
admiral, general, the instructors, and everyone else were
not far behind.

"You did it!" It was the voice that broke his attention.
Evan was still lying on the ground and smiling, watching the
mass of spectators run to find his ball. He was laughing at
their backs, but when he turned his face to the sound of the
voice, he found Amanda standing and looking down at him.
He gained his feet, showed his biggest smile, and laughed
like a little boy.

"Did you see that?" he asked. "It worked! It cleared the
trees. I cut the corner!"

"I know," she said, joining his laughter while taking his
hands. "You did it!"

Evan's joy for the moment was contagious. He pulled
her to him, and she leaned until her forehead touched
his. He then lifted her and spun her around in a high
circle, right there on the tee box. She clung to him, her
eyes looking down into his, and he held her by the waist,
looking up at her. They spun and laughed as though they
were the best of friends during the best of times. Evan did
not think of her beauty. She did not consider his strength.
They simply enjoyed the shared happiness of the moment.
He spun her back down to the ground, releasing her with
a dancer's twirl, and the two then went off hand-in-hand,
laughing, stumbling, and rushing to find the others.

"Will you win?" Amanda asked, breathless.

"That depends on where the ball landed. If it's in the
bushes, there's no way I can win."

"That's not possible. I saw it myself. What if it's in the fairway?"

"What if?" Evan asked.

She turned and looked at him because, as she would later recall, his question had struck her as asking more than what was obvious. "Well," she smiled, "then you win."

CHAPTER 19

~ THE BALL PLAYS HERE ~

Evan and Amanda strolled down the eighteenth fairway and together reached the bend in the dogleg. As they rounded the corner, they could see to the par five's distant flagstick. They saw the flag hanging motionless in the still air and saw what caused Evan to jerk to a stop. His smile disappeared, he released Amanda's hand, and then he took off, sprinting down the fairway without saying a word.

Amanda saw it too, and her eyes widened, jaw dropped, and then she, too, began running full speed after Evan. There was a commotion in the center of the fairway, and in the middle of the melee were two MPs restraining Major Akerly by his arms. His face was badly bruised, his nose bloodied, his shirt torn, and dirt stains covered both knees of his uniform. His eyes were downcast and he was gasping for air, as though he had been running. Soldiers everywhere were shouting and pointing in opposite directions.

Evan caught up with the admiral and the general. There was an immediate increase in the volume of soldiers explaining everything at once, only now there was a common authority point to which they began directing their explanations. This happened, that happened, over here, and over there, they shouted, along with the name, "Major Akerly."

"Quiet," the admiral yelled, looking about to identify his highest-ranking subordinate.

"Tell me what's happening here," the general said, also shouting to be heard.

The quiet that followed included sounds of heavy breathing and shuffling boots. Several men shook their heads.

"Now, someone tell me what is happening here," the general said.

Several junior officers began explaining at the same time, restoring the noise and confusion of uncoordinated explanations. Fingers again pointed here and there. The general turned to a second lieutenant. "You," he said, "tell me what happened."

"Yes, sir," the officer began. "Evan's ball was in the center of the fairway. It cleared the dogleg and stopped in the very middle of the fairway. It stopped right here."

The lieutenant pointed to the ground near where he was then standing, and the admiral and the general followed his finger to where each saw nothing on the ground. There was no ball.

"After the ball stopped, Major Floyd Akerly, there, well, Major Akerly, he was hiding in the bushes, waiting for the ball. When it stopped here in the fairway, he ran out, took the ball, and he threw it back into those bushes over there. We caught him in the act."

Angry shouting ensued while the admiral and general again followed the lieutenant's pointed finger back toward the foliage surrounding the dogleg. Both looked sternly to the bushes, the fairway, the lieutenant, and then to each other.

"Can this be true?" the general asked, reducing his volume while increasing the level of disappointment in his voice.

"Unquestionably," the lieutenant said, "Just let this young man tell it." He pointed at Cedric. "He was the first to arrive, and he's the one who saw it all happen. He followed Akerly and caught him red-handed."

Everyone quieted and gave their attention to Cedric. The general turned to him with a command that sounded deflated of excitement. "Young man, tell us what just happened."

"Back on the tee box," Cedric explained, "just as Evan was getting ready to hit his drive, I happened to see that soldier over there. Something didn't look right, like he was crazed and angry. He looked at Evan like he hated him, like he could kill him. Anyway, when Evan was about to hit, just after he turned to hit over the trees and everyone was looking up at the tops of the trees, I kept my eyes on the soldier. I watched him run off into the bushes. I thought he might be frightened or maybe something was wrong. He ran straight along the line Evan's ball would take. I was unsure what was occurring, but I had never seen anything like it. I followed him."

The admiral and the general then looked at Floyd, who stared at the ground in front of him. His demeanor justified a presumption of guilt.

"I followed him through the brush, and right when he reached the edge of the fairway, he spotted Evan's ball. It was rolling and stopping out in the middle of the fairway. The soldier ran out to the ball, picked it up, and threw it back into those bushes. He threw it back just as I was coming out onto the fairway. He nearly hit me with it!" Everyone followed Cedric's extended finger back to the brush. "He tried to run away when he saw me coming. I tried to stop him."

The loud commotion that ensued was quieted by one soldier from Battery B. "It's true," he said, also speaking with wide eyes. "We found Major Akerly in a scuffle with this kid. We stopped them, but when we heard just what it was the major had done, we all decided to defend the Army's honor."

"What?" the general yelled. "Can this possibly be true?"

Cedric, upon hearing the authoritative, angry, and dominating voice, turned and looked anxiously to Evan for help.

"Is this true, Cedric?" Evan asked.

"Just as you heard it," Cedric answered.

"Then where is Evan's ball now?" the admiral asked in a tone equal to the general's irritated and angry one.

No one had yet thought to find the ball, but everyone looked back to the bushes where a large group of determined men was heading to search for it.

"Wait!" Knudsen shouted, startling and stopping the search party. "Don't touch the ball until we can figure out what really happened."

His insinuation brought about another round of shouting, and a quick conference was held right then in the center of the fairway.

"What do you mean, 'what really happened?'" the general asked. "We know what happened!"

"What we know for certain," Knudsen said, speaking after receiving a subtle nod from the admiral, "is that the Army is playing a round of golf against the Navy. The Navy player hit a ball straight up this fairway. The Army player tried to cut the corner of a dogleg. He hit a risky shot. My ball is in the fairway. Private Wilkins' ball is not."

A tumult of offended voices arose, but Knudsen ignored them in favor of continuing his attempt at a rational explanation. "I find it both a convenient coincidence and a suspicious circumstance," he said, "that the Army's ball is alleged to have cleared the dogleg and to have landed in the center of the fairway. Then it was picked up and thrown by an officer, an Army officer, no less, and that a fifteen-year-old boy who just happens to be Evan's caddie detained the officer. Finally, the ball in question is to be retrieved from the bushes and placed ahead of the Navy's ball, way up here in the middle of the fairway. This is unbelievable!"

"But it's true!" Cedric said, widening his eyes in defense.

Bentley did not bother to look at Cedric, for just then there was another round of excited yelling over in the bushes. Everyone turned to look. While Knudsen was making his case, the search party, after initially being stopped by Knudsen's protest, had continued to move one step, then another, and several more until they were well into the brush and searching for the ball. They found it right away and left it untouched. A crowd formed around the little ball where it was found lying among the brush and branches. The searchers shouted to those on the fairway, and when the players, the admiral, and the general arrived, a soldier stood pointing to the ball and offering his excited explanation.

"Look!" he said. "The ball is up against the trunk of this tree. It could not possibly have landed there unless it came from the direction of the fairway."

The ball was, in fact, close to the base of a large tree on the opposite side from where Evan hit it. It was obvious it had come from the fairway side.

"It might have hit one of these small bushes and bounced back against the tree," a seaman said, but his words were speculative and devoid of enthusiasm, as though he did not believe his own explanation.

Knudsen was about to offer his thoughts that the idea warranted consideration and that a solution might be for Evan to hit again, but the admiral, after looking at the ball, contemplating Cedric, and staring at the accused who stood beaten and dejected between the MPs, just shook his head.

"Young man," the admiral said to Cedric. "Where did you say that ball was out in the fairway?"

The admiral picked up Evan's ball and followed Cedric to the very center of the fairway. He placed the ball on the exact spot indicated by the caddie, spoke quietly with the general, and the two commanders then walked over to Floyd.

"Is this true?" the general asked Floyd. "Look at me!"

Floyd lifted his eyes no higher than the general's cluster of chest medals. He nodded his agreement and hung his head like a horse.

"And is this where you found Evan's ball?" the general asked, indicating the golf ball that had been returned to the fairway.

Again Floyd gave a pathetic and helpless nod of agreement. The general moved close, stood threateningly with his heavy breath falling on Floyd's face, reached for the rank insignia on Floyd's shirt and ripped it off in one violent motion.

"Get him out of here!" he said, turning his back while two MPs roughly grabbed Floyd.

The general turned to look at the admiral, who was pointing to Evan's ball lying there in the fairway. The admiral stepped forward and looked into the eyes of his counterpart.

"I'm sorry," he said. He pointed his finger to the ground at their feet, right there in the middle of the fairway. He nodded his head and said, "The ball plays here."

CHAPTER 20

~ LIFTING AND LOWERING GLASSES ~

Confusion often departs as quickly as it arrives. With the Navy's acceptance and agreement that Evan's ball belonged in the center of the fairway, after remarkably cutting across the dogleg, uncertainty cleared to reveal a tremendous moment of clarity. Everyone present returned back up the fairway and assembled behind where Bentley Knudsen's ball lay with its perfect view to the green. They watched Bentley take his second shot with a two iron to send the ball flying low and fast. It returned right back to where the crowd had just come, and it stopped only one yard short of where Evan's ball had been placed. The game then reduced to one of reaching the green and making a putt. Because Evan stood one stroke ahead of Bentley, if both reached the green and made his putt, the result was academic: Evan and the Army would take the field.

"It's not over," Fletcher said. He was standing beside Chadwick and both were watching as Bentley readied to hit. "What if he reaches the green and makes his putt? If Evan does not match him, they would tie. They would have to play a tie-breaker."

"What makes you think that will happen? Look around. Listen. Everyone's smiling and no one is hushing. It's over."

When Bentley hit long and reached the green, Fletcher began pecking a finger on Chadwick's shoulder. "See?" he said.

"Shh. Let's see what Evan does."

Evan, too, swung hard, hit long, and reached the green. Instead of stopping at a convenient distance from the cup, though, his ball rolled. From where he stood back up the fairway, Chadwick added his voice to the chorus of cheering voices. "Look at it roll. It's still going," he said.

"I can't see it!" Fletcher yelled. "What's happening?"

"Come on!"

The two joined everyone else who took off running toward the green. The ball looked small in the distance, but those with a vantage point saw it roll onto the green like a steel bearing drawn to a magnetic cup. The ball was moving, the crowd was running, and then it happened. The ball disappeared.

"It's in! He did it!" Chadwick yelled.

He made his call while running beside Fletcher. They stopped when they reached the green and found it alive with cheers, handshakes, and pats. There were soldiers and sailors surrounding the hole, and they waited while Evan came to retrieve his ball. Bentley came with him, looked down in the hole, and then he smiled as Evan removed the ball and held it high for everyone to see. They sent a great cheer echoing across the course. Both the soldiers and sailors tossed their caps high into the air.

"Two hits on a par five," Fletcher said, bouncing as he spoke. He mirrored Chadwick's expression of wide eyes and open mouth. Both stood with their hands held open in disbelief, and they looked as though they had witnessed a miracle. "That was unbelievable. What happened? Did Evan just shoot an albatross?"

"He did," Chadwick said. "He shot a two on a par five. He shot an albatross. He just won the game for the Army."

"What's the final score?"

"Let me see," Chadwick said. He looked at the ground while figuring the numbers. "It's hard to think out here," he said, "but I got it. The Army won by a score of sixty-five, seven under par, to the Navy's sixty-seven, five under par."

The moment became an instant classic memory for Evan. He was not allowed to walk from the eighteenth green. Instead, he was surrounded by over two hundred cheering, laughing, celebrating fans. They clobbered his back with pats, passed his left and right hands from well-wisher to well-wisher, hoisted him off of his feet, and carried him from the green like a hero.

Amanda watched it all happen from where she stood to one side of the green. Because of the men, she was unable to get anywhere near Evan. The contingent of young men and women joined her, and they stood surrounding and congratulating her as though she had played the game herself. She heard so many cheers at once that she could only turn her smile from one voice to the next.

"That was incredible," one young lady said.

"Yes it was," Amanda said, laughing and meeting the smile of one of her friends.

"Can you believe it?"

"No," she said, turning to smile at another friend. "What he did was amazing."

"We did it!" She turned and discovered the male voice behind her belonged to Charles Ambrose. He greeted her with a smile. "I plan to play just like that at UCLA," he said.

The Army owned the last evening in August, 1943, Los Angeles, California. The Navy contingent departed the clubhouse, the golf course, and LA, and many left the state of California. They went right after the Army's victory. A large number of motivated young men can accomplish remarkable amounts of work in a short period of time. They emptied, cleaned, and brought in tables and chairs, refreshments, and a dance floor by that evening. A thirty-four piece band that was a local favorite in the Los Angeles area came early to set up for the night. Invitations had been sent earlier in anticipation of the victory, so it was that a stream of guests later arrived in groups of four and five, scented, swishing, smiling, sweatered, and laughing. They found clusters of young men dressed in their formal military dress, and without formality, the soldiers and the guests mingled. All victory celebrations are pleasing to hear. The music played and mixed with the sounds of couples laughing, smiling, and dancing. People everywhere congratulated each other.

"I haven't seen Evan. Where is he?"

"I have no idea," Amanda said, turning and seeing Charles Ambrose. He stood leaning on her chair, a hand positioned by her shoulder. Before he could ask the obvious, she cut him off with a smile. "I told you before," she said. "I'm saving my first dance for Evan."

An hour had passed since the celebration began, but Evan had still not arrived at the party. Consequently, the band was the focal point of attention in the room. Couples swayed to the fast sounds of brass and string music, stirring a cloud of smoky air that hovered above them. Facing the dance floor were four-sided tables that were surrounded by triple the number of chairs, and these were filled with loud groups of celebrants, laughing, toasting, smoking, and recounting the game. All watched for Evan to arrive.

Beside Amanda was an empty chair. She listened to those at her table wonder about Evan's whereabouts, recount events of the golf game, and discuss the war, which was the prevailing topic. As the night progressed without Evan, Amanda found herself disengaging from every conversation.

"Amanda? Did you hear me? He should be coming any time."

She turned from where she had been watching the door, and laughed. "I'm sorry," she said. "What did you say?"

At the time, Evan was walking toward the clubhouse in the company of the general and his entourage. None in the group were smiling, none were talking, and all looked unusually serious, given the day's events. Evan walked with the proud formality of a man of war, and he held himself taller, looked smarter, and strode with a nonchalance that gave the appearance of lightness, as though he were on the verge of floating. He was tethered, though, for in between the swipes and glances he made to the fresh new military insignia on his uniform, his eyes and the slant of his expression revealed he was troubled by deeper thoughts than golf and officer insignias.

Still, when he entered the clubhouse, he did so like a conqueror. People shouted his name, came forward to bombard him with accolades, and stopped him by the door with countless words of praise. He gave in to a smile. The general smiled, too, and both laughed at the instant appreciation. A space opened between them as they received the congratulations of all who came forward. They shook hands, nodded, smiled, and thanked the smothering crowd. The general leaned to peer around a group of soldiers so he could nod and give Evan a reassuring smile. The general also waved for him to come closer.

"Would you look at this?" Evan yelled. "I see nothing but smiles."

"It's for you!" the general shouted back. To the crowd, he called for silence. "Quiet. Quiet. Listen up. I have an announcement to make."

The sound of shushing filled the room, but complete silence was never fully achieved. The volume of noise simply decreased.

"I present to you," the general continued, nearly shouting, "the day's champion, Lieutenant Evan Wilkins."

The general followed his announcement by putting his right arm around Evan's shoulder and using his other hand to touch the clean new lieutenant insignia that was visible to all on the upper part of Evan's arm. The announcement registered with the crowd and brought another round of clapping and cheering. Evan had congratulations nearly beaten into his shoulders, but he managed several times to search to find Amanda. So enthusiastic was the support for him that it took nearly an hour before he proceeded farther into the room than his initial few steps. After what seemed like every soldier, instructor, and supporter had a turn registering appreciation, he was able to see well enough to find a central table with two empty seats. Standing behind and touching one of the chairs, he saw Amanda looking at him. He stopped as though stunned and stared without smiling. She stared back at him. People spoke at his shoulder, hands touched his shoulders, but she retained all of his attention. From the moment he saw her, he lost sight of everything else in the room. She stood out, poised against the peripheral blur.

As they gazed across the distance, Evan noticed the slow manner in which Amanda lowered her eyes to look at his new badge of rank, and then he saw her lift a brow, narrow her eyes, and nod her head while her lips formed a grin. At the same time, they began walking toward each other and gained momentum as they moved. They came together hard, like two waves colliding. She flew up high, placed her hands on his shoulders, he held her by the waist, and they twirled together for the second time that day. Their spin ended just as it had earlier in the day with Evan slowing as she slid down his length until she had regained her feet. Without letting go or moving apart, she looked up at him, and he kissed her. Their kiss was a fast, little touch of the lips, but that touch conveyed reassurance, connection, and acceptance. Complexity is often found in the simplest of sentiments.

They talked, danced, laughed, and celebrated. They enjoyed an evening both wished could last forever. After everyone present looked to have had an excellent evening, just before the general was about to depart, he moved in front of the band, motioned for his aides to join him, and asked the music conductor to cease the music. Those who were dancing stopped and looked at him.

"Listen up," he said. "Quiet now. I need your attention." He waited while everyone gave their attention to him. They quieted in that same way crowds quiet for important speakers that want the full attention of an audience. Voices stilled over time, until the room silenced as much as it would. The general then cleared his throat.

"Forever, this day will be remembered by the Army," he said. "Never forget what it was that Evan Wilkins did for us today." He looked over at Evan and added, "Lieutenant Wilkins, thank you. The Army owes you a great deal of gratitude."

"Here, here!" someone shouted, and then people everywhere lifted their glasses and offered toasts of their own. He waited for the room to quiet again before he continued in a somber tone. "This is a time of war. We must never forget that American men are dying. Today we beat the Navy on the golf course." He elevated his sober expression with a smile at Evan. "Remember, though, we did not beat an enemy. We played a friend. We do have enemies, though, and they have not been beaten. Not yet, at least."

As he spoke, those in the room quieted. They listened for him to add a "therefore," "as a result," or some other prefix to a conclusion.

"Orders have arrived," he continued, "for the 170th Field Artillery Battalion to leave California. They want us to get over there and help end this damn war. We are to begin a journey to the east coast, and from there we will travel to the European theater of operations. The details of our orders are still unknown, but we will be going, and we will receive further details as we go." He delivered his final words with an increase in volume and enthusiasm. "We won the golf game. Now let's win the war!"

For emphasis, he swung a clenched fist sideways across his midsection, but the response he elicited from those who heard his words lacked enthusiasm. The room remained hushed, and the obvious reaction the general received, though not desired, was one of introspection and a quiet exchange of eye contact between the soldiers.

"Today is the last day of August," he continued. "We leave on the third day of September. Men, you have two days to prepare." He paused, then concluded, "All officers are to be here tomorrow for a briefing at oh six hundred."

The room lost the merriment of carefree celebration, like all rooms do when unanticipated and disappointing news is delivered without warning, when musicians stop playing and begin packing their instruments, and when partygoers begin departing in groups. The general and his staff were the first to go. The soldiers followed, looking sober, tired, and without emotion. A group of expressionless young ladies left next, their lips tightly sealed as they went toward the door. Several of the 170th's officers walked among the tables and encouraged their men to get moving. In minutes, the clubhouse was empty, and all that remained was the silence that followed the celebration.

CHAPTER 21

~ *TILL DEATH DO US PART* ~

Following the general's announcement about the upcoming move from the golf course, all of those who were present began departing the clubhouse as though they were leaving a funeral parlor. They went in twos and threes, spoke in whispers, and looked with somber expressions to no further than the back of whomever they followed. Evan and Amanda went out with the rest. Like everyone else, they remained quiet and contemplative. They neither smiled nor looked at each other, and it was only when someone gave Evan a "way to go," "good game," or "nice job," that either appeared to acknowledge anything outside of their own world of thoughts. When they did look at anyone else, they saw that the earlier, unrestrained enthusiasm for the day's game had already departed with the general. Each person's attention seemed to be on matters such as packing, saying goodbye, traveling, and fighting the war. They were undergoing the extreme emotional change of war. One moment they were living; but now, in this new moment, they were simply alive.

That last August evening in Los Angeles, California was splendid. The night air was warm, calm, and bright. There was a harvest moon, and its light illuminated everything that was dark outside on the golf course. Evan and Amanda were able to make out tee boxes, fairways, trees, bushes, pathways, and each other's gray silhouettes. An infinite sky full of stars shined above and covered them in the universe of black and white—the binary simplicity of on or off and yes or no. He was there and she was too. Neither bothered looking high enough to see above their view of gray. They saw all color gone from their sight, and so, too, were the obvious little truths of their time spent together. She did not want him to leave, and he wanted only to stay with her. Each wanted the other, but they had only lived the truth. Their first look had gone with a first kiss, and now it, too, faced the oblivion of goodbye or the first of something greater.

Night walks on golf courses are unmatched for inspiring words to go with emotions. Experiences of the day get relegated to something that happened much earlier, and the moments of the night become everything. Evan and Amanda felt this change when they stepped out from the stuffy gloom inside the clubhouse. They felt the warm night air. They saw the bright darkness. They woke to the finer sentiments of the soul.

They brought their hands together without thinking about doing so, as though the touch of the other would preclude their pending separation.

"I'm glad the game is over," he said, speaking more than talking. "I'm surprised by how much emotion it drained from me."

"Game?" Amanda said. "Oh, yeah, the game. Was that just today? It already seems to me like a distant dream."

"I know what you mean."

"Look up," she said, speaking as though she had never before seen such a bright, dark sky. "You can see everything."

"It's the harvest moon," he replied. "It helps farmers see everything in the night just when it's time for them to harvest. Because the sky is so bright, they can run their combines all night. They even get to work when it's cool

204

outside, instead of working in the hot part of a summer day." When Amanda said nothing, Evan continued to speak as though he needed to keep talking. "I call these 'American moons.' Twenty years after American independence from England, the British decided our little experiment with lofty ideals had run its course."

"Really?" she asked, without looking at him or sounding interested in his point.

"Yes. England came to take back what it still considered to be its own. They returned and launched a coordinated attack. They went south through the Great Lakes, north through New Orleans, and west into Washington, D.C. They burned our White House. In defense of New Orleans, Andrew Jackson led a night attack under a sky just like this."

"Oh?"

"Yes. Jackson's men surprised the British and made them run. We paid for the fight with our White House, but we won. Because the moonlight helped us, I call harvest moons American moons."

"Oh," she repeated, "now you're going to give me a history lesson. Maybe I'll call it a 'History moon.'"

"I'm sorry," he said, grinning in the grayness. "I heard your tone. You do not want to talk about the moon and neither do I." He returned to where they left off in an earlier conversation. "Are you sure about walking? You know I can drive you home in one of our jeeps."

"No," she said, "it's not that far. Besides, I would rather walk with you."

He had heard her speak the exact words back at the clubhouse, but outside they sounded different. They carried emotion. As he breathed in the warm night air, heard the fading sounds of the men become the night sounds of the golf course, saw moonlight shading their way in white, and felt her hand in his, he repeated his consent. His voice joined the everywhere sounds of a thousand crickets.

"Okay, we'll walk," he said.

They began by walking across the tee box on hole number one, and then they walked the entire length of the front nine. Neither suggested cutting over at number four—the hole with the sloping green that provided a much more direct route to the Nichols home—and they began their walk without saying anything at all. Both were silent, feeling everything that happened in the past thirty days. There was the buildup in anticipation of the golf game, the friendship they developed, all of the time they spent practicing with the instructors, the party, Floyd's behavior, and the game against the Navy. There was the victory celebration and Evan's promotion to lieutenant. Like the space behind all of the stars, there loomed darker sentiments. He and the 170th would leave in just two days to join the fight. They faced parting, perhaps forever, the horrible possibilities of war, and the certain loneliness that always follows separation. Their intertwined fingers held these confused emotions in check, but only until they stepped onto the green of the fifth hole. Like a jumble of logs succumbing to the force of a flood, their emotions were overwhelmed by the moment's truth. Amanda stopped on the green and turned to face him.

"What am I to do when you're gone?" she asked.

He looked down into her eyes. Though it was night, he saw her question. The moonlight allowed him to see in her eyes what he heard in her voice. He used a finger to wipe a tear. Moving closer to her, he softened his voice and nearly said the wrong thing in his attempt to console her.

"You'll be fine," he said. "Things will return to normal for you. If anything, I'm the one who should be worried. I could be killed!"

"That's what I mean," she said. "We've spent so much time together—almost every day since we met—that I now feel as though you have been here forever. And yet, the time has been so little. I want more. I do not want you to leave."

"I feel the same way." The tone of Evan's voice was soft and serious. "I feel the same way," he said, looking down into her moon-gray eyes. "I have to go, you know. I'm in the Army, and the Army is needed." She saw his grin form a shade in the dark. "That's how I will think of the war. I will be fighting for you. I feel better already."

"But if something were to happen to you," she said, "I don't know what I would do. You say you gain comfort from thinking you're fighting to protect me, but that doesn't help. It only causes me pain. Don't you see? You've gotten into my heart."

"Pain is a strong word," he said. "You'll be fine. Nothing will happen to me. When I return, I think we should talk about your heart."

"Even if nothing happens to you," she said, "something will happen to me."

Amanda pressed her body against his and her face under his chin. He put his arms around her, she squeezed, and they both stood there on the green holding each other. He felt her tears on his shoulder, heard her draw a deep breath, and felt her tightly squeezing against him. Both remained silent for a period of several minutes, until Evan cleared his throat.

"I'm sorry I have to leave," he whispered.

If he had been required at that moment to further explain what he was sorry for, he would have mentioned her hurt, his leaving, and the trouble he caused her. He would have talked about Amanda. He would not have mentioned the reality that he felt her same feelings. He was sorry they could not have more time to be together. He did not want to leave her. She felt this truth in the heave of his chest. She pulled her face from under his chin and looked up at his eyes.

"When will you return?" She asked the question more to hear him talk than to elicit a date or time. He smiled because he knew she knew he had no idea when he might return.

"Just as soon as I can get back here," he said. "It should be obvious that I intend to return to you. I feel we belong together, and I think if my battalion was not leaving, I would want us to stay together forever."

"Forever?" she repeated, the wistful whisper of her voice carrying the sound of impossible hope. Yet, she clung to the word. "Just how long is that?"

He closed his eyes. Crickets were everywhere. He considered his answer while squeezing her against him, and then the words of his heart formed in his mind. He opened his eyes to find hers waiting. She was looking so deeply into his eyes that she appeared to be seeking his soul.

"How long is forever?" he repeated her question. "Till death do us part?"

He felt her soften in his arms, as though she were yielding to both gravity and the truth in his voice at the same moment. Their silence turned serious—charged with emotion—but lasted for only a moment. Their holding, looking, hugging, and thinking ended in the meeting of their lips. What might have been quite a passionate kiss ended just as suddenly as it started. Amanda stopped and leaned her face from his, and she turned her eyes up to look in his.

"What did you just say?" she asked. "Can you please say it again?"

"You heard me," he said. "When I return from the war, I want to marry you." While she cried, he squeezed and held her head under his chin.

When they finally separated, they walked with their arms around each other and talked about a new world of possibilities. They talked about plans, ideas, their future, where they might live, what they would do, and shared the dreams that come at such a time. They walked until reaching somewhere deep on the back nine—somewhere near the green by her house—and then Evan stopped. She stopped too.

"I want to make this official," he said.

Though neither could clearly see the other, they saw enough. The light from the moon met their faces and cast shadow profiles right there at their feet. Each saw only what they needed to see. On the golf course green, under the light of the moon, accompanied by the everywhere sounds of crickets, and feeling more than the warmth of the last night of August, Evan dropped to one knee. He held Amanda's hands in his and looked up at her. He cleared his throat.

"Miss Amanda Nichols," he said, sounding less formal than emotional, "will you marry me?"

"Yes," she said, answering so quickly that she gave no doubt. She could not have said the word any faster. She then repeated her answer through a smile. "Yes. Yes. Yes. Yes." Four times she said it, and then she, too, dropped to her knees, where she lay down on her side, turned flat on her back, and accepted Evan on the soft bed of grass.

Later that night they said goodnight by the back door of her house. They came together, kissed, said goodbye, separated, said goodbye again, and then repeated the parting all over. They shared the laughter of knowing they could finally be totally at ease with each other, and the feeling was intoxicating. Amanda saw in Evan's eyes, his smile, and in the manner in which returned to her again and again that he was much happier and more relaxed than she had ever seen him. His emotion infected her. He was being silly, and she liked it. They spent nearly an hour saying goodbye, but Amanda finally entered her home and Evan departed.

Once he cleared the bushes and was out on the fairway, he walked far enough to turn back and see the upper windows of her home. There, he stopped and looked back a final time. He saw the moon first, big and bright, behind her house. There were no lights on in the house—not even in the one dormer he sought to distinguish from the others, but he remained there alone and waited for her to reach her room. He stood staring up at her dark dormer and grinning at how the moon seemed to have stopped directly over her house. He waited and, without seeing her light, walked away from a dark dormer.

Let her sleep, he thought. He looked at the big house, nodded his head, and added, *Hold on to her for me. I'm here forever.*

Evan walked back to his barrack and thought about the long day. It had been a day during which everything had gone right for him. It had been his day. He would remember it all. He made memories for life. Nothing had gone wrong.

How is it that some days are like this? he wondered, *where everything is right? And not just right, everything is perfect. I won the game, received a promotion, the dance was in my honor, I admitted my love to Amanda, and she accepted my proposal. Everyone should get a day like this one, at least once in their life.*

He wore a smile when he climbed into his narrow cot that night. Everyone was asleep, and at the moment he finally lay his head on his pillow, he was gone too. He might have dreamed, might have laughed out loud in his sleep, might have tossed, turned, or just lay unmoving, for when he awoke the following morning, he remembered nothing but that he was happy. He woke entirely alone in his barrack, too, and the effect was that he woke uncertain as to where he was, why he was alone, and why it was that the day was already so bright outside. He felt entirely uncertain as to what he was supposed to be doing at just that moment. Golfing was over, his CO had been demoted and thrown in the stockade, and his battalion was soon leaving to join the war. After dressing and forming tight corners with the scratchy wool blanket on his cot, he heard the door to his barrack open. Instantly he was surrounded by all the men of his Battery B. They burst in upon him with the energy and laughter of those who have already had a full morning. They greeted Evan on behalf of the day, all spoke, and several jumped onto his cot.

"We let you sleep. You looked exhausted, and we thought you earned the break. Besides, we still don't have a CO. No one else has been assigned to Floyd's position. We're in limbo."

"What does that mean?" asked Evan. "We don't have a commanding officer? Great. Where is Floyd right now?" His question brought back to him the darker memories of the previous day—they returned in detail.

"The MP's took Floyd to the guardhouse. He's still in there," said one soldier who was anxious to share information. "The general demoted him to a private, but because Akerly got into trouble during a round of golf—a game we were not supposed to be playing, especially while the rest of the Army is out fighting and dying—the general cannot court-martial him. He needs to keep the whole thing quiet." Several laughed at the general's predicament.

"I heard Private Floyd Akerly is now just one of the men on a gun crew."

"In which battery?" Evan asked.

"I heard he's a gunner in Battery C," the man said. "Can you believe it? Now he's a private, just like us!"

Heads nodded and everyone laughed and exchanged eye contact with each other and with Evan.

"Who will be our new CO?" Evan asked.

"They're still meeting in headquarters. The general's there with the officers. They've been in there for over three hours. We still don't know."

The general and all of the officers of the 170th met in the clubhouse for the morning's three-hour briefing. While he and his staff left the meeting and departed immediately for the east coast, the battery commanders assembled their men and gave briefings about the battalion's planned movements. The men of Battery B were more interested to learn who would be their new CO, but Evan's main concern was finding a way to see Amanda. He looked for opportunities to get away.

The new CO turned out to be a major from Battery A, known as a doer, a pusher of men, and a man without friends. He was matter-of-fact and kept the men on a strict military regimen of maintenance, planning, drilling, organizing, and preparing for their departure from the golf course. Evan and the men were so busy, they had time only to prepare for war. He could find no opportunities to slip away to see Amanda. Nor was there any opportunity for him to look for her out on the course because he could no longer play golf. Even though he was constantly busy, he found plenty of time to feel miserable about not seeing her. At nearly every opportunity of his day, he felt the urge to see her. She had become his constant thought, his reason for doing. While he performed his duties to ready the battalion for its departure, he did so with withdrawn attention, a distracted demeanor, and an unsettled heart. He wanted to see her, and he felt the desire like a basic need of his soul. Neither the men nor the new CO had time to notice Evan's burden, though, because such feelings were for idle times. Over those few days after the golf tournament, preparations for departure consumed every minute. For the battalion, orders were simple. There was too much to get done too quickly. Between the new CO's need to take charge and the men's need to comply with his orders, there was no time for emotions. Orders were given and men acted. Both required the strict discipline of military obedience.

For her part, Amanda had plenty of time to be miserable for Evan. She kept herself fully engaged in the ill-advised pursuit. The morning following the golf game, she took her usual early morning walk to the tee box of the second hole, where she and the others always met. She sat alone for over an hour before she gave up and faced the reality that Evan was not coming. That truth was not good enough for her. After taking the miserable walk home that morning, she went straight to the desk upstairs in her room and wrote from her heart to his. Later that afternoon, she made the same two walks—one hopefully there and the other miserably back home, and she reread her note several times alone.

"Is something the matter?" The family's maid discovered Amanda sitting by a window, holding her letter and looking out at the golf course. "Can I get you anything?"

"No. No," Amanda said, making a quick wipe of an eye. "I'm just wondering about a word."

"But you look so sad. Forgive me."

She returned to the bench on hole number two the following morning, where she experienced an even greater disappointment than she had on the first day. She sat and looked at an envelope she held in her hands where she had written "Lieutenant Evan Wilkins" in her best handwriting. She tore the seal, reread the letter, and remained for some time while she ran her fingers across the smeared pages of ink. She left feeling empty, but the following morning was worse.

On that last day, Amanda made her way from the back nine, took the shortcut at four, and arrived at the second tee in time to catch sight of a nearby movement. For a moment, she felt the first hint of relief, and she opened her mouth. But the feeling left just as quickly as it had come. Hope was replaced with disappointment when she saw the movement was that of a heavyset man in work boots and dirty cotton work pants watering the tee box. Because she had at first thought he was Evan, she had approached him with aggression, and stopped so close he reacted with surprise. She startled him as much as he disappointed her.

"Hi-ya, missey," he said. "Whacha doin' out here?"

"I'm sorry," she said, backing away. "I was looking for the Army. I thought I could catch a glimpse of them practicing. They're usually out here every day. Forgive me." She turned and rushed to leave.

"The Army's gone!" he shouted after her. "Isn't that great? They left about four this morning. It's our golf course again! They're gone for good."

That morning was Amanda's last on the course.

~~~ PART III ~~~
THE HOLE

CHAPTER 22

~ JUST ONE DAY AT A TIME ~

Floyd spent two miserable days and nights locked in the battalion's makeshift stockade, right there on the golf course. The steel door of the small room did not have bars, but the deficiency was hardly a lack. There could have been no door at all, and still he would not have gone anywhere. He was held captive by the turmoil of his mind. The only window was a small one in the door. The room contained a six-foot cot and a seat-less pot, and there was no sink, shower, mirror, or any other means for him to consider anything outside of his dark interior. He had gone straight to the cot at the moment he had entered the cell, lay fully dressed on a stiff wool blanket, and remained unmoving as though he was delirious from fever. He closed his eyes for the few hours during which he lost consciousness between three-in-the-morning and when he heard the sound of his cell door opening at six.

He did not turn to see who was there. He lay unmoving on the cot and listened to the sounds of the guard opening the door, pushing something into the room, and then closing the door and walking away without saying a word. Floyd lifted himself just enough to see what it was that had sounded to him like a brick sliding at him across the concrete floor. He saw a meal tray sitting beside his bed, but he refused to touch it. He also refused to move the tray and, during one of the mindless breaks he took during his day of lying on the cot, staring at the ceiling, and thinking in the dark, he stepped on his plate of food.

Oh, that, he thought, continuing toward the pot and smearing creamed corn with his foot.

Dirt and blood remained on his face, the underside of his fingernails were puttied with black earth, his clothes were grass-stained, and threads remained hanging from where the general had torn the rank insignia from his shirt. They hung like broken legs on a horse. The cuts and bruises on his face and the unwashed dirt on his hands, arms, clothes, and boots smeared the once white pillowcase. When the guard returned to bring Floyd's evening meal, he saw the morning meal scattered about the floor and observed that Floyd had spent the entire day on the cot, where he still lay with his eyes open, his face creased by a scowl, and a vacant, stupefied, numb stare. He looked as though he belonged right where he was—locked up.

"You made a hell of a mess," the guard said. "Look at me when I talk to you." He stood holding the door open while waiting for Floyd to answer. "What is this? You can't even talk. You must have been one hell of a major. It's no wonder you're in here."

Late in the night, hunger compelled him to venture from the cot to retrieve the tray and take it to where he lay on his bed. He ate in the dark. Eating broke his stupor. He spent another dark night on the cot, but he no longer restricted his thoughts to his mind. He began speaking out loud. With an angry voice, he spoke the same thoughts he had formed over the prior two days.

"Sure, they can demote me," he said, lying on his side and speaking into the dark, "but they cannot demoralize me. It was not my fault. Evan is to blame. This cannot stand."

He spoke himself awake the entire night, and he stopped talking only when he heard footsteps approaching out in the hallway. Again, he did not lift himself to look at the arrival until he heard the gruff sound of a command.

"Akerly, stand at attention. Get up now before I come over there and drag your sorry ass out of bed." Floyd looked and saw a battery commander instead of the guard he thought had brought his morning meal. "That's better," the man said. "Look at you. You're a mess. Is that potatoes and gravy in your hair?" Floyd neither looked nor answered. "Listen up. I am the CO of Battery C, so that makes you mine. Everyone wanted you thrown out of the Army, but the general said he could not do it. He said it was politics. You are the first demoted officer I've had under my command. I had to decide what to do with you. Can you guess what I've done? Do you know what that makes you?"

"A private?" Floyd guessed.

"You'll wish you were a private!" the CO said. "No. That's not it. You're not good enough to be a private in my battery. Instead, I'm making you a runner. You are the new Battery C runner. Do you hear that?"

"Yes, sir."

"Did you hear me?"

"Yes, sir."

"Then say it out loud. Tell me who you are."

"I am the runner for Battery C."

"That's right. Now get yourself cleaned up and ready to go. We leave the golf course tomorrow morning. You be ready." As the CO was turning to leave, a guard arrived. He slid Floyd's breakfast tray inside the doorway and left before the CO stopped and looked back in the room. "One more thing," he said. "Everyone knows what you did. You are a disgrace to your old battery, to my Battery C, to the 170th, the entire Army, and to everything else on earth. You had better learn how to keep your mouth shut and stay out of the way."

"Yes, sir."

As a runner, Floyd was charged with doing everything that needed to be done in Battery C. Everyone was his superior, and anyone could command him to perform the most menial tasks. Runners were excluded from membership on any of a battery's four gun crews. During a battle, the runner's duty reduced to both driving and running. All four of the battery's artillery pieces required that orders be brought from headquarters. Each gun crew had six men who were responsible for emptying shells, cleaning barrels, repositioning the pieces, loading the guns, performing maintenance, aiming, firing, and then repeating the entire operation again and again. Heavy backpack radios facilitated communications between headquarters and the battalion's three batteries, A, B, and C. As a backup, each battery had its own runner, whose responsibility it was to drive between headquarters and each of the four guns. The runner delivered the instructions to each gun crew, ran back to his jeep, drove back to headquarters, and then repeated the circuit, as fast as he could, until either a battle ended or he was killed on the rutted back roads that surrounded a good fight. In essence, runners were human backups to the radio. Because of the visibility of their constant activity, runners also faced the greatest risks and suffered the lowest life expectancies in the 170th.

A runner always had duties, especially when his battery was between battles and sitting tight in camp. These duties included little more than running this to here and that to there, be they orders, mail, laundry, or packs of cigarettes. In peacetime, runners could be seen hurrying about as harried little messengers, always alone and always carrying out some trivial duty.

After his new CO departed the cell, Floyd returned to his cot and lay with his thoughts. *What a mess,* he thought, staring at the wall across from his bed. *So that's how it is. I'm a runner. And why not? I no longer matter to anyone. They've demoted me from major to runner. Yes, they've done it, but they made a mistake. How dare they do such a thing? I know a runner is nothing, but I'm a major. I will not let them humiliate me.*

In the afternoon of his second day, an MP opened the door to the cell and stepped inside. Floyd did not see the MP when the man stood turning his head in disgust, but he did feel the pile of folded clothing the MP tossed on his bed. Without looking at Floyd, the guard turned, closed the door, and locked it behind him. Floyd glanced down at the pile at his feet and used the toe of a boot to kick and scatter it across the concrete floor.

"They give me a private's clothes," he said, speaking his thoughts. "Those clothes for me? Ha! I am a major in the United States Army. Do they really think this will stand? Well, it won't."

As he spoke, his voice grew louder, and his little eyes narrowed until they were wedge slits like the defining axe shape of his face. The short hair on his head was disheveled and matted with gravy on one side, and he looked around the little cell like a cat trying to evade its owner's grasp. He did not look frightened though, for he pressed his lips in the convex manner of a staggered boxer.

"It's true. It's true," he laughed. "I did it. I am the one who threw Evan's ball, but is this what I get? Demoted? It doesn't add up. 'Throw a ball and lose your rank.' No, no, no, or ...." He stopped and squinted through the distance then lifted the corners of his mouth until he achieved a full-blown grin.

"Yes," he spoke. "This will not stand." He glanced at the window in the door. "This cannot last. I will get revenge."

221

The range of emotions he experienced after his demotion was narrow. He skipped denial and went straight to blame and anger. He took no responsibility for his situation and considered nothing to be his fault.

"It's Evan's fault. Evan caused everything. He played golf every day while the rest of us worked. We were working together. I was building a unit. I was preparing to fight for our country. But not Evan. Oh, no. While we were working together, he was out playing. He prepared only himself, and at the same time he was also helping himself to Amanda! Right in front of my face. How dare he? He knew she was mine. He's the one who should be locked up, not me!"

He sat up on his bed and stared at the white wall in front of him, to where he spotted a single ladybug taking a sideways walk. He saw her make a flying fall to the ground and watched her flapping her nearly helpless wings all the way down. She struggled to regain her legs, folded her wings, turned first one way, then another, and started walking toward a tiny crack of light under the cell door.

"Oh, and he was innocent about it all," Floyd said to the insect. "He was just doing his duty, a duty I hadn't even given him. It's his fault this happened. And that damn general shares the blame too. Hmm. I'll have to fix them both." He nodded his head and smiled. "Fixing the one will fix the other." He went too far by laughing, because the sound brought to mind his new CO. "What a joke. When he came into my cell, I stood up and saluted him, but that was it. I never listened to a word he said. But something was important. What did he say?"

Floyd took an hour of silence before remembering that the CO had ordered him to be ready to go in the morning. They were moving, and he was being released. He would join Battery C at oh four hundred, just before the entire battalion departed the golf course. He knew he was not being included in Battery C's travel preparations, and he knew this would cause further problems for him.

They'll try to treat me with resentment because I did nothing to help prepare for departure, he thought. *The men hate it when they do all the work. They'll call me a slacker. It will be worse than being demoted, but there is nothing I can do about it.*

He watched the ladybug as she lumbered across the room. Her progress was slow, but steady. Floyd's eyes went from the ladybug to the small gap under the door. Seeing her goal, he straightened his lips and narrowed his eyes.

"You're going to make it," he said aloud. "You're a determined little bug."

Floyd laughed at the ladybug's determination, but then he saw that the clothing he had kicked from his bed would block her path. The realization and the sound of his laughter startled him. He jumped up, gathered the scattered clothing from the ground, threw it back on the bed, and sat back down before she could reach the door.

"There," he said, whispering as though he was alone with a friend. "Now you can make it. While you're going forward in time, I'm staying behind." Looking at the private's uniform beside him, he added, "No. I'm wrong. You're going forward and I'm going back in time."

Just as the ladybug reached the gap, Floyd again jumped from his bed and ran to the door. He stood with his right knee lifted and his boot poised directly over her, as though he would stomp her with several thousand times too much force. He abandoned his intention of crushing her and, instead, he dropped to his elbows and knees to watch her proceed. He went all the way down until he was prone on the concrete floor. He turned his head sideways as he pressed his cheek against the cold surface, and there he watched the back of the escaping bug. When her journey took her under the dark width of the door, he saw her contrasted against the light coming from the other side. She made her way into that light and colorfully disappeared out into the world.

So that's it, he thought, climbing from the floor. *She made it. Little her. She just needed persistence and endurance.* He grinned. *I have those. I have persistence and endurance.* He returned to his bed, made slow turns of his head, and laughed. *Quitters quit, but I persevere. I'll take it one step at a time. That's all I need. If they think they can treat me this way, when I'm not even the one to blame, they've got something else coming. I'll show them.* He looked toward the empty space under the door.

"Thank you for showing me the way, little ladybug," he said. "We'll both make it, just one step and one day at a time."

Floyd looked down at the pile of clothing lying where he had tossed it on his unmade bed. He set the clothing aside, and then he methodically made his bed, giving his greatest attention to military formality—bedding stretched taut and folded into military corners. He stretched the green wool blanket, and he shook and smoothed the one flat pillow that was inside its dirty white pillow case. He placed the pillow under the blanket at the head of the bed and again stretched and flattened the top blanket.

"Now those are military corners!" he said aloud. "I could bounce a nickel on this bed."

He folded his wad of officer's clothing, arranging them into an organized little pile, and smiled. His clothes were nicely folded against the backdrop of the bare wall, and the entire room looked tidy. The MP came later with his meal tray and a box containing all of Floyd's personal effects from his trunk back in the officer's barrack. Floyd stood stiff and respectful while the MP dumped the entire contents of the box at his feet, and then he went to work organizing everything he owned—a small collection of clothing, personal effects, one writing pad, a pencil with a broken lead, dice, and nothing else. There were no pictures or letters.

He took one of his discarded socks, dipped an edge into his tin cup, and used the wet sock to wash his face, hands, and arms. He dipped his comb and raked white potatoes from his black hair. Once clean and dressed in his new private's uniform, he looked through his belongings. He took one of the dice, dropped it on the bed, and watched it bounce. Satisfied, he tossed the die across the concrete floor. It collided with the near wall and rattled before stopping, and he saw that it had landed with the up side showing only one black dot.

"That's right," he grinned at the sight. "I agree. One day and one step at a time."

He arranged the rest of his belongings before sitting on his bed to eat. In mid-bite, he stopped, went to the dice, and turned them both so only one dot showed on each. He then returned to his meal, stared at the dice, and laughed out loud.

"Snake eyes," he said to the room, stretching his mouth, narrowing his eyes while hissing the words. He said it again. "S-s-s-snake eyes-s-s-s," and this time he ended with laughter. He nodded his head up and down, and then he repeated his earlier words: "Just one day and one step at a time."

The following morning, he was released and placed under the supervision of his CO. He was placed in a cramped corner of a large transport where he endured the eyes of the strangers from Battery C. The battalion departed El Rancho Golf Course with the sound of rumbling engines and grinding gears. Plumes of billowing exhaust blew off in the wind, and, in only a moment, the golf course was left abandoned, looking like a lush ghost town.

The battalion spent fifteen months traveling and training at various camps. There was Camp Cooke in California, Camp Sill in Oklahoma, Camp Polk in Louisiana, and Camp Shanks in New York. From Camp Shanks, the battalion departed for Pier 90 for "service in the European theater of operations," as it was documented in the official Army record. The 170th boarded the born-again HMS Queen Elizabeth and sailed across the Atlantic.

Their travel time at sea was a mere six days. While the men were naturally apprehensive about approaching closer to war, the sea time dragged. They were not used to having so much idle time. They became restless with days filled only with the distance, the sea, and the sky. Every one of them used their idle hours to do nothing more than think.

After his short stay in the stockade, Floyd had been faithful to his "one day, one step at a time" resolve. He did anything and everything he could to be helpful to the men. His tidiness was the first piece of his plan. The second was his readiness, willingness, and virtual eagerness to do just about anything for the men. It defined the new Floyd. From the camps in the states, across the Atlantic to the staging area in England where they readied to cross the channel, Floyd ran to be helpful. If a paper was on the ground, he would fetch and dispose of it. If something needed to be carried, Floyd would come running. If something was spilled, it was Floyd who came fastest. And if someone wanted a tool, Floyd brought it. He swept, mopped, cleaned, ran errands, and listened for opportunities to do something, anything that was helpful to anyone. He was even known to voluntarily empty the battalion's camp buckets, a horrible job even for the willing.

One evening at dinner in the giant tent that served as their dining hall, all of the privates from Battery C were discussing the day's rumors about the upcoming invasion of the continent, trying to guess where they might land. "Of course it's going to be in France," Private Carl Mathews said when his turn arrived. "Even Hitler knows that. I want to know where in...."

Mathews was cut off by the sounds of a tin plate, silverware, a cup full of milk, and bowl full of soup as they collided with the floor. The sound was violent and unexpected, and Mathews and the other privates snapped their heads toward the site of the landed mess. They saw Private Chris Knowles standing with one end of his tray squeezed in his hand and the other end held angled toward the mess on the ground.

"Damn you, Knowles," Mathews said. "You got it on me. And look at that. You got pudding on my shoes. I'm giving you until the count of zero to get it off."

Private Knowles looked at Mathews' shoes, and then turned as though he intended to bend down, place his empty tray beside him on the ground, and clean up his mess. Before he did, though, Floyd arrived. He came so fast that all were surprised. The liquids were beginning to spread, but Floyd used his hands and arms to contain the mixture. Down on his knees, he returned the serving items back onto the tray and scooped the food from the floor. Private Knowles looked from Floyd to Mathews, and he saw Mathews and the other privates watching and grinning. Mathews signaled to Private Knowles.

"Make sure he cleans my shoes," Mathews said, whispering and pointing to the food on his boot.

"I got it," Floyd said, overhearing the comment. He finished with the floor, dropped at Knowles feet, and cleaned pudding from the private's shoes. He rubbed them until they shined, and then he stood up, saluted, and went back to where a damp spot remained on the floor.

He returned the tray to the soldier, looked at no one, and then dropped back to his knees to wipe the floor clean of residue. He stood, swiped his hands together, and remained looking to where he found soup on his palms and a smear of pudding that he had accidentally wiped onto both pockets of his pants. With the men intently watching, grinning, and peeking at him, Floyd took the sopping napkin and cleaned the mess from his clothes. Satisfied, he turned and left the room without saying a word to anyone, without looking at a single person, and without hearing the men's comments.

"Can you believe that guy?" Private Knowles asked. "Was he really a battery commander?"

"Damn right he was," Mathews said. He turned and joined the outburst of laughter that came from the others sitting at the table. He lifted his fork and wagged it at Private Knowles, who was still on his feet and looking like an eager dog eyeing a waving stick.

When Mathews threw the fork, Knowles ran to it, bent down onto his hands and knees, sniffed at the utensil, and grasped it between his teeth. He returned the fork by dropping it from his mouth onto the table from which it came.

"My name's Floyd," Private Knowles said. "Aren't I a good dog?" He panted and stuck his tongue out of his mouth, but then he adopted the pose of a soldier. "Forget about dogs," he said. "I'm too well-trained. You have to remember I used to be a battery commander."

"You may have been a commander in Battery B," Mathews said, "but you're a buffoon in Battery C. Actually, you're fine. It's Floyd. He's the buffoon."

Floyd heard it all from where he stood outside of the tent. He heard the increase in their laughter, and he reacted by squeezing his hands and lifting the ends of his grin.

CHAPTER 23

~ THE RUNNER AND THE ARRIVAL ~

On that voyage across the Atlantic, there was another besides Floyd who lingered at length with difficult thoughts. Evan had not gotten to say goodbye to Amanda before leaving and, though he had written countless letters to her, he had not received a single reply. He was troubled by the lack of any correspondence from her. It was difficult for him to believe she would not write to him, even though that thought had occurred to him once back in the States, resulting in his experiencing a particularly lonely time. His passionate heart and practical mind smothered his doubts. He knew she simply would not abstain from writing.

He wondered why it was he had not received a single reply to the numerous letters he had written. The reality contradicted his senses, and so he found that, over time, he withdrew his expectation. When he expected a letter, none came. When he did not expect a letter, still none came. He watched as the mailbags arrived, waited with the others, and then walked away from the empty bag, despondent and wondering. The 170th had not stayed in any one place long enough for him to get to the bottom of his correspondence failure. At each stop, there was no opportunity to cable or telephone her. At his level, in the 1940's, military communications were terrible at best. All he did on his voyage across the Atlantic was think of Amanda, miss her, and think more of her.

Though time heals all wounds, Evan was not wounded. He was hurt. He developed a strong determination to get done with what had to be done and to get back to her as soon as possible. He needed the war to end. Until then, he could not see Amanda, hear her voice, or feel anything but frustration over their lack of communication. Yet Amanda remained the resting thought of his mind. Fortunately, the demands of his daily responsibilities kept him from immersing himself in his despair. Training, daily briefings, meals with the officers, charts, plans, enemy deployments, gun positioning, and the risk of death soon occupied his attention as much as returning to Amanda had. The demands required nothing less than his full attention.

Absorbed in his daily activities—distracted from thinking about and pursuing that which was greatest on his heart—Evan took one day at a time because he had no other choice. Consequently, he was judged solely on his past. He had won favor throughout the Army, appreciation from the Air Force, and was considered to be a first-rate hero among the Marines, the Navy's wayward son. Only the Navy wanted to dislike Evan, but in the military, and in the Navy especially, there was such a deep respect for golf that Evan was disliked in the manner that siblings dislike a beloved younger brother. The reality was that Evan received both favor and appreciation. He was welcomed to every meeting, worked diligently at his responsibilities, and was even given command of Battery B's gun crew number four. He would be directly responsible for the lives of those six men, which resulted in spending his fifteen months in U.S. training camps, two months assembling at Wallasey, Cheshire, England, and all of those anxious hours crossing from Portland, England to Le Havre, France, planning and coordinating the successful invasion of the continent, and ensuring the survival of each of his men.

After so many months, it was only at night that Evan allowed himself to think of Amanda. As he dozed off, she floated into his mind, and he always recalled her first as he had seen her last. After those several times they said goodbye, separated, and again and again came back together to embrace, Amanda had finally stood waving through the framed window of the back door. The light from inside that shone behind her, dimmed with time. Amanda had remained, though, and Evan smiled when he recalled their shared laughter, standing with just that pane of glass between them. He thought she had the brightest white teeth he had ever seen, and he remembered how her eyes seemed to reflect his deepest feelings. But over time, as though a dimmer switch had removed her light, Amanda's eyes, her smile, and all of the wonderful features of her face began to darken. Details changed. Her lips blurred into a flat line, her high cheekbones rested, her eyes settled, her brows relaxed, her color shaded, and Evan's memory of her became one of beautiful Amanda, framed in her window, searching for him in the shadows of night. The image continued to dim with time, until it eventually became Amanda looking out of her back window with her two hands pressed against her cheeks.

Don't worry, he would think at night, just before sleep came to him. *I'm still here. You're still there for me, and I will always be there for you. We have each other.*

The truth about the mail is that it worked back then. Deficiencies in its delivery were overrated, even though its exceptions were proclaimed to be its rule. "The mail works just fine," Kenneth Calloway, the runner for Battery B, said one day to Evan. "The mail gets through. Why do you ask, lieutenant? Is there a problem?"

"I'm asking because I've never gotten anything, not one letter," Evan answered. "I don't know about a problem, but

I do know I never get mail. I have been expecting letters to arrive for months now, but I've received nothing."

"Yea," Kenneth said. "You and everyone else. 'Where's my mail?' and 'When's it coming?' I've heard it said a thousand times. 'You must have lost it.' Everyone says the same thing. They blame the runners, they blame the mail, they blame the military, they blame the government, but they never blame themselves. I think a man gets no mail because no one writes to him."

"Is that so?" Evan said, his inquisitive expression changing to one of disappointment. "But what if that's not true? What if a man has someone back home who writes to him?"

"Then he receives his mail when it arrives," Kenneth said, speaking in his matter-of-fact tone of certainty. "No mail, no one writing."

After leaving El Rancho Golf Course, Evan had many similar conversations with B's runner. His first twenty or so inquiries had been irritations to Kenneth, but somewhere about the fiftieth time, Kenneth began to expect and appreciate the lieutenant's persistent hopefulness. Though runners were lowest on the military's chain of command, they were eagerly received at mail call, and they often observed the deeper emotions in soldiers' hearts. They saw both delight and disappointment. They inevitably developed an inflated image of their own importance and mini power bases from which most were uncaring, disinterested, and unconcerned. Kenneth was this way with Evan, but over time even runners can be won over to a cause. Kenneth began searching his mailbag for letters addressed to Lieutenant Wilkins, and he even began to feel Evan's weekly disappointment when nothing arrived.

Kenneth's responses of "nope," "nothing," and "not today," became "sorry," "I didn't find anything," and "maybe next week."

"Is there any chance my letters are getting lost?" Evan asked one day.

"Anything can get lost, but it's unlikely that letter after letter would do so. You really think she would send you so many letters? Are you that positive?"

"I would think so. Yes, of course she would. We're engaged to be married, and besides, I've written to her time and again. If she's getting my letters, then she would answer them. Is it possible she's not receiving mine?"

Kenneth was an angry man who at times appeared bitter. Like all men of his ilk, though, once committing himself to another's cause, he was one of the more loyal and determined friends anyone could have. Kenneth eventually gave too much to the effort, for he was determined to figure out just why it was Evan was not receiving any return mail, especially because Evan remained so true to his belief that at least some note would have come. Kenneth had personally handled the countless letters Evan wrote, addressed to Amanda, sealed, stamped, and mailed.

"If you put your letters in the mail drop," Kenneth explained, "then we send them once a week. If a letter comes for you, it comes with all of the other mail. We sort outgoing mail by where it's heading. We sort it into headquarters, Maintenance, Medical, and the three batteries, A, B, and C. After that, we deliver it. There's no other way."

"Can it be getting sorted into the wrong group?" Evan asked Kenneth at another time. "Is it going to another battery?"

"After this many months, it's not likely. Someone would have returned it to us by now. Undelivered mail is rare. In fact, as far as I know, we've never had any."

On a day of heavy seas, a day when the darkened sky made it impossible to venture onto the rain-soaked deck of the tossing battleship, Kenneth found an opportunity to investigate the mystery of Evan's lack of mail. Weathering rough north Atlantic storms was always tiresome, but the experience in December during World War II was especially unnerving. All knew a chunk of ice or German torpedo might end their journey without a moment's notice. The wind was fearsome, and heavy rains pelted the ship with a level of force that a century earlier would have had captains yelling to lower the gallants and furl the jibs. Though she was so huge that she mitigated the worst of the sea's waves, the Queen Elizabeth still moved to her left, tilted to the right, plunged, splashed, and barreled her way forward without cease. Kenneth was below deck like everyone else when Evan handed him a letter he had written to Amanda. Kenneth carried it as though he were a doctor bringing a newborn to its mother. He deposited the envelope, not in the mailbox, but directly into the mailbag that he knew would be taken ashore as soon as the ship arrived in Scotland. He made sure Evan's letter was in that bag, pulled snug the leather drawstring, and then glanced around the large mailroom. Compartments deep down in battleships often serve multiple purposes, and the Queen Elizabeth's mailroom shared space with laundry, an assortment of supply boxes, military equipment, heavy tools, and a collection of boxed supplies the battalion would need to engage in battle. Kenneth stood alone and perused it all. *If mail were lost,* he thought, *where would it be?*

He looked at a table that was used for sorting mail, at a bucket of empty mailbags that were used for delivery, the big laundry sinks, and then at the supply boxes that were sealed and stacked here and there. He got down on his hands and knees to look under the mail table, stood on his toes to look up on some shelving, and wandered around the mailroom while considering everything in his sight. Deep at the bottom of the ship, dim lighting made seeing difficult, and the plunging and tossing motion of the ship made walking a test of balance. Kenneth felt seasick.

"There's just no way anything's here," he spoke in the dark. "We do not lose mail."

He walked out, but rather than feeling as though he had satisfied his curiosity, he felt only the relief of being out of the compartment. He had checked for the lieutenant's mail, but he had come up empty-handed. He left in frustration.

As he walked through the opening that served as the entrance to the mailroom, he bumped shoulders with another runner who was just going in. "Watch it," the arrival said, mumbling and disappearing into the dark of the mailroom.

"Sorry," Kenneth said, and after taking a few more steps down the ship's passageway, he stopped mid-step without looking back. *What does he want down here?* he wondered. *There's no mail today, there's nothing to do down here, and he had nothing in his hands. What's he doing?*

Kenneth returned to the mailroom and peeked around the opening, quickly withdrawing his head to avoid detection. He took another quick peek, withdrew again, and then stood considering what he had seen. Though the light in the mailroom was dim, he could see past the stacks of boxes to where he saw a distant cabinet with its door ajar. The runner that had bumped into him was rummaging around inside the cabinet. Kenneth saw the runner withdraw a large box from the highest shelf and then take a furtive glance over his shoulder. Kenneth had avoided detection, but the runner had not. He knew the man was Private Floyd Akerly, the runner for Battery C. Ever since the golf game back at El Rancho Golf Course, everyone knew about Floyd.

Both heard the sound of approaching voices coming from the passageway. Floyd froze. He replaced the lid on the box he had been examining, placed another box on top of it, pressed the cabinet door shut, and went to the mailroom table. He began moving the empty pouches, envelopes, and stamps that lay there, as though he was busy doing a duty. Unconcerned men passed the mailroom. When their voices faded to silence, Floyd returned to the cabinet, withdrew the second box from the top shelf, and pulled an envelope from a front pocket of his pants. He placed the letter into the box, withdrew a different envelope, and placed it in his pocket. He had made an exchange. Once the new envelope was deep in the pocket of his pants, he checked to ensure that it was hidden from sight by smoothing the pocket to ensure the bulge from the envelope was not visible.

Once done, Floyd again froze. He stiffened just like he had done earlier when he heard the men approaching out in the passageway. He remained rigid and turned with wide eyes to examine the doorway. He did not hurry to the mail table. Instead, he remained unmoving and intently staring, listening, evaluating, and separating the sounds of the groaning ship from those that men might make. He heard no one coming his way, but he remained watching and listening while he returned the lid to the box. Standing high in the cabinet, he stared at the empty mailroom beyond his shoulder.

Floyd finally returned the box to the cabinet and closed the door. He walked over to the mail table, shuffled papers, and then walked out of the mailroom. Though Kenneth had been out in the passageway watching Floyd earlier when the group of men approached and passed the mailroom, he had ducked and crawled just inside the mailroom's entry to avoid being found spying. He had crawled to where high stacks of boxes provided protection from discovery and had scrambled behind the boxes to avoid being seen. When the men passed, he found he could peek around one low edge of the boxes and continue observing Floyd. Unfortunately, though, he accidentally touched one of the big boxes with the toe of his boot, and Floyd tensed and listened. He never saw Kenneth crouching and moving to where he could hide deeper behind the boxes.

Once Floyd put everything back in place and left, Kenneth stood, bent at his waist, rubbed his knees, and found he was alone in the big compartment. He looked around while evaluating, and dismissed every creak and groan of the ship. Discovering no sounds that were made by men, he went straight to the far cabinet, extracted the same box Floyd had, removed its lid, and peered inside. The dim light seemed dimmer, but it was not so dark that he could not see. He knew what he had found. He saw over a hundred letters, each addressed with the looping cursive that, in 1943, was still a mark of a fine education. There was a smell of old paper, but it still emitted the subtle fragrance of perfume. He lowered the box to the floor, got down on his knees, held its sides with his hands, and lowered his nose down close to the letters. He took a deep sniff and smiled, as though he had smelled a flowering and heavily scented rose, fresh on the vine.

There are much worse scents to take to death. The draw of his breath, lungs full of perfumed air, the smile on his face, eyes closed in pleasure, and the satisfaction of a mystery solved provided at least some consolation for the disturbing whack he took to the back of his head. Instantly, his skull opened, and blood mixed with liquid pewter and gushed from the wound. His head dropped into the open box, spattering and soaking most of the letters.

Floyd dropped an over-sized pipe wrench and pushed the dead man's body aside. Private Kenneth Calloway's skull cracked against the metal floor, but Floyd cared only about protecting the letters. He picked up the box and set it down.

"Oh, no," he whispered, wildly looking about and subduing his feelings of alarm. "There's blood on the letters."

Even though fresh blood was no longer soaking the letters, a new puddle of it began forming near Kenneth's head, right beside where Floyd had set his box. The ship's rocking caused the puddle to flow toward the box. It ebbed and flowed with the motion of the rough sea, and continued its sticky spread. Floyd again grabbed the box and held it between his hands. With his eyes widening and heart pounding, he listened, glanced around, watched the moving puddle, and then rushed to set the box on the floor next to one of the large concrete laundry sinks. He jumped over to where bins of dirty laundry awaited the next morning's detail, and returned to his box with a handful of soiled linens and clothing. He wet several dirty towels and used them to methodically wipe blood from each of the envelopes.

Unfortunately, his effort caused him further alarm and agitation, because every time he returned a wiped envelope back to the box, the blood on the other letters only soaked it again. *Damn that Kenneth! Why did he have to come snooping around anyway?*

Floyd poured all the envelopes onto the floor, cleaned the inside of the box, wiped each envelope, and returned them wet and stained to the box. He split his attention between cleaning and listening and watching for anyone who might walk into the mailroom. He feared discovery less than he feared ruining Amanda's letters.

"Stupid!" he mumbled. "I should have left them in the box. Now there's blood everywhere. I've got to clean it up."

Panic caused irrationality. He chose to clean the floor by the box when, across the mailroom, a lifeless body was lying and oozing even more blood. Giving up, he stood, trembling with indecision about what he should do. He looked at the entrance to the mailroom, at his box, and then at the bloody pile of laundry. At least the letters were wiped. He looked at them where they were back in the box, wiped it, replaced its lid, stopped to listen again, and then rushed to place the box inside the cabinet. He frowned at its placement. The wet side was showing, so Floyd rotated the box to its dry side. He placed another box on top of it, and then he stood, looking for signs that others on the ship might see and then investigate. He did not want blood to give away his secret. After closing the cabinet door, he examined it too, for signs of blood.

Nothing. Anyone who sees this mess will never think to look in the cabinet. Why would they? There's not a hint of blood there. There's not even a smear on the door.

He allowed an ironic chuckle to lift the right side of his lips, and he looked around the dark mailroom before he peered at the floor. *They'll see the blood, alright, but no one will find the letters.*

He could see the slow, sticky motion of the puddle at his feet, but it touched only an edge of his boot before he moved. He was less concerned about that than the sound of the men he heard approaching out in the passageway.

CHAPTER 24

~ *SOME SORT OF A CRUEL MISTAKE* ~

"Look at all the blood!" Floyd whispered in alarm when he saw the thick puddle that had spread while he was cleaning the letters. "He was full of it! Who would have known a body held so much?"

He feared another hour of the ship's swaying motion out in the rough Atlantic would spread the sticky mess over the entire floor. He checked his boots and saw only a smear. His relief was short-lived as he held his hands before him and examined them.

Of course they have blood on them, he frowned. *Not much, though. Cleaning the letters cleaned my hands. There's just a little on the hair of my wrist.*

He rushed back to the concrete sink and furiously scrubbed his hands and arms. He again returned to the mess on the floor, picked up the heavy pipe wrench, and returned it to where he had first found it hanging back by the supply boxes. His worst fears were realized when he heard men walking in his direction. He froze.

Maybe they'll pass, he thought. *I think I hear two people. What do they want? Supplies? Yes, they want something down in here. Oh, no. They're not passing. They're coming in here.*

He rushed like a dark cat at night to hide where the aisles of large boxes were stacked. He hid behind the stacks and, once there, placed both of his hands and one of his cheeks flat against the high stack nearest to him. He peered around the corner but saw no one. Two men had already entered the mailroom, and their voices blared in Floyd's ears, even though they spoke in normal tones and were actually getting farther from him.

"All of the supplies are kept down here, private," one of the men said. "Always keep a box of carbon paper close at hand when you're typing. You need as much of it as you need of plain paper. In fact, every time you re-supply one, get the other. Extra trips down here are just a waste of everyone's time."

The men did not turn toward the mail area where Floyd was hiding. Instead, they went deeper into the mailroom to the cabinet that held the box of letters.

It's Rudy, Floyd thought when he recognized the voice of Battery A's runner.

"You should never need to come here, though," Rudy continued. "It's my job as your runner. If you need anything, all you have to do is ask, and I'll bring you your supplies."

Floyd rolled his eyes. He, the runner for Battery C, was watching Rudy, Battery A's runner, while lying on the floor was Kenneth, Battery B's runner. The three runners were normally together only at times when they retrieved their mailbags. They cared little for each other, and acknowledged each other with no more than a series of grunts. *The irony,* Floyd thought.

"I know right where to go," Rudy said. "There's never much light in here, and you have to hang on because the ship tosses so much. That's another reason to use me." The ship lunged to the left, forcing them to hold onto a shelf before proceeding.

"Why isn't there more light in here?" Jim asked, colliding into the back of Rudy, who had stopped with a jolt.

"My God!" Rudy yelled. "Look. It's a body."

"What in the hell?" Jim said, looking down at the lump on the dark floor. "Look at it. Look at all of the blood! He has to be dead."

"I think I'm going to be sick!" Rudy said. "Let's get out of here. We need to go for help." He turned to leave but found Jim blocking him.

"Wait," Jim said, pushing to get past Rudy. "Why is that pile of bloody laundry tossed over there? Whoever did this must have used those towels afterwards. Why?"

"I don't know, I don't care, and neither should you. Let's just get out of here. We need to find an MP, right now."

"Whoever did this must have cleaned something," Jim continued, ignoring Rudy's frightened insistence. "He must have cleaned something with the laundry. Look! Over there by that sink. There's another pile of bloody clothing."

"Oh, my God," Rudy said. "Someone cleaned the blood from his hands and clothes. He's a killer, but he's not stupid. You can't walk around a ship with blood on your hands now, can you?"

"That's not it," Jim said. "Look at this. The towels are wet, as though they were dampened—and look how many of them there are. The guy's skull was obviously busted open, but it doesn't look like he's blood-spattered. It looks like he fell and bled into that puddle. Whoever did this must have cleaned more than his hands. That is the only explanation for why there are so many wet, bloody towels."

Jim squatted down and held one finger against the victim's throat. Both remained silent while he felt for life. He turned his eyes up to Rudy's and shook his head. "Nope. He's dead. There's no question about it. But what's this? His neck is still warm to the touch. This must have just happened."

Alarmed, the two men stood together and turned their heads in all directions. Each braced his back against the other. Floyd heard it all, and he listened with a growing sense of alarm. With shaking hands, he remained hiding, listening, and scheming for a way to escape. Though he could not see the two men, he could hear them and was able to discern their movements. He understood they were scanning for threats, but then he was able to see Jim drop down and out of sight.

"Look," Jim said, "the puddle stopped growing. I was wrong. His death could have happened a while ago. The blood is sticky. The reason I thought the puddle was still growing was because of the ship's movement—see how it has spread? No, this did not just happen. It could have happened as much as thirty minutes ago. Let's go and find help. We have to report this right now!"

Floyd remained frozen until the men's voices faded down the passageway. He snuck from behind the boxes, peered around the mailroom, rushed to the doorway like a roach fearing light, halted, listened, glanced back at the filing cabinet, and then rushed out of the mailroom. He was fortunate not to encounter others, for anyone who saw him would have sensed something was amiss. Floyd ran with his hands open and his arms away from his sides. His eyes were wide and scanning. He knew he looked as though he were fleeing a threat from deep within the groaning and swaying ship. Anyone he encountered would have slackened his jaw, looked back with alarm, and joined him to make his own fleeing escape from the unknown deadly threat.

At the end of the passageway was a metal companionway that rose to the next level. Floyd raced to the top, peered furtively in both directions, and then climbed up and out. He found himself in another empty passageway. He took a deep breath of air and exhaled, feeling the first moment of relief. To stop his hands from shaking, he put them flat against his legs, took another breath, quickly shook his head, and forced himself to walk slowly to the far end of the new passageway. He consciously forced himself to refrain from making backward, over-the-shoulder glances by staring down at the ground before him. He continued to walk at a fast pace. He went through an opening, through another, climbed two levels higher, and not once did he make eye contact with any of those he began passing on the upper levels of the ship. No one seemed to have noticed him at all, as was usual for the attention given to runners.

Floyd went straight to his bunk without talking to anyone. It was still daylight outside, but the sky was darkened by the slashing rain still pelting the ship. Lying on his back gave him a momentary feeling of relief, but he still felt his hands shaking. When it became obvious to him that he would not sleep on his back, he turned to lie on his side with his face toward the bulkhead. He tried not to linger on any one of the multitude of disturbing thoughts that terrorized his mind. Each time one idea began to form into an image he would rather not see, he cleared his mind by shaking away the form. Instantly, another disturbing image began forming. As soon as he recognized what it was—a box, wrench, skull fragment, pool of blood, handwritten letters, or men coming at him from behind dark objects—he would shake off the image, stare again, and repeat the unnerving pattern of haunting himself again.

After lying still with his eyes closed, he began to calm. He felt the forward propulsion of the ship, felt its rocking motion, and even considered that he could actually feel his blood pumping through his veins like pressurized liquid passing through narrow tubing. He stayed in his bunk until all the men who were not then on watch fell asleep. Every few days, bedding was changed between the sleep shifts, and it had been done that day. He lay for nearly two hours with the back of his head feeling the clean, starched cover on his thin, flat pillow. Flailing his right hand, he encountered his pocket and remembered the letter. He opened his eyes.

Oh, yes, he thought, *another letter. There you are.*

He removed the envelope he had retrieved from his box and, just as he had done eighty-two times before, took a covert glance around him before tearing it open to read Amanda's words. He had read all of her letters in empty corners of tents of the camps back in the States, but this one he intended to read right there in his bunk. He at first held the envelope flat between his hands—as though it were a prayer—turned on his pillow to be sure no one was watching him, and then tore open the envelope with as much care as he could muster. None of the sleeping soldiers heard the soft rip.

Floyd turned away from the bulkhead to read where he could. A man sleeping in the bunk across from his twitched with periodic spasms. He lay on his side, facing Floyd, and his mouth remained open, though his eyes were shut. At irregular intervals his body jerked, and Floyd would stare at him until he was convinced the man's eyelids would not unexpectedly pop open. He then opened the letter and held it so that the only light in the berthing compartment hit the page. Floyd had a problem seeing the words, but his desire and motivation overcame the obstacle. He angled the paper to the light's advantage and moved his squinting eyes to within a few inches of the paper.

This one should be good, he thought. *She's finally losing hope. It was inevitable. I don't understand why she never saw it coming. He's gone. He's not coming back. He doesn't love you. Give up. Forget about Evan.*

He grinned and laughed to himself. Without realizing it, his quiet grinning caused him to relax even further, and his hands shook less. Floyd noticed the covered lump at the foot of the bed of the man sleeping across from him. It was his covered feet, and one of them jerked with a spasm. The movement had caught Floyd's attention, but it simply prolonged his grin.

He recalled that letter four was a good one. They hadn't been gone from the golf course for barely a week, but already Amanda had been so passionately lonely.

What groans of agony she had written, he recalled. "Return to me," she had written. "I will wait for you forever." *Well, we'll see about that! Letter thirty-eight was another good one. It was even better than number four, because she had finally begun to get it, and it was about time. It took her long enough.*

He had read every word in each of her letters. He remembered them all. Another favorite of his was letter thirty-eight. He grinned at that memory.

I finally understand now that you cannot write. The war is terrible, but it is enough to know that you are getting my letters. I will keep writing so you can know how hurt I feel by your last letter, the one Major Akerly, God bless him, wrote for you. He did exactly as you requested. I say it again, God bless Major Floyd Akerly, but what should I call him now? Private Akerly? No! That sounds entirely too disrespectful for such a good man. I'll just call him Floyd. Well, I received the letter you instructed him to write and sneak to me. He was faithful. The risk of writing on your behalf was all his. You have a good friend. But you must know the words more upset me than they brought relief. Can it be true? Are we through? Is it over? Why? What happened? I simply cannot accept your decision until I see your eyes and hear the words come from you. I am not ashamed to admit that you have devastated me. How can this be? What has happened to you? I simply will not believe it! There has to be some sort of a mistake, some cruel mistake.

Floyd stopped grinning when the sleeping man next to him parted his lips and made a gurgling sound. His eyeballs moved under his closed lids, but he twisted his head, scratched himself, let out a sigh, rubbed his nose, and finished by burrowing the side of his head deeper into his thin little pillow. Floyd watched and waited until the sound of deep breathing returned, and then he brought the new letter, letter eighty-three, up against his nose. He took a deep whiff of the perfume Amanda had dabbed on the paper. The scent, just released from the freshly opened letter and still fragrant after fifteen months, was the second most enjoyable pleasure he got from reading her letters. Her words were first, but her fragrance remained a strong second. It helped him by beautifully drawing him into her emotions. It helped him feel her words. She had gone from passion, at first, to heartbroken confusion over why Evan had not written to her, to a loneliness that caused her to cry in the night, to several surprises about which she had written—using entirely too many exclamation points—and finally to the staggering disappointment after the letter she thought Floyd had written on Evan's behalf. She changed from writing about uncertainty to writing news, news, and more news. Always, it was the perfume that Floyd enjoyed more than her news. He drew another deep sniff, held close the paper, checked the sleeping man across from him, and then read letter eighty-three, beginning with the same form of endearment she used to begin every letter Floyd had seen:

My Dearest Evan,

He has begun saying your name! You wouldn't believe it. It's beautiful. You just have to hear him. You'll love it! I told you I took him out of his crib after only a month of being home—I just had to—and since then I have been putting him to bed with me every night. Anyway, the two of us were in bed earlier tonight, and he was squirming and laughing, just like he does every time I blow on his stomach. Both of us were laughing, and our eyes were just wet with the fun. You would have laughed too … it's infectious with him.

He was lying next to me, and his eyes were squeezed shut by his laughter. When he began to recover himself, when he first opened his eyes in that careful way he does, as though peeking to see if I would notice and then return to get him again, there you were! I caught you in his eyes! Ricky looks just like you! It took my breath away. He only peeked, but in that peek, in his shining and happy eyes, along with that little sideways grin the two of you make, I saw you. The sight of you in him just stopped me cold. It took my breath away, and I think I must have frightened him, poor little guy. I immediately became lonely for you and sorry for us. We simply cannot be over. Why would we be? I still don't understand and never will. Like I wrote before, I reject those words. Somehow, there just has to be a cruel trick being played on us. Please return and relieve me. I am yours, you are mine, and Ricky is ours. This makes us a family, and families should forever be together.

When Ricky settled down, he left his plump little hand over his eyes. His fingers were spread and interlocked over his eyes, and he thought himself then to be well hidden. Because of my startled reaction when I recognized you in him, he peeked at me, but all Ricky could have seen was my expression. In it he must have noticed the change. My smile dropped, my eyes became distant and longing, and there was even a drop in my tone when I said the words, "Oh, my." I saw you, but Ricky only saw me, and he began to feel sad himself. At one moment, we had been playing and laughing, and at the next moment, I had soberly fallen onto my back. Ricky immediately quieted, and he squirmed his way onto his knees so that his head was looking down on my face. He wiped and rubbed the tears that had fallen on my cheeks, and then I began to pull myself together.

"Mommy's alright," I told him. "I miss your father. I miss your daddy, and I want him home. I want Daddy."

Our little Ricky looked at me as though he were trying to understand my words! Can you believe it? But listen to this… he spoke your name! I am positive he tried to say his father's name … your name. He said "Du," and I so quickly changed to the happiest, most excited, and encouraging mother a child could want, that he said it again, again, and again. Ricky said, "Du, Du, Du, Du." We stayed awake saying your name, and by the time I lost him to sleep, he had begun to make your name sound more like the word, "Dah." He's getting it!

I simply could not wait to tell you, so the moment Ricky went to sleep I started to write this letter to you. He is just right there on the bed sleeping. He is beautiful and resting at peace right now. He is a perfect version of you. He even knows you, too. Even though you are not here, even though he's never seen you, he knows you. He knows you are his father, and he knows you are the most important person in our lives. I tell him this all of the time. I am always telling him just how important he is in your life. I tell him that his father will return and kiss, hug, squeeze, wrestle, play, teach, love, and adore him—just as much as I do. Don't you see? We're a family. He knows you. He wants you here with us, just like I do. I've taught him that you are the most important man in his life, and this makes him want you here now. We both do. Both of us love you, Dah.

Love always, all ways,
Amanda

"What is that damn smell?" the man across from Floyd asked, propping himself up with an arm and looking dumbly through the darkness.

Floyd had finished reading the letter well over an hour before, returned it to its envelope, and pushed the envelope deep into his pants pocket. After, he lay awake and angry about Amanda's failure to give up on Evan. She was not devastated, as he had wanted. Rather, she was hopeful, more hopeful than ever! Sure, she was lonely for Evan, but she was expecting and awaiting his return.

She's even infecting that kid, Floyd thought while tossing, turning, and plotting, but then the sleeping man awoke.

The soldier who had spoken had smelled the perfume from Amanda's letter, but after peering at Floyd for an instant, he dropped his head back onto his pillow and said nothing more. Floyd remained quiet and not another word was spoken. Amanda's letter had distracted him, but he found he was calm enough to think rationally. He thought about what he should have done back in the mailroom, and that thought led him to more practical plotting for the next time.

Eventually he felt calm enough to brave eye contact with others. He left his bunk and went to find something to eat. *Food will settle my stomach.*

He rose and went to the ship's mess deck, where he sat alone among a few groups of two and three. *Did that one look at me? I can't tell. I'll wait and peek.*

He ate with his eyes directed downward and his left arm extended out around his meal tray. Alone at the end of a long table that dark night, he overheard enough conversation to know something had happened on the ship. Someone had died, and the MPs were looking for the killer.

He returned his empty tray to the rack near the scullery, stacked his cup, plate, and ditched his utensils, and, as casually as he could muster, walked from the mess deck. That night Floyd slept like he was sick with a fever.

CHAPTER 25

~ WHO'S THERE? ~

Following the golf tournament, Evan gave little thought to Floyd. So far away were those memories that they received nothing more than an occasional shake of his head as Evan remembered and wondered what had occurred back on El Rancho Golf Course. Floyd, on the other hand, from the day of his capture, right up to the day he took his first step onto Nazi soil at Le Havre, France, thought quite often about Evan. He had spotted him only once, and had ducked out of sight to avoid detection.

The near-encounter occurred two days following the alarm caused by Kenneth's murder on "that ghost ship," as Floyd later referred to the Queen Elizabeth. Evan and Floyd's batteries were housed on different levels, so there was little likelihood of their encountering each other. This was especially true because their battalion was a small part of the nearly thirty-four hundred troops crossing the Atlantic on the Queen Elizabeth.

While the artillery pieces and munitions of the 170th's three batteries were transported on another ship, all of their field command maps, tents, shovels, radios, supplies, and other such necessities traveled along with the men. This gear was kept in supply rooms deep below deck. High above the supply rooms, officers of each battery held regular briefings. For the briefings, all of the men from a battery assembled just before the officers arrived. While they sat on metal chairs deep within the battleship, hearing the low rumbling sound of big diesel engines and feeling the subtle, back and forth rocking motion as the ship moved forward—the group experiencing entirely too much motion for men quietly assembled in a dimly-lit compartment—all craved gulps of fresh air. Down below, the air was tart. The almost constant flow of men in and out of the large briefing compartments created a certain warm, heavy, smelly, and nauseous stuffiness. Though slight, there was always a light smell of sickness in the air. The smell was discernable for the entire trip, and the worst part was that no one knew for certain if the odor was fresh. Several of the troops were so motion sick that the ubiquitous hint of vomit was simply the taste of their accumulating saliva. The majority of the men were kids making their first trip at sea.

Just before Battery C was to hold a routine planning briefing, one of the men assembled became sick. The soldier made it into a nearby narrow, metal passageway, but once there, those assembled heard him heaving. Back in the briefing room, Floyd quickly acted.

"I got it," he said, leaping from his seat in the back of the room and running to a nearby maintenance locker.

He retrieved a pile of towels, and then did a meticulous job of swabbing the mess. At each end of the passageway, he opened doors to allow air to flow through and carry away the freshest bite of the odor. When he finished cleaning, he carried the offensive load of towels down to the ship's lower level. He took the vomit towels down to the laundry and a supply room that was also that same mailroom in which he had hidden his box of Amanda's letters. On his way Floyd was determined not to glance in the direction of his cabinet. He planned to go no further into the supply room than the concrete laundry sinks.

254

I know that damn cabinet is back there, he thought, *but I'll ignore it. I won't even look at it. But what's this on my hands? Vomit? It stinks. It's on my hands. I deserve another of Amanda's letters for having to do this. I should take one.*

He abandoned his plan and walked quickly to see where the cabinet stood in the darkest part of the room. *There you are, but no!*

In his line of sight from the compartment entrance to his cabinet, he spotted a soldier and recognized instantly the form of Lieutenant Evan Wilkins. He made an instantaneous, abrupt, jolting mid-step stop, much like a rider on a horse who sits back in the saddle and pulls hard on the reins, or an automobile driver who locks the brakes and screeches to a skidding halt. He instinctively ducked and, at the same time, let the stinking laundry fall. With his hands opened before him and his shoulders hunched, he looked for an escape.

I'm too far from the passageway, he thought. *I have to hide. Move now? Where? Those boxes! I can make it. Yes. The boxes! I can make it.*

He lifted his face from where he had landed on the towels when he fell to the deck, and then made a crawling scramble to get behind the stack of boxes nearest to him.

I made it. Listen, though. Evan is not making a sound. If I peek past the edge of this box, he will not be able to see me, but I can see him. Yes. There he is, but what's this? He knows someone is in here. He's looking for me.

Floyd frowned and touched his arm where he felt his nerves reacting to what he was considering. When he saw Evan, he was surprised to feel tingling and a sense of fright—not for himself, but for Evan.

Evan stared at length toward the place where Floyd had first spotted him. He appeared to have seen nothing, though, for he did not advance or retreat, but stood still and waited, staring intently toward the compartment's opening.

While he spied on Evan, Floyd felt the sensation of electricity pulsing through his nerves. His limbs stiffened, and he began shaking. The cabinet with the box of letters was right behind Evan. In the dim light, to Floyd, it appeared as though Evan was wearing the cabinet as a backpack. Both men stood completely still, staring intently.

"Who's in here?" Evan called. "Announce yourself." He remained unmoving, searching, and listening, but he appeared to have seen nothing. He remained staring toward the doorway, silent, still, and wondering. His aim was perfectly placed, for if Floyd had not earlier taken to hiding—had he not immediately recognized Evan, ducked, dropped his load of towels, and then crept behind the boxes—he would have been seen. The two would have had to face each other for the first time since the golf game.

After the passage of two minutes of silence, except for all of the subtle creaks, aches, and groans of the ship's lowest level, Evan moved. He took slow, deliberate steps toward where Floyd had been. "Who's there?" he asked, raising the volume of his voice to a threatening level.

Floyd remained unmoving, silent, and watching Evan move toward the compartment's entry. *He knows he's not alone,* Floyd thought, pressing against the wall of boxes, stifling his breathing, and watching. *Look at how he's walking, trying to pick up every sound and movement. Careful now. He's doing that on purpose. There is nothing in his hands, but he's spreading his hands and tensing his arms. He looks ready for a fistfight.*

Floyd frowned while taking tiny side-steps to get farther behind the boxes. While peeking as little as possible, he gave his nose, ears, hair, shoulders, and even his eyebrows individual consideration. Such ancillaries can give away the presence of the most careful watcher. As Evan neared, the thought occurred to Floyd that Evan might hear his beating heart or his gasps for air after he could no longer hold his breath. He widened his eyes and, for the first time, removed them from Evan long enough to consider a possible course for escape.

What was that? What did I see? Floyd searched across an aisle from where he was hiding and identified what he thought he had seen. *Yes. There you are. I might need you again.*

The same pipe wrench he had used to crack the skull of Kenneth Calloway, the runner for Battery B, was hanging across the way. Its jaws were coated in black grease, and no one had examined it and found the drops of blood smeared in the dirt and grease.

I cannot believe they missed it. And look, there's still hair on the jaws. I can easily reach it again. He smiled. *I proved how well I can use that wrench.*

Floyd saw that Evan was still focused on whatever was in front of him. He was standing still and looking about in wonder, but then he started glancing around in several directions, sniffing the air, and frowning with disgust.

The towels! Floyd realized. *I left them right where they fell. He must smell the vomit. There he goes. He's found them now.*

Evan looked down to examine the pile of vomit-soaked towels, but then he lifted his head in alarm. He looked everywhere around him and spoke again, using a quieter, more threatening tone of voice. "Who's there?" he asked.

Evan waited, but he received no response. He waited several moments, and then he began taking slow steps backward, as though he anticipated a surprise attack. He scowled and shook his head at the stench. Floyd withdrew during a moment when Evan stopped and stared straight at the spot where he was hiding. He remained silent, watching and listening, for nearly two minutes.

"I heard you," Evan called. "Identify yourself. You're over by those boxes. What was it I heard? Metal? What do you have? Are you hiding from me? Come out and let me see you. Why don't you answer me?"

Evan waited, but Floyd did not speak a word. At length he accepted the silence, retrieved his small box of papers and maps, and turned to leave. He scanned the area one last time as he left.

Floyd remained hidden, silent, and clutching the large wrench long after Evan left. Alone in that compartment, holding the heavy piece of steel across his chest like it was an axe, Floyd began to tremble. He shook at the possibility of what he could have done to Evan.

I would have crushed him, he thought. *It's what he deserves. I would have gone further than simply hitting him hard and cracking his skull too. A good whack would have been nothing. I would have hit, hit, hit, again and again, until I cracked and crushed his skull. Yes, that's what I would have done.* He nodded his head up and down then laughed out loud.

"Who's there?"

Oh shit, Floyd thought. *Damn him. I should have kept quiet. He heard me.*

The voice brought him back to reality, and he cursed himself for laughing. The question had come from just outside the compartment. It was Evan.

"I heard you this time," Evan said. "I know you're there. Who are you and what are you doing?"

Floyd froze in surprise. He squeezed the wrench against his chest like a magnet holding onto a chunk of steel. Evan may have walked out, but he was waiting in the passageway. When his suspicion became reality, he stepped into the opening and called out. He waited for a reply that never came.

"You cannot pretend you're not in there. I heard you laugh," he said, speaking in his deepest tone of authority. "Who are you? Who's there? I heard you. Speak up like a man."

Floyd was still well out of sight behind the boxes, but his light shaking was now a heavy tremble. He looked around him and said nothing. He listened as though he were the one facing a threat. He could hear over the loud thumping of his heart, but he discerned only silence.

"This is Second Lieutenant Evan Wilkins," Evan said, following a period of utter silence. "Since you choose to remain hidden and won't speak, I'm left to assume you are up to no good. Speak up."

Floyd was surprisingly alert, and he felt increased pressure in his pulse and in his stifled breathing. He could hear agitation in Evan's tone, but it was the challenge, the threat, that had him squeezing the wrench. He had never before heard Evan's challenging tone. After a period of continued listening to nothing more than silence, Evan re-entered and began a slow, sweeping walk past the boxes, past the laundry facilities, past the mail table, and all of the way back toward Floyd's cabinet.

Floyd remained unmoving, but as he watched the back of Evan, he ever-so-carefully set the wrench on the floor. He did so without making a sound, and then he moved. He slipped to the opposite side of the boxes, and from there he took another look and saw that Evan was still walking in the opposite direction. He then dashed out as quietly and quickly as he could move and sprinted down the passageway. By the time Evan rushed toward the sound of fleeing footsteps, Floyd was nowhere to be seen.

Evan returned to the briefing compartment where all of the officers from Battery B were waiting for him. He placed his box on a table and spread maps of France, Belgium, and Germany before the group. They then took turns tracing their index fingers across the top of France. They traced from Le Havre to Cambrai, onward through Aubel, Belgium, and finally to where their first incursion into Germany would be made at Neiderbreisig. The 170th's maps were not in color, so what might have appeared to be veins flowing on the continent rather looked like the cracks in an old painting. What should have been healthy reds and blues were the grays and blacks of death. Each officer took his turn talking and running his index finger along their intended route. At one point, the CO warned his officers about the many little towns through which they would be traveling. The towns appeared as round blood clots along the route of veins.

"We must be especially careful in these," the CO said, indicating the many named dots along their route. "You never know where danger lurks. Just know it's there waiting for you."

"It lurks in the supply room," a junior officer said. He was just returning from below, and the CO frowned to let him know the discussion was serious. The young man explained himself.

"I just left the supply room, where I found something curious. Laundry shares the space, as you know. While I was in there retrieving this map of the English Channel, I encountered a horrible smell and found vomit-soaked towels on the deck. That was strange enough, but then I found a big wrench lying on the deck by the supply boxes."

"A wrench?" Evan asked.

"Yea, one of those giant ones. A wrench you could use to crush a skull, like what happened to Private Calloway. I just gave it to an MP."

"It's like I said," the CO interjected, thumping his finger on the map of their route. "You will never know where danger lurks. Be ready, warn your men, and keep on the lookout."

CHAPTER 26

~ HIGH AND TO THE LEFT ~

The Nazis fought with desperation during the first half of 1945. With the Soviet Union coming at them from the east and the United States coming from the west, they fought like an animal defending its home, like a grizzly defiant on its hind legs, a rabid little four-legged creature snarling before its den, or a swarm buzzing around its hive. They were desperate. By the time the Allies landed on the continent, though, the Germans had been so weakened from fighting that they could do no more than strike out and retreat while the Allies pushed, pursued, surrounded, and squeezed them like the closing jaws of a vice. The Nazis defended against annihilation.

From their beginning in Le Havre, France, the 170th never knew desperation. They had been fortunate to step onto the continent neither facing nor giving fire. After beaching in Le Havre, they trucked to the devastated Dieppe Airstrip, crossed the entirety of northern France, and bivouacked in Aubel, Belgium. From Aubel, the battalion then approached Germany, and it was on German soil, near the vicinity of Neiderbreisig, that the 170th formally engaged in the deadly art of war. The second gun unit of Battery C fired the battalion's first artillery round in combat, but that first shell missed its target.

"Incompetent!" Floyd had yelled after hearing the news of the miss. He was driving alone in a jeep and carrying new orders from headquarters to the four gun crews of Battery C. "How hard can it be? I gave them the exact coordinates. They're idiots. I should be in charge."

In war, confusion reigns, and accounts have been preserved century upon century, millennium upon millennium, where the side with the greatest control over such confusion takes the field, wins the day, and ultimately prevails in war. Battery C took that first shot on March 19, 1945. The 170th had been sent to support troops establishing the Remagen Bridgehead. Two days later the battalion—losing two of its men on the same day—matured into an aggressive fighting group. On that day, the 170th determined to kill on its own.

With four guns to a battery and three batteries in the battalion, there were twelve artillery pieces in the entire battalion. These were strategically arranged for combat with alphabetical simplicity. Battery A's guns were on the left, B's were in the middle, and C's were on the right. Headquarters coordinated their firing, and when all twelve guns fired in concert, the battalion was a deadly force.

So it was Rudy, was it? Floyd thought as he drove, nodding his head in understanding. *Well, someone had to be the first to die. It's always a runner, eh? But why was Rudy over there? As A's runner, he should have been near his battery. C did the firing, but the coordinates I gave them should have had them hitting Battery B. They're incompetent.*

That first morning of battle, the four guns of Battery A fired non-stop, and Rudy was busy running constantly between headquarters and the gun crews. Like Floyd, he had rushed in his open-topped jeep to deliver orders for targeting the guns. He then returned with ammunition requests, maintenance needs, calls for medical equipment, and other such incidentals. He had not stopped for the three hours before his life ended that day.

"Rudy didn't know what hit him," Private John Thorburn said, looking at each of the men in his gun crew. He made a slow back-and-forth turn of his head and spoke with disbelief. From where they sat reclining, smoking, and listening, the others of his gun crew looked at Private Thorburn with interest. They were dirty and tired. "None of them knew what hit them," Thorburn continued. "I doubt they even knew they were being targeted. It makes no sense."

Thorburn looked off to where he heard the distant sounds of guns firing at the Germans. He turned to look in the direction where Rudy and Battery A had been positioned when they were hit, and then he took a deep sucking drag from a cigarette he held pinched between his thumb and index finger. His plump fingers were dry and cracked, and they were soiled with grease. He held the drag of smoke deep in his lungs, and then sent it out in one strong blow. "The shell that hit them came out of nowhere."

"It had to come from somewhere," one of the men said.

"You bet it did," another said. "Where'd it land?"

"Right on Rudy's head," Thorburn said.

"Really?" another asked. "Did anyone else get hurt?"

"No. They were lucky," Thorburn said. "But here's the thing. Battery A was positioned a good half-mile away on our left, and the Krauts were where they are now—straight ahead and shooting at us." He pointed his finger straight before him. "The Germans are there. Now watch this." He pointed his finger while turning forty-five degrees to his left. "There," he said. "That is where Rudy was when he was hit. The Krauts were not really shooting over at Battery A. They were shooting at us."

"But they shot at B too."

"You're right," Thorburn replied, pausing after taking another drag from his cigarette. He did not hold the smoke this time, just blew it out and added, "But they never shot at A. Someone else hit them. Someone else killed Rudy."

"Sure they shot at A," the first man said. "I saw them Krauts walking their shells right up the hill. What are you saying? If the Germans did not hit A, then who did? Us?"

The men all laughed at the notion, finished their lunches and cigarettes, grabbed their helmets, and then turned together just in time to watch a jeep come sliding to a stop on the green grass around their gun chief. They saw Floyd jump from the jeep and watched him run with a slip of paper in his hand. He handed the field note to the gun chief, a first lieutenant in Battery C, and then he ran back to his jeep, started the engine, and drove away as fast as he had come. New orders had just arrived from battalion headquarters. After scrutinizing and showing the piece of paper to his radio operator, the chief looked over to the gun crew.

"Lunch is over," he yelled. "We've got orders. Let's go. On the double!"

The men moved and repositioned their gun and spent nearly two hours lobbing artillery shells onto the distant positions of the Germans who were defending the bridge at Remagen. Thorburn examined the trajectories of the shells and found them to be similar to that of a good six-iron shot—low and hard. Floyd returned five more times during the barrage, but only two of his visits resulted in the men repositioning their gun.

The 170th lost its second man later in the afternoon. With his frequent visits to field headquarters, and his speeding visits between Battery C's four gun positions, Floyd had managed to stay on top of everything occurring on the battlefield that day. If a gun was moved, he brought the order. If shooting stopped because of a maintenance need or a simple break for a meal, Floyd arrived with the authorization. And whenever ammunition was needed, it was Floyd who returned to headquarters with the request. He knew everything happening that day. Because field radios were huge contraptions in 1945—big, heavy, and difficult to handle—they were a source of complaint for the men. They were unreliable, too, so the battalion's radio men often tossed aside their backpack radios and took to relying on positioning orders supplied by their runner. The officers of C's four artillery pieces relied on target coordinates Floyd delivered.

They're not even confirming orders with the radios, Floyd thought after leaving battery headquarters with another set of coordinates for the guns. *Since Rudy died this morning, everyone just wants to shoot at the Germans.*

Floyd laughed at the thought, drove his jeep to the next gun position, ran out the new orders, ran back, drove to the next gun position, did the same, and continued until completing the circuit and returning to field headquarters. He stomped on the brakes, slid to a stop, jumped out of his jeep, and again raced into headquarters. When he returned to the jeep, he again ran and carried a new set of firing orders for the gun crew. He sat with the jeep's engine running and examined the orders, frowning.

"What is this?" he asked aloud. "Fuel? They are ordering me to refuel my jeep? What do they think I am? An idiot? Do they think I don't know when I need gasoline? I'm surprised they don't order me to take a leak." He glanced down at the jeep's fuel gauge, and found it was nearly empty. *Well,* he thought, *I would have noticed I was out of gas without their telling me. I can take care of myself. They treat me like an imbecile.*

He drove to a nearby fuel depot and began refueling his jeep. The fuel was stored in elevated tanks that could hold five hundred gallons each. There was a fuel nozzle

that ran from each tank, and Floyd inserted one of these
nozzles into his jeep. There was also a shut-off lever that
was manually turned, allowing the fuel to flow by gravity
alone. He lifted the lever and stood close by the nozzle
as fuel flowed into the jeep's gas tank. He stood near the
fuel tank's opening, bent and listening to hear when the
tank was approaching full so he'd know when to manually
disengage the fuel tank's shut-off nozzle, but after a few
minutes, wearied of listening.

Damn the sound of fuel, he thought. *I can hear the guns
firing. Those are C's guns, but listen over there. Are those Battery
B's guns? Is that where Evan is?* Floyd lifted his head and
stared to where he heard the distant sounds of Battery B's
guns. He recalled the position maps he had seen back at
headquarters. He closed his eyes and was able to distinguish
one specific sound from among the many others, which
required him to entirely dismiss the sound of the flowing
fuel. He knew where all gun positions were then assigned
on the field, and because several minutes had passed
between firing each gun, emptying a spent shell, cleaning
and lubricating, reloading, checking the gun's aim, and
then firing again, he was able to determine what he sought.

That's got to be them. He opened his eyes and stared off to
the left of his battery's positions. He had the coordinates,
he had seen the maps back at headquarters, and he had
checked the position several times over.

"It won't be like this morning," he said, whispering
through a grin. "That damn Rudy. It wasn't my fault! The
coordinates were wrong." While relaxing his grin into a
frown, he retrieved gun number one's new orders from a
breast pocket of his shirt. "Damn it!" he said. "Where in the
hell is that pencil? It had a good eraser."

It must have fallen, he thought. *Let's see. It's got to be here.*
He went to the door of the jeep and leaned in to find the

pencil. With his backside sticking out of the open doorway, he ran his hands over the seats, the floor, in-between the seats, and finally down to the floor.

"There you are," he said, smiling at the pencil he held up like a prize.

He examined the new orders, thought for a moment, and carefully erased the order and added new coordinates by erasing a few sharp edges and adding curves and lines. *Perfect,* he thought. *Sure they've been changed, but these look real. These are the coordinates I saw back at headquarters.*

He checked and rechecked the positions during a later stop for new orders for his gun crews. He knew the exact location of Battery B's gun number four, Evan's gun. All he had to do to hit that position was change one of his gun crew's firing directions—change the coordinates to go high and to the left.

"No," he said aloud, "It won't be like this morning. Not at all. I missed him, but the coordinates were all wrong. That was not my fault."

This time, he grinned at the thought. I've got him.

He was still sitting in the jeep when the sound of running gasoline came to him like the rustle of leaves in a tree. He jumped from the jeep and rushed to get to the fuel tank's shut-off nozzle. The tank had filled, and fuel was overflowing down the side of his jeep. He heard fuel splashing onto the dry ground. He was so alarmed that he reacted without thought. After racing and reaching the shut-off nozzle, he pulled it from the jeep too quickly, and fuel splashed on the side of the jeep, his pants, shoes, hands, and down to where it soaked his socks. He hurried the nozzle back onto its holster, drew back his hands as though they burned, and began wiping off the fuel, soaking his pants. In his alarm, he forgot about the orders he had carefully revised. The order was in his left hand, and he had partially soaked it with the gasoline nozzle he had held in his right. "Damn it all to hell!" he shouted. "It's wet."

He searched the inside of the jeep but failed to locate a towel, napkin, or any other article with which he could dry the stinking order. He then pressed the order against a sleeve of his shirt, patted it, wiped it against his pant leg, and held it by its driest corner to wave it in the air like a cloth handkerchief.

Floyd climbed back into the jeep, angry, wet, and smelling of fuel. He examined the order and saw that, though it was still wet, the revised instructions were clear. The distant sounds of the guns were mute to the noise of his frustration. "Damn it," he spoke aloud. "I got dirt on it."

With his attempt to dry the order, he had gotten dirt on a corner of the paper. He held it before him to examine it with wide eyes, but then he smiled.

"Nice touch," he whispered, nodding his head. "The dirt adds authenticity. It will be impossible for anyone to know the coordinates were changed."

He laughed before leaving and driving the course in reverse, traveling from gun four to gun one, thereby allowing more time for the order to dry before he delivered it to where it would be used. At his first stop, the gun crew ridiculed him for smelling like gasoline. They yelled at him like at a stray dog.

"You stink!" a private in the fourth gun crew yelled. "Get out of here before you blow up and kill us all."

"Runner!" the gun chief yelled, coming forward to discipline the private. "Whoa! You do stink. Get back to your jeep. I will send someone out to meet you. I'll send a runner to meet a runner."

Floyd was laughed away from the first gun position, and the same happened to him at his next two stops. As he drove to the last position, to gun number one—to *the* gun position—he stuck his wet arm up in the air.

That will help, he thought. *My shirt is already dry. The smell on the note is probably gone too. It should have blown away.*

Floyd was not alone while driving the supply lines. He passed ammunition trucks, fuel trucks, spotters returning from up front, other runners, medical units, mechanics, and reinforcements for the units assaulting the bridge. Because the Americans were taking the position, the roads behind the bridge were filled with traffic. On the way to the position of gun number one, Floyd avoided looking at other drivers and struggled to calm himself against the excitement he felt could give him away.

I must look composed, he thought. *Calm's the word. They cannot suspect me, or I'll be found out. I will not be caught! Not this time.* He frowned at the idea of getting caught, and he decided he would practice avoiding suspicion. *Laughter, that's how. I'll laugh. If I appear happy, I will not draw attention.*

He practiced laughing while he drove, but he closed his lips to make an instant frown. *Wait! That's not right,* he realized. *I would be the only one laughing. They're all so serious at the guns. They're trying to kill and someone else is trying to kill them. I'll laugh later. I'll just have to be serious, like them. That's what I'll do. But there's a fine line between appearing serious and looking suspicious.* He frowned at the thought. *How do I hide suspicion?*

He stopped the jeep further from the gun chief than on his previous visit. He sat there, considering his dilemma and speaking softly to himself. "It's the eyes. Don't let them see the truth in the eyes. I will rush like I'm in a hurry. That's it. I have no time for trouble. Why hang around? I'll just hand over the order and leave."

His decision made, Floyd jumped from the jeep, ran the short distance to where he saw Second Lieutenant Milton Baker, III. He made a hurried stop.

Lieutenant Baker extended an arm and repeatedly opened and clenched his hand to rush Floyd along. Floyd drew heavy breaths, wore his practiced expression, and looked at Baker's outstretched hand rather than at his eyes.

"What is this?" Baker asked. "Where are my firing orders? Where's the damn order?"

Floyd reacted by widening his eyes and allowing his mouth to fall open with the drop of his jaw. He looked down at his empty hands and patted his pockets. Still determined to avoid the officer's eyes, he ended his confused search for the order and spoke as he turned. "I must have left it in the jeep," he said. "I'll be right back."

Floyd ran back to the jeep, jumped in, started the ignition, and found the order lying there on the passenger seat. The sight of the note startled him. He made a quick glance at the officer and turned off the ignition, but remained sitting while he again examined the coordinates. He climbed from the jeep and ran to meet Lieutenant Baker. Baker's hand was still extended, but he had begun curling his fingers to make a patting motion against his palm, as though he were clapping with just one hand.

"What's so damn funny?" he asked when Floyd returned. "Why are you laughing? Is something wrong?"

Floyd tensed. *Serious*, he thought. *I need to look serious. Don't laugh. Frown.*

"I was laughing," he said, placing the order in the officer's hand, "because I had left the order in the jeep. That was a mistake. It's the whole reason I'm here, isn't it? I'm here to deliver these orders without making a mistake, eh?"

"A mistake?" Baker said. "Leaving the order in the jeep? That was just plain stupid. But wait a minute! What's this? What's wrong with this order? What in the hell did you do? This is a mess."

Floyd felt a rush of fear tremble his hands and take his breath. He tensed and again widened his eyes and lowered his jaw. Outwardly, he failed in his role as a serious innocent. Instead of meeting the lieutenant's eyes, he watched Baker pinch the order between his finger and thumb and wave it in the air.

"What's wrong with it?" Floyd asked.

"Wrong?" Baker repeated. "It stinks to hell of gasoline. Just a spark would ignite it. Did you do this?" He handed the order back so Floyd could examine it. "Damn!" he said. "Even you stink."

"Yes," Floyd said, "I mean, no. Those fuel nozzles at the depot do not shut off by themselves. Gasoline spilled on me and the order." He positioned his hands as they had been when he spilled the fuel—holding the order in his left and a pretend fuel nozzle in his right. "It's smells from the gasoline that spilled."

Floyd avoided making eye contact by staring at the order in his hand. He was aware that Lieutenant Baker was watching him. *No,* he thought, *I cannot look suspicious. Everything is fine. It's just a little gasoline.* He smiled, but he looked more suspicious than happy. *That's wrong too. War is not a happy time. Death is serious business. Look serious.*

"I really have to go," Floyd said to Baker, speaking just under the volume of a shout. "I need to get back to headquarters." He turned to rush off.

"Is that right?" Baker asked, grasping the back of Floyd's shoulder. "You did not look to be in a hurry when you arrived here. I saw you sitting over there in your jeep doing nothing. You just sat there and stared at this firing order. Why the sudden hurry now?"

"You have your orders," Floyd said. "Mine are to get away fast."

"Get away?" Lieutenant Baker asked, lifting his brows.

"Get back," Floyd corrected himself. "I have to get back to headquarters."

Baker removed his hand, and Floyd took off running for his jeep, but the lieutenant shouted after him. "Stop! Don't you dare leave. Get back here on the double!"

Floyd stopped abruptly, but he waited before turning to face the officer. He stood unmoving like he had been stopped by police. When he turned, he found Lieutenant Baker walking toward him with one of his big arms extended and pointing at him.

"Leave me the damn order!" Baker shouted.

Floyd looked down and realized he still held the order in his hand. In his rush, he had not given it to Baker. He cursed himself, looked Baker in the eyes, extended the order, and laughed. "Oops," he said. "I forgot. You can see I'm in a hurry."

Lieutenant Baker watched as Floyd departed, racing off in the direction of headquarters. Baker called out the new coordinates, and his crew repositioned the gun to hit the precise coordinates that had been written on the dirty, stinking order. Just as they were about to fire a round, the private who had earlier described Rudy's death stood back and examined the direction of the artillery's aim.

"It doesn't look right," Thorburn said.

"What doesn't?" Lieutenant Baker asked.

"The aim. There ... look. The German's are in front of us, but look how the gun is pointed toward the left. And it looks too high."

Baker looked at the direction of the gun's barrel, turned toward the direction where they had been firing all day, and then looked back at Private Thorburn.

"Remember how far away we are from them," he said. "The Krauts must have brought up reinforcements. Headquarters knows exactly where they are. That is why we're always moving the equipment. Orders are orders, and we're going to follow ours, exactly as they're written. Let's hit 'em hard."

Baker reread the coordinates, the gun crew re-checked their aim, and they left the gun positioned as was ordered. With that, the men began firing. They fired once, reloaded, fired again, reloaded, and fired yet again. In all, they sent three explosive artillery shells flying high and to the left. The shells flew along a path similar to that of a decent wedge shot. While the gun crew was loading a fourth shell, Lieutenant Baker gave them an order to stop.

"Hold up," he called, pointing at a jeep that slid to a stop next to the hot gun. Two MPs were in the back, and they jumped out shouting and waving their hands. "What do they want?" Baker asked.

CHAPTER 27

~ SOMETHING DEADLY THEIR WAY CAME ~

Battery B had heard the news of the battalion's first loss earlier that morning. The reaction from the men had been one of anger, rather than the numb feeling of acceptance that usually follows the loss of a young companion. The lieutenant commanding the fourth gun watched with satisfaction as his men cleaned, positioned, loaded, and fired their big artillery piece. They were perfect. The morning's news and Evan's training of his men inspired them to achieve an efficiency that was deadly for those across the river. The combustion in the weapon, compression in the chamber, and the concussion in the air, at just the moment of firing, somehow helped them to grieve the battalion's first loss. The gun became an extension of their emotions. The explosion of each shot was like the clenching of their teeth and shaking of their fists. They felt each pounding hop of the gun like the stomp of a foot, and the spit of flame that followed each fired shell was comforting, too, for it spewed forth their anger, Evan would hurry to meet their runner and, without fail, would intercept him before the man could climb from his jeep. He would then call out the new orders, his men would follow his instruction, and this same coordinated work efficiently continued throughout the day. His gun crew's work ethic was a model for the entire battalion.

Later in the afternoon, just when Battery B's runner was about to depart, Evan received the news that he should be ready for a significant change in orders. Something was coming.

"I'm not exactly sure what's happening," the runner had said, grinning and speaking louder than normal. Evan understood the young man wanted to be overheard by the rest of the gun crew. "It appears in headquarters that something is up. I think the Germans are withdrawing."

"No kidding?" Bernard Caprillia said, turning away from the gun and looking at the runner.

The rest of the gun crew joined Bernard in looking over at where the runner and Evan were talking. The men's faces were dirty and expressions were sober, but their eyes looked hopeful. They had done a day's work, and each listened to hear what they thought the man had just shouted. They sought to hear what they expected could recharge their enthusiasm. The day of monotonous routine around the artillery wore on their emotions. They wanted to hear results.

"Did we lick 'em?" Private Caprillia called.

"Not yet," Evan said. "We still have orders, and until we hear otherwise, we sit tight and wait. The runner did say that something is coming, that he thinks the end is near. He thinks the Germans are leaving, but he was not sure. He'll check with headquarters and tell us when he returns."

The crew's enthusiasm increased following the runner's departure. They fired at the Nazis as though they had returned well-rested after a long break. For thirty minutes, they shot without stopping, but during one lull in the shooting, when the men were hurrying to clean, position, and reload the gun, they paused in appreciation of the sound of the guns off to their left.

"A's givin' 'em hell," Private Caprillia said. "So is C. Listen to those big guns."

They heard the sound of guns pounding out shells to their left, and they heard C's guns doing the same back to their right. Evan and all six men of his crew stood listening to the thundering sounds around them, and they smiled in appreciation for what they knew to be happening to the Nazis.

Artillery guns launch shells with loud, controlled explosions. The pieces jump on their wheels, flames shoot from their barrels, and the noise is deafening. What follows a shot is a low, stunning absence of air for only a moment, but it is the sound during that moment that infests the moment with the ringing tone of deafness. Because of the great distance between the artillery pieces and their targets, there came too, after every shot, a moment of uncertainty about what it was they hit. They were certain about loading, aiming, and firing a shell, but they had to wait for the result. They could only hope for dead-on hits. When they heard the three shots from Battery C's closest gun crew, they turned as one and looked into the distance before them. They watched and smiled as they waited to see to where the shells would land. After the news from their runner's last visit, they expected victory.

Evan looked at his men like he was examining a portrait. They were poised beside the gun, staring off into the distance, looking through tired eyes, and watching intensely to catch the explosion of the shells they heard shot back to their right. Shell casings were scattered on the ground behind the artillery piece, a neat stack of unused ammunition stood nearby, smoke from their last shot still lingered above the gun's barrel, their faces were coated with the dirt and grime of their full day of working the gun, their uniforms were worn and dirty, and the very black and white of their expressions resembled an image captured for posterity. They stood fascinated, exhausted, and full of wonder. All searched together. Something was out there. Something was happening. In a manner similar to how marines were memorialized around a flag on Iwo Jima, the crew could have been memorialized around their gun in Germany.

If pictures could come to life, Evan's gun crew would have done so slowly. He watched them turn together as a unit, slowly, and he joined them turning, frowning, and looking back in the sky. They looked over to where they heard one of C's guns fire, and their expressions changed as they watched. They sensed that something was wrong. The realization began vaguely at a first split second, but then confusion reigned. They understood something deadly their way came.

"Oh, shit!" Private Caprillia yelled. "Here comes a shell."

"Everyone down!" Evan shouted, but his words were lost among the cursing, groaning, and panic of the others. All jumped toward the nearest piece of ground that gravity provided. Because the shell traveled so fast, the men had only an instant following realization of the threat before the shell hit, obliterated their gun, created a crater where they had been standing only moments before, eliminated every sound within hearing range—a quarter of a mile or so—sent dirt and dust flying everywhere, knocked down nine nearby trees, and killed every member of the crew, including Second Lieutenant Evan Wilkins. Limbs, flesh, bone fragments, and traces of blood flew everywhere, but once the second shell arrived, right on top of where the first had landed, nothing moved but the dusty, smoke-filled air. All that remained was a smoldering crater surrounded by husky chunks of earth. When the third shell landed on the spot, the site became devoid of all traces of humanity.

Just before the first shell hit, Evan was posed with his men and looking off into the distance before him. He had turned with the group, knew the truth for only a second before the first shell hit, tried to utilize the nine-point-eight meters-per-second-squared of gravity, and simply ended with that first explosion. There were no dying memories of what had been, no flashing scenes from his early life, no gallant struggling for some little bit of hope, and no dying speech to sober sentiments. Evan simply died. The second two explosions cremated him.

* * *

Amanda Nichols, at the moment of the first explosion, was twenty-one, still living along El Rancho Golf Course in her parent's Los Angeles mansion, and awaiting Evan's return. She was downstairs in the house and, with that first explosion, she curiously paused what she was doing, jolted in an unexpected manner, and stared with wide eyes at nothing at all. She placed both of her hands against the corners of her mouth and began to cry. Her forehead creased with lines that would remain for her lifetime, and she allowed herself to slump down into a red-cushioned chair behind her. She sat there for nearly an hour, lost in thought, wondering about the unexpected onset of the feelings that had overwhelmed her. Something had happened. She knew it. She could feel it, and she knew it was Evan.

While she sat where she landed, looking without seeing, she thought only of him. She felt overwhelmed by the sense that something horrible had happened to him. She sensed it, but she also sensed him. She felt he had just passed her, that he had gone in a hollow moment of desperation. Evan had been gone for nearly two years, but only then did she feel he had truly left her, as though she had lost him forever. She extended an arm before her, and she called for him with both her heart and mind, but then she wailed for him. She said his name deep in her mind, but all that came back was the echo of an empty forever. She hurt for the want of a lie, but Evan was forever gone from her.

Six weeks later—and what a long, emotional, and exhausting time those six weeks had been—news of his death reached her. It came in a terse little note that was mailed from Germany. At the time, Amanda had not seen the irony. With the arrival of her second letter from the 170th, after all of those months and months of the unanswered letters she had mailed to Evan, the letter she finally received back was the one she did not want. It came with nothing more than the news of his death. The note was heartless, but it was clear.

"Private Evan Wilkins," it read, "was killed in action in Germany."

On her sixth reading of the note, Amanda saw the two mistakes. The first was his rank. Evan had been promoted to lieutenant on the last night he was with her. The mistake in the death notice of calling him a private was small, but like all small mistakes, it added hurt to her heart. The mistake also gave her the relief that comes with the feeling of offense. As small as it was, she could forever dislike whoever had written the note. The second problem with the death notice was the handwriting. Instead of being typed, the note had been handwritten, and she noticed the similarity in the handwriting with that of the letters Floyd had written about Evan.

Up in her room, she withdrew her letter box and compared each letter to the death notice, one by one, lifting a letter, comparing it, tossing it aside, going faster, grabbing another letter, and another, and then pushing them all into the pile on which she slapped the death notice.

"The writing is identical," she whispered. "Floyd wrote the death notice. He wrote with a cold heart. Floyd will never be my friend."

Turning her head against tears, Amanda saw Evan's letter. She held it to her chest and cried. Evan was dead, or was he? She feared trusting in Floyd's truth.

"This is real!" she said, loud and angry, opening Evan's letter to read her proof.

My Dearest Amanda,

Finally, it has happened! The battalion boarded the HMS Queen Elizabeth last week, left New York, and we are now crossing the Atlantic on our way to help put an end to the war. Something is coming. Can you feel it? I do. I feel the end is nearing.

I have written you nearly two hundred letters since leaving the golf course and, in addition to telling you where I went and what I was doing, I also told you that I felt something like an elastic band had tethered my heart to yours. The farther I traveled, the more I felt the band pulling me back to you. In Oklahoma, it felt stretched so taut that I wondered if it might break. Remember? I wrote that instead of a band, I felt the squeeze of a noose choking my heart to death. But it's gone now! Suddenly, and for the first time since leaving you, I feel relief. Instead of a line stretched taut to the point of either breaking or slinging me back to you, I feel relief. I feel slack in the line. We are finally on our way to fight and end this war. Everyone expects us to be done and home in less than a year. One year! As soon as the war ends, I expect the stretch in the band to sling me back to you. I plan to fly to you like I was shot.

Just now, sitting alone at this table in the smallest briefing room on the ship, I laughed out loud. I wish you could see me. I'm smiling because I just thought of the moment I return to spend the rest of my life with you. What will we do first? Get married? Of course we will but what then? We never talked about what we would do after we were married. I want to give you a home where we can start a family. Imagine spending our lives together and having children. Imagine a son. I grew up without a father, but our son would have one. He would have me, and I would teach him everything. We would build a legacy.

I am still waiting for a reply from you. I've not gotten a single letter, but instead of losing faith in you, I have begun losing faith in the Army's mail system. I have finally found someone who will help me with the mail. He is the runner for my battery, and he is planning to hand-stuff this letter into our mail bag and make sure it gets off the ship. Even though the runner cannot explain why I never get letters from you, he insists you will get this one from me. He said he would die before losing it.

Now and forever, I am yours. In the same way everything gets worse before getting better, I have to fight in the war before I can come home to you. Do not worry, though, for I feel certain that the German guns will never find me. The feeling gives me peace. It allows me to plan for how I will spend the rest of my life with you, and that is how I end this letter—thinking of my life spent with you. I am yours for life.

Always, All Ways,
Evan

After the day of the death notice, a sadness, emptiness, and loneliness took possession of Amanda's soul. Evan was gone forever, and while she tried to hide her pain, there was always the truth that came in the form of tears. Nights were the worst. She adopted a wistful demeanor, known for her manner of remaining distant, watching and wondering about the world around her. Mr. and Mrs. Nichols saw something else in her watching. They saw her intense, focused, and always anxious watch for Floyd to return and tell her about Evan's last moments. She was certain he would know what had happened. She might have endured a sorrowful existence, and she might have forever remained on the melancholy side of sanity but for her two passions—her little boy and her writing.

CHAPTER 28

~ *LIVE IN YOU* ~

It was at that time, just after finishing with Floyd's heartless death notice, that Amanda began clinging tighter to her fifteen-month-old son, Ricky. Since the night when he took his first breath in the Nichols' home, the baby had slept in his mother's bed. Every night Amanda would smile and play with him, and after Ricky fell asleep, she would use one of her fingers to lightly touch his lips, press his cheeks, straighten his fingers, smooth the little brows above his sleeping eyes, caress his forehead with kisses, and come to know every square millimeter of his precious face. Ricky was hers, and he was entirely Evan back then. Just holding him at night in her bed helped relieve some of her loneliness. Throughout the fifteen months of Evan's absence, she had visualized the precious moment when he would see their son for the first time and the three of them would become a family. She conjured the image daily, until all her senses were alive with it, and she hugged Ricky tightly each time as she visualized Evan doing the same. Now the arrival of the Army notice had snatched that dream away as though it had never existed.

The infant became a toddler, and the toddler proved to be one of those watchful children who sometimes unnerve adults with the way they observe—as though they know more than is yet possible. When tears quietly fell from his mother's eyes, fell at night while lying in her bed and watching her, little Ricky would remain quiet, showing no expression at all. He could understand no more than that his mother was unhappy, and several times her tears brought the same unhappiness and tears to him. Mothers, too, like fathers, must be emotionally strong for their children.

In the mornings, little Ricky always awoke first. Though he would not remember that his mother had grieved in the night, he would wake and stare at her sleeping face in the mornings and pat, stroke, and even rub her cheeks. He did this until Amanda awoke, seeing his eyes there awaiting hers. Ricky watched without expression, and such quiet watching by a young child always imputes some impossible understanding on his part. As time went by, she would wake to find him simply staring into her face, staring without patting. She would see his father's eyes in the boy, and she would squeeze him just as though she could still feel the father. Amanda was a lonely lady, but regardless of the depth of her loss, as long as she had her son, she could never remain lonely for long.

Her deep sense of sadness eventually retreated behind the maternal veil of purpose, and she went on to spend her life as a beautiful woman alone with her adored and adoring son. From the observant toddler, Ricky became the thoughtful and energetic Rick, an understanding young man, Richard, an outstanding father, and finally a comfortable man in his sixties—fit, handsome, intelligent, successful, and grayed at the temples. Richard's only son gave him a grandson.

"Your father would have been proud of you," Amanda told Richard at each stage in his life.

She was especially careful to remind Richard of his father at each of those significant events in a man's life, moments when paternal affirmation is most needed, most helpful and, for Richard, most desired. His graduation from college, his wedding day, the birth of his son, his son's college graduation, the trials of his career and marriage, the birth of his grandson and, even on that last day when Amanda was saying goodbye, Richard missed for his father.

"I missed him, of course," Amanda said, "but you know that, don't you? I've told you so many times. Wouldn't he have been proud of you? Oh, yes! You would have been like a jewel to him. You know that, don't you? Say it again. Tell me again you know your father would have loved you. Say it to me."

"He would have loved you first, Mother," Richard said, using the most reassuring tone he could muster while sitting beside a hospital bed. "I know he would have loved us both and, yes, I know he would have been proud of me. I know he would have loved me."

"Do you?" she then asked, whispering, smiling weakly, tears wetting her eyes.

"Of course I do," Richard had whispered back to her. "But I have always had you, and you were and are more than enough for any son. I have you now, Mother ... we all do. You will forever live through me, through my children, through your grandchildren, and even through their grandchildren and their grandchildren's grandchildren. You will live forever."

Amanda gasped, and she smiled while looking up into Richard's loving eyes. "And so should your father," she whispered. "Let him live. He was your father ... that is enough. God allowed him to be taken before he even knew about you. Please don't let him die here and now with me. Keep Evan alive in you."

"I will," he said, turning his head in the slow manner of disbelief and pressing the back of his hands to his eyes. "I will do whatever you say. The man you loved is my father, and so I promise you that I will never forget him. I will learn everything I can about Evan, and I will grow his legacy."

"There is one more thing," she said. "You know how much I have written in all these years."

"Of course I do," he said, rubbing the moisture on his moist fingers into the dry wrinkles of her hand.

"I never allowed you to read what I wrote because I thought you might react by doing something terrible."

"Why would I do that?"

"Because he was so terrible."

"To you? Who? Who was terrible to you?"

"A man named Floyd Akerly. Yes, he was horrible to me, but he was even worse to your father. After I'm gone, you can read my journals. They're all in the library, and everything is in them. But wait. Do that later, after I'm gone. What I want you to do right now is promise to keep alive the memory of your father. You've seen his only letter. Memorize it. Add to the legacy of your father."

"I promise I will," he said.

Words such as Amanda's do not simply die once they are spoken to a son. They have a haunting way of remaining forever in his consciousness. They linger at length, until the man either obeys or denies them. Richard chose to obey them. The very day Amanda was laid to rest, he resolved to learn what he could about his father, feeling committed to the promise he made his mother, and frustrated by the gaping voids in his knowledge of Evan. At that time, he knew his father's name was Evan Wilkins, he had come from somewhere in Idaho, he was a very good golfer, he died fighting in World War II, he fell in love with his mother, proposed to her, and then he missed out on having and enjoying his family. Evan missed spending his life with the one he loved, and he missed enjoying the patriarch's reward following maturity and family success. Evan missed life.

In Amanda's journals, though, Richard discovered his mother's horrors. He found more than enough to fill all of the voids in his knowledge of his father.

CHAPTER 29

~ ANCILLARY PASSIONS ~

From the first moment I entered Floyd's house, I was surprised by its cleanliness and its missing odor. I expected it—a distinct smell I would not like. Upon my arrival, Floyd had again neither seen nor heard me. Just like all of my previous visits, I found him sitting in his brown recliner, and staring out of his front window. Over the weeks of visits with him, I had learned what to expect from both of us.

For his part, he always sat waiting in that brown recliner, wearing his thin grey sweater, and smiling at me like I was his son. For mine, it was the same thing. My craving for information about Evan had contained most of my feelings of repugnance for him. On that last day, my last visit to his home, though, both of us defied convention. He was sitting in the recliner, but for the first time since I knew him, he was not wearing the sweater. Instead, he wore a shirt with buttons, and he had a colorful, hand-knitted quilt wrapped around his thin legs. I thought the quilt made the old man look even older.

My change was internal. Instead of approaching him to gain knowledge, as was my custom, I came the final time to be done with him forever.

The quilt warming his legs looked like one of those small blankets church quilting groups make. The women probably said a ceremonial prayer over a whole bundle of quilts, and then, as a group, they came to deliver Floyd's

prayer blanket in person. I supposed them to have come
unannounced to deliver their cloth of many colors.
I imagined the women standing before him with the quilt
stretched hand-to-hand, and Floyd watching in silence,
unemotional, as each took a turn praying for the blanket,
for God's favor on the old man, and for Floyd's eternal
peace. Even if he wanted to, he could not decline the quilt,
for such deliveries come with insistent kindness. At his age,
what could he do? Besides, his legs surely were cold.

On that day of my last visit, Floyd's housekeeper, Maria,
had gone out to run errands and to shop for groceries.
I knew this would be the case, and so I purposefully arrived
when I knew he would be alone. No one answered my light
tapping on his door, and when I pushed it open, there was
no one to hear the sound or notice the movement.
I entered alone, remained silent, and went to where I knew
he would be sitting and staring out of his window. I peered
around a corner to observe him before he saw me, and I
was then struck by just how feeble he looked. As on all of
my earlier visits, I thought ninety-four was terribly old.

An old man's age does not much matter, though, for
a number is just a number. What matters to an old man is
what he can still do in those late years. Foremost, he can
live even longer. He can love, laugh, cry, take part in the
dénouement of his life, remain quite helpful to his family,
glimpse what he will be leaving behind when he is gone,
and, if nothing else, he can be kind. Even with the aches
of age, the opportunity to be kind remains a decision.
Kindness is a choice, and kind old men are priceless
treasures in every family. Floyd had no family, and so I
observed him doing what old people do when they are
alone without family—he watched the world through his
window. Because there was nothing to be seen through that
front window, he appeared to me to be watching without

emotion. He possessed the knowledge of what he had done with his life, the good and the bad. He had outlived most of his contemporaries. Now he was old, alone, and without family. He simply stared. He did not even enjoy the pleasure of hopeful thought. The hopes of his life were, already, long gone.

He knows what he has done, I thought, standing behind him, recalling his stories of Evan, and trembling with rage for what I had read about him in Amanda's journals. *I wonder at ninety-four if he realizes the consequences, not to himself, but to me. He has taken too much, way too much! He must have known his actions would come back to him. Trouble always returns.*

Floyd remained staring out of the window, but I could not tell if he wore any expression at all. His back was to me, and the recliner dwarfed his shrunken frame. From where I stood, I could see the same picture I had seen on my first visit—the photo of him as a twenty-six-year-old officer posing with his Battery B gun crew. Rather than look at Floyd in the black-and-white photograph, I sent my eyes straight to Private Evan Wilkins. I found him, and there I saw a young man of twenty-one, eager, grinning, and ready for life's adventures. He looked destined for a full life of love. He stood tall, and he looked young, athletic, and confident. I noticed a dimple in the muscle that ran the length of his right forearm and thought it the result of his playing countless rounds of golf. I saw, too, that he had been a good-looking kid. I returned his smile. Though I had never known him, I recognized myself in the distorted reflection. I saw, too, Floyd in the photograph with his dark little eyes, black hair, and wedge-shaped face. His lips formed into a line that was probably a grin, but the visual effect of his being agreeable failed with his eyes. The first time I had seen that picture, I had seen only an officer with his men. Seeing the photograph on my last visit, I saw Floyd with Evan, something altogether different.

"You killed my father," I said to Floyd's back.

What strange words I spoke in that quiet little room. They sounded surreal, as though made up and spoken by a stage actor. They sounded impossibly far-fetched. Who dares to kill another man's father? Floyd had not heard what I said, for he did not start, turn around, look at me, or say one word in response. He remained staring through his window, and I remained staring at him. I also continued to seethe, because the truth I had spoken served to agitate my emotions. I grew angry all over again. I wanted to snap his thin neck. Instead, I spoke again.

"I'm back!" I yelled at the back of his head while I moved to get closer to him.

Floyd heard me the second time I spoke. I saw that my voice caused him to start, as though he had just then awakened from an old-man nap, and I watched him turn from the window to where he found me fixed on the back of his skull.

"Oh!" he said. "It's you."

Floyd appeared to have been startled by my sudden appearance behind him. He had not heard me and had not even suspected anyone was standing so near to him. He was caught defenseless. Previously he was warned of my arrival by either Maria or me. With her out, and me silent and staring, he reacted with alarm. Before his mind could acknowledge me as an acquaintance, he widened his eyes and narrowed his lips. He saw me as a threat. He looked frightened of me. Once he identified me, he reacted by attempting to smile. His lips curled. His teeth showed, but all I saw was the man who had gotten away with more than murder. I had read Amanda's journals. Instead of smiling at him, I gave him an expression devoid of everything kind.

"What's the matter, Richard?" he asked. "Is something wrong?"

"Not at all," I said, pressing my lips and narrowing my eyes. "I was just thinking about everything you told me about Evan Wilkins. I want there to be more you can tell me. I'm upset about how your story ended."

Floyd had grown accustomed to my sitting on his sofa, smiling, and asking him for specific details. I had been so anxious, but that was before, back when he was unknowingly testifying in his defense. While I remained standing, I saw him sink into his big recliner and peek at me through questioning eyes. He saw my mood.

"Anyway," he said. "I'm glad you came back." He spoke with his loud, raspy, old-man voice. "Sit down at least. Don't leave me alone."

It was when I sat down that I finally smelled it. I smelled something other than cleanliness. I had caught a whiff of the odor on my last visit, and I recall thinking that even the best housecleaners miss subtle, ninety-four-year-old smells. The odor was light, but it was there. It was faint, and reminded me of the scent resulting from an odd combination of dust, age, inactivity, musk, medicines, the cooking of salt-free foods, all underlain by the weak scent of some lemony cleaner. Old books get that smell—minus the cleaner—and there is nothing to be done about it. Age has a distinct smell.

On that last visit with Floyd, I was struck most by his being alone, especially at his age. Ninety-four was much too old to be left alone. Where was his wife? His children? Their children? Or even their children's children? He should have been a great-grandfather. At the very least, his housekeeper should have arranged for someone to be with him. What if something happened? What if he needed help or required assistance?

When I placed a glass of water in front of him, he either did not notice or he chose to say nothing about the lack of ice or the small amount of water in the glass. I had filled it no higher than a finger or two above its bottom. I did this so he would need me to go to his kitchen for a refill. This I wanted to do. I then sat on the sofa in front of him, squeezed his two sofa pillows, and started by indicating the photograph from his Army days. I began with a question that held a nonchalant sort of interest. I asked as though my interest was from little more than an indifferent curiosity.

"Tell me again," I said, taking the photograph in my hands, "who were are all these men?"

"Those were my men back in Battery B," Floyd said.

"You mean Battery C," I said, making my first attempt to shake him a bit.

"No. All of the men in the picture were in Battery B. I was an officer, and those were my men."

"But you were in Battery C, too, right? That's what you told me." I frowned and pretended to be confused.

He looked as though I had just ruffled the cover of some well-stowed memory. I stared into his eyes and, before he answered, found myself distracted by the whites of a ninety-four-year-old man's eyes. They were yellow, glassy, and permanently streaked by broken red lines that looked like scattered sticks after a storm. I thought of broken neurological synapses. I thought of impulses from the brain scattering into the abyss of old brain matter.

"That's right," he finally admitted, "I did tell you I was in C too."

Floyd frowned and glanced over at the old photograph. I thought I caught him looking at the eyes of Evan Wilkins, who now appeared especially young. Floyd could not have seen more than an innocent young man. He twisted at both of his ears at the same time, and he led me to consider that the small devices in his ears hindered, rather than aided, his hearing. After completing his adjustments, he again glanced at the photograph and looked out the window. I thought he might be waiting for me to speak, but I remained silent, watching, and waiting. I stared at him like he had raped my mother.

"Why do you ask?" he said. "I was in the Army. We won, and it was all so long ago."

I ignored his question and returned his attention to the old photograph. "Was this one Evan?" I asked, as though I had chosen Evan at random.

"Let me see," he said staring at the picture. "Hmm, is that Bingham?"

He glanced out of the window, twisted at his ears, and then turned back to me. He noticed me peeking at his water glass. It was nearly empty, so I reached and held it as though I would refill it. He stared at the glass in my hand.

"No," Floyd admitted. "That's not Bingham. It's Wilkins. You're right. That man is Evan Wilkins."

Floyd stared at me like a ninety-four-year-old man watching a crowd, revealing neither interest nor disinterest. He waited for whatever would come. World War II had become a simple black-and-white archive, the war department was the defense department, and artillery rounds that hit one's own men—resulting in accidental deaths—were labeled "friendly" fire. Floyd had grown old alone, Lieutenant Evan Wilkins had been dead for decades, and the time had come for me to act on my resolve. I returned to the kitchen to refill his water glass, but I first took and crushed ice from the freezer. I placed the frozen shards into his drinking glass and added the two drops I knew would end his life.

My decision to act was, until then, undecided, for when I arrived earlier that afternoon, I came with the purpose of telling him who I was. I wanted him to know that Evan Wilkins was my father. Knowledge without action, though, is the foundation of a hollow, pacifist, pathetic, and haunting legacy. I was forever resolved to give my family more than I had received. At my age, one either gives up on, or gives in to, his resolve. I made my decision quickly and easily. Ninety-four-year-old men slumped in recliners with church quilts wrapped around their legs are simply gone. They have grown old and died of natural causes. No one asks questions. Without slashes, bruises, cuts, or gashes—when there is no blood and there are no signs of struggle—ninety-four-year-olds are simply gone. As a cause of death, old age is as convenient as friendly fire.

When I returned from the kitchen, I looked at the two cushions sitting on his old velvet sofa. They were the deep crimson color of blood, just as blood is drying. I found myself unnerved by those pillows. They had been my first choice, months earlier, but I had decided to dismiss them. If I was younger and then in possession of the knowledge of what he had done, I have little doubt his last breath would have been drawn through those cushions. How tasteless. Who could smother an old man? Who could live with himself after performing such a violent act? There was too much to lose. The act would have been Floyd's victory. He would have ruined both father and son, and I would have become just like him. Instead, I returned with his water glass, intending to watch him sip himself to death.

I sat down and remained silent. After he took his first drink, Floyd stared at the photograph, and I stared at him. My silence must have gotten to him, though, for he eventually turned to meet my gaze. He saw that I was glaring more than watching him, and I saw how this unsettled him. He dropped his eyes away from mine and turned his head down to a side, in the manner of a scolded dog. After two large gulps from the glass, he resumed his submissive pose where he waited for me to say something more. He had already said enough.

"You killed Evan Wilkins," I said. "You killed my father."

Floyd's reaction surprised me. He grabbed at his throat, mouthing like a carp, his eyes wide and wet, arms flailing and knocking the water glass onto to the floor, but then he moved as though he would rise and stand. I watched him cough so hard that he fell back onto his chair, where he sat looking at me with perspiration forming along his hairline.

"You?" he said, squeezing his throat and mouthing a hoarse whisper. "Hel—"

I watched his frail body convulse.

"You know who I am," I said, remaining calm in my seat. "Think about it. I told you my name long ago. By now, you should have connected the names Evan and Nichols with Wilkins and Amanda. I am their son. I am Richard Nichols."

I was unemotional as I watched him die. One or two of his wide-eyed gasps were unnerving, but I neither moved nor savored the moment. There was no joy. There was no satisfaction. I did not extract my vengeance. There was no violence. Revenge came in the form of a thin, frail old man, alone and slumped in his recliner. Somehow, though, that was enough for me. I nodded my acceptance, stood, adjusted my tie, collected the remaining ice from the floor, dropped it in the kitchen sink, rinsed and refilled his water glass, and met Maria returning from her shopping trip. She walked with me to where we discovered Floyd sitting slumped in his chair.

"Oh, my," she said, rushing to where she manipulated him like a nurse.

"It looks like he just slumped," I said. "You had better call an ambulance."

"He's not moving. I call now."

301

I left later thinking about my mother. She had been an outstanding woman who never married and, instead, gave her heart to ancillary passions, one of which was me. I replayed the familiar words she had spoken throughout my life. They had been important for her to repeat to me.

"Your father would have been proud of you," she had said, and on that last day, I finally agreed.

The library in my home on the golf course held my mother's lifetime of writing. Her prose and poetry filled numerous journals, and I returned home from Floyd's carrying one of them, the journal that led me to pursue and punish him. In that journal I read about Floyd returning from the war and visiting my mother. She had been home alone with me at the time, but I had been too young to defend her. Her written words instilled more than one passion in me. Besides punishing Floyd, she gave me the passion to perpetuate my father's legacy.

As I returned the journal to the shelf by slipping it between two dusty notebooks, I was stopped by the unexpected words I found scrawled on the cover of her next journal. I removed it from the shelf, sat, and read in the library until the earliest hours of morning. When I left home the next day, I went on my way to shoot one last albatross.

Made in the USA